A WINTER WEDDING AT PRIMROSE HALL

JILL STEEPLES

Boldwood

First published in Great Britain in 2024 by Boldwood Books Ltd.

Copyright © Jill Steeples, 2024

Cover Design by Head Design Ltd

Cover Images: Shutterstock

A CIP catalogue record for this book is available from the British Library.

Paperback ISBN 978-1-78513-369-5

Large Print ISBN 978-1-78513-370-1

Hardback ISBN 978-1-78513-368-8

Ebook ISBN 978-1-78513-371-8

Kindle ISBN 978-1-78513-372-5

Audio CD ISBN 978-1-78513-363-3

MP3 CD ISBN 978-1-78513-364-0

Digital audio download ISBN 978-1-78513-367-1

This book is printed on certified sustainable paper. Boldwood Books is dedicated to putting sustainability at the heart of our business. For more information please visit https://www.boldwoodbooks.com/about-us/sustainability/

Boldwood Books Ltd, 23 Bowerdean Street, London, SW6 3TN

www.boldwoodbooks.com

For Nick, Tom and Ellie
With love, as always

1

Pia Temple held the wreath, which was brimming with pinecones, whole dried oranges and cinnamon bundles along with an abundance of dried flowers and leaves, and placed it carefully onto the outside of the kitchen door. She took a step back to admire its beauty, the burnished copper tones lending a flavour of the forest floor. The crisp nip to the air was another indication that autumn had well and truly arrived. She smiled, knowing that her handiwork would provide the perfect welcome for her guests, who would be arriving in a short while.

The magnificent seventeenth-century Primrose Hall had a grand front entrance with an imposing stone portico and a regal front doorway in glossy black, but regular visitors to the hall knew to use the side entrance that led directly into the heart of the home, the large and welcoming country kitchen. It was the setting for so many special occasions, charity coffee mornings for the villagers, working brunches for the team, long leisurely lunches with guests, family conflabs and, best of all, romantic dinners. Pia relished those times when it was just her and Jackson, sitting together at the oak table, sharing intimate chatter and delicious food usually whipped up by Jackson. Bertie, the Dalmatian, and Teddy, the scruffy mongrel, were a constant presence too, as they were never far behind Pia, padding around after her at the hall and in the grounds in expectation of their next big adventure. Now, they larked about on the gravel driveway as Pia made some last-minute adjustments to the wreath, shifting it one way and then the other to make certain it was in exactly the right position.

'Come on, you two,' she called to the dogs, once she had finished tinkering with the door decoration. The pair of them were wandering further away, ever hopeful that they might be in for their second walk of the day, but an incisive whistle from Pia had them bounding over immediately. She rewarded them with a treat, which could always be found in the pocket of whatever outfit she happened to be wearing that day.

Inside, she poured herself a glass of water and sat at the kitchen table, enjoying the peace and calm. It had been a hectic couple of weeks. Scrap that, she thought with a wry smile. It had been a challenging few months, not only with the busy calendar of events at the hall, but also with the unexpected dramas that had made this last summer one that none of them would ever forget. Sometimes she couldn't help her mind entertaining thoughts of what-ifs, but when she caught herself thinking that way she tried to snap herself out of it. Much better not to dwell on what had happened and instead focus on everything they had to be grateful for and to look forward to.

That's why she had so enjoyed her impromptu crafting session this morning. A chance to properly unwind and let her mind switch off from everything else while her attentions had been focused solely on the different materials she'd gathered on the table in front of her, feeling the texture of the bumpy pinecones, hearing the crinkle of the leaves as she applied them to the wreath. The scent of cinnamon mingling with citrus tones had reminded her that Christmas really wasn't that far away. And, with a bonfire night display, the Christmas Carols by Candlelight evening, and her wedding, just a few of the events planned in the coming months, she knew that this morning's brief respite wouldn't last for long.

'Are you all right?' Jackson asked. Pia had been lost in thought, her gaze drifting off through the leaded windows of the kitchen, taking in the beautiful view of the well-tended grounds that swept around the hall, the towering trees of Primrose Woods visible in the distance. She looked towards the door, her heart lifting at the sight of her fiancé, thinking how handsome he looked standing on the threshold. He was wearing black jeans and a cream half-zipped cable-knit jumper, his hair curling onto his collar. His dark eyes appraised her, the tilt of his head expressing his concern.

'Fine! I've been making the most of the lull.'

'I don't blame you. Where is everyone?'

'Rex and Ronnie have headed into town. They're going to do a bit of shopping and then stop for some lunch.'

'Poor Dad. Ronnie can't be buying yet another outfit for the wedding, surely?'

Pia laughed. It had been a huge source of amusement to Pia, and a source of dismay to Jackson, that Jackson's mum had been fizzing with excitement ever since she'd found out the date for her son's wedding to Pia. Ronnie had been eagerly making plans over possible outfits and accessories ever since, changing her mind several times in the process.

'They're looking at shoes today, apparently.'

In the absence of her own parents, who she'd sadly lost in recent years after acting as their carers for the best part of her twenties, Pia appreciated having the presence of Jackson's parents in her life. Both Ronnie and Rex were larger-than-life characters with captivating personalities who had shared a brief and tempestuous marriage years earlier before they had divorced and gone their separate ways. When Jackson fulfilled his childhood dream and bought the neglected and derelict Primrose Hall, restoring it to its former glory and making it his home, his mum Ronnie had taken residence in the grounds in her cherished camper van, refusing on several occasions Jackson's offer to have her own rooms within the hall itself. She always said that she liked the independence and freedom the van offered and with it the possibility that she could take off whenever she wanted to, although in recent months Ronnie's wanderlust had waned.

Ever since Rex had turned up at the hall unexpectedly last year, after several years living abroad, wanting to make amends with Jackson, the son who he had largely neglected while he had been growing up, the dynamic at the hall had changed immeasurably. Had Rex known his ex-wife was living there too, he might never have turned up at the hall that night, but after the initial shock of coming face to face with their pasts, and some heated and revelatory conversations, Jackson and his parents had found a closeness and a bond between them that wasn't always apparent in earlier years. Ronnie had been delighted to rekindle her romance with Rex and now the pair of them were like a couple of lovestruck teenagers, spending every available moment together, making up for lost time.

'How many pairs of shoes can one woman wear to a wedding?' asked Jackson despairingly.

'You'd be surprised. Well, especially as far as Ronnie is concerned,' said Pia, still chuckling. 'She's been talking about heels, sandals, flats and wellies. She likes to be prepared for every eventuality.'

Jackson wandered across and placed his hands on Pia's arms,

gently massaging her shoulders with his thumbs. She wriggled in her seat, stretching out her muscles, enjoying the sensations his touch evoked. The familiar scent of his aftershave, earthy with undertones of citrus fruit, reached her nostrils and her eyes closed as she relaxed into his touch. He leant down, his breath on the back of her neck sending shivers down her spine. She turned to look up into Jackson's dark brown eyes, recognising the intent within his gaze.

'I told you we should have eloped, then we might have avoided all these issues. And we'd be married by now too.' There was a gleam of amusement in Jackson's scrutiny, but Pia knew he wasn't entirely joking.

'Yes, but it wouldn't be the same without our families and friends around us. After the year we've had, it will be the perfect celebration. Not only of our marriage, but also everything we've achieved here at the hall, the friendships we've made, your family coming back together and, of course, you getting over the accident and Rex recovering from his heart attack.'

'Don't get me wrong,' said Jackson, who pulled out a chair from the table, turning it one hundred and eighty degrees so that it was facing Pia. He straddled the seat, his clasped hands resting on the back of the chair. 'I am very grateful for all those things, but I don't want our wedding turning into just another event on the Primrose Hall calendar. Indistinguishable from all the other events that we've hosted here.'

'Oh, but it won't be. I know we've held a couple of weddings here before, and they were both gorgeous celebratory days, but ours will be all the more special, because... well, because it's our wedding! And a Christmas wedding too.' She clapped her hands enthusiastically, a familiar flutter appearing in her chest. Every time she thought about it, she was gripped by a mix of emotions: excitement, anticipation and a sprinkling of trepidation too. She supposed it was only natural to harbour some doubts; getting married was a life-changing event, after all. She looked across at Jackson, gauging his reaction. Underneath his confident front, she knew he was a private person who would much prefer to exchange his vows with her in an intimate ceremony with only a handful of people present. Had she been wrong to insist that they share their big day with all their friends and family?

'It will be wonderful, but hey, it's not too late to call the wedding off if you're really not that keen on the idea?' She forced herself to say the words brightly, even if she shuddered inside as she heard them roll off her tongue. Maybe they needed some extra time.

'Now, did I say that?' Jackson was quick to reassure Pia, cupping her face in his hands. 'Nothing's going to stop me marrying you, not even these gammy legs.' He gave a wry smile. 'We just need to remind Ronnie occasionally that it's our wedding and not hers. Honestly, to hear her talking, you might be mistaken for thinking she was the blushing bride. I don't want you feeling that she's pushing you out, taking over, as she likes to do.'

'Not at all. I love having Ronnie's input. She's excited for us and why shouldn't she be?'

Jackson shook his head indulgently and rolled his eyes. As a young boy he'd had a strained relationship with his mum, not understanding why she would often take off in her camper van to go off on her adventures, leaving him to live with her sister, Marie, with whom, admittedly, he'd had a very close and loving relationship. It didn't stop him feeling the hurt and betrayal of being left behind by his mum, though. In recent years Jackson and Ronnie had grown closer, but those old wounds weren't far beneath the surface, and Ronnie still had the ability to infuriate Jackson, with something as simple as a wrong word or a questioning glance. Still, these days Pia liked to think of them all as one big happy family, even if they still had their fiery moments from time to time.

'What are your plans for the day?' Jackson asked.

'Abbey and Willow, Ruby and Freddie, and Katy and the children should be arriving any moment now. I want to try little Rosie in her bridesmaid dress to see if she's grown into it or if it will need altering. Then we'll have some tea and cakes, and a catch up.'

'Ah, of course, I remember! In that case, I probably need to make a dash for it,' he said with a wry grin. 'Delightful though all those babies are, I really don't want to intrude on the wedding talk, and I can just imagine the racket that lot will make.' He grimaced exaggeratedly. Jackson liked to pretend that he wasn't fond of small children, but Pia knew it was only an act. 'Besides, I need to catch up with Tom. I want to have that long-overdue conversation with him about making him a permanent fixture on the team. I'll take the dogs with me, save them from getting underneath your feet.'

'Thanks, Jackson, although I know Rosie will be disappointed not to see you and Bertie and Teddy.'

'Well, I'm sure the excitement of trying her dress on will keep her distracted. Send them all my regards, won't you?' He stood up, leaning down to deposit a kiss on her lips. 'Love you, see you later,' he called, heading outside.

'Love you more,' Pia called after him, a smile lingering on her lips. It was true. She did love him, but there was still a part of her that wondered if she was really making the right decision in marrying Jackson.

2

Rex and Ronnie had spent all morning mooching around the shopping centre, stopping for coffee in the big department store before heading to the old town where they wandered, hand in hand, along the cobbled streets. Ronnie loved the array of specialist shops there, including an antiquarian bookshop, a record shop selling all the old vinyls they knew from their younger days and a wool shop where Ronnie stocked up for her latest project, a patchwork bed blanket for Pia and Jackson's wedding present. There was also a choice of independent boutiques which Ronnie gravitated towards as they stocked the unusual colourful clothes that weren't readily available on the high street that so appealed to Ronnie's eclectic tastes. Although today it was Rex's attention that was caught by one particular treasure in a shop window.

'Oh, look at that, Ronnie! Didn't you have a dress similar to that one back in the day?'

Ronnie turned to look at the display in the window of a shop that sold vintage clothing and accessories. The cream dress on the mannequin was long and flowing with a smocked front and embroidered daisies dotted over the lace skirt, evoking memories of long-ago summers, flower power and the sounds of strumming folk guitars.

'I think I may have done,' said Ronnie with a smile, transported to another place and time. 'I was always a bit of a hippy, even long after they were a thing.'

'What do you mean "was"? You still are!'

'You're probably right there. Okay, so I might be stuck in the past, but everything seemed so much better when we were young. Don't you think?' Ronnie took a step forward to admire the dress in closer detail. 'It really is beautiful, but more suited for a bride, don't you think?'

'Well, I can just imagine you in something like that.' Rex's eyes sparkled, no doubt conjuring up images of Ronnie in the dress.

'Besides, I've already bought two outfits for Pia and Jackson's wedding so I certainly don't need any more. Although...' She gave a final lingering glance at the dress, clearly considering the idea, before breaking into laughter. 'I couldn't! It's not the done thing to wear cream to a wedding. Come on, before you lead me into trouble. Let's go and find some lunch,' she said, taking Rex by the hand.

They found a little café in a secluded cobbled mews that served a selection of quiches, wraps and sandwiches. Rex chose the healthy option as he was on doctor's orders after his recent health scare, opting for a seafood salad, while Ronnie went for a slice of salmon quiche with salad. Ronnie loved the time she spent with Rex, just the two of them, enjoying each other's company. They'd always got on well, sharing a similar outlook on life and sense of humour, but in their younger days, they'd both been spontaneous and fiery, which would often result in broken promises, hurled insults and screaming rows. These days, they were wiser, kinder and mellower, and while there was still a delightful spark to their relationship, it was a relief to everyone concerned that there were no longer the dramatic fireworks of before.

'I'm so pleased I've picked up the rest of the wool for Pia and Jackson's blanket. I was almost running out and I really need to keep going with it so that it will be ready in time for the wedding. I can hardly believe it's only a few weeks away now.'

'This year has certainly flown by, but then I suppose we've had a lot going on.' Rex gave a wry chuckle, shaking his head. 'I don't know what I'm supposed to get them for their wedding. What do you buy the couple who have everything?'

'We can say the blanket is a present from us both. How about that?' Ronnie leant over the table and squeezed Rex's hand. 'Besides, I bet they'd say you've already given them the best gift ever by still being here!'

'Well, nothing was going to keep me from a good old shindig at the hall, not even a heart blip. It will take a bit more than that to get rid of me.'

'I'll hold you to that, Rex, and don't go getting any more ideas about taking an early check-out,' she joshed, although any reminders of that time were enough to stir dread in her heart. It had been more than a blip. Ronnie and Rex had been on an extended trip to Europe in the camper van when Rex fell ill in the south of France. He'd been rushed into hospital and underwent emergency treatment while Ronnie struggled to cope with the idea that Rex wasn't infallible as she'd thought. She'd always looked up to Rex, admired him and loved him, and having only just found him again after several years apart, she couldn't bear the thought that she might lose him so soon. Now, her gaze drifted around the café, appreciating the mundane normality of the moment, knowing it could quite easily have been denied them.

'Do you ever think that if we had stayed together we would have been married for over thirty years now?'

'Crikey, there's a thought! You know me, though, Ronnie love. I don't like to look back with regret. What's the point in that? I'm all too aware of the mistakes I made, the bad decisions I took and the people I hurt in the process.' He tilted his head and scrunched up his mouth in apology. 'I was young. Selfish. More interested in the cars and the booze and the next big deal than acting like an adult or being a good husband and father. I can see where I went wrong, how I could have done things differently, but no amount of hand-wringing and soul-searching will make a jot of difference. You can't change the past. All you can do is learn from it.'

Ronnie nodded, observing Rex closely. He might have aged, as indeed she had. His dark chestnut hair, so recognisable in his sons, was entirely grey now and there were laughter lines around his eyes and mouth, his skin a ruddy bronzed colour from all the years spent living in the sun, but he was just as handsome as ever. He still had the ability to set her heart alight and to make her laugh, deep down in her belly, in a way that she had never replicated with anyone else.

'I like how you hold your hands up and admit to your mistakes. Not everyone can do that.' She fell silent for a moment, her lips pursed together. 'Obviously I would if I could, but then, as you know, I don't make mistakes.' Ronnie lifted her chin high, trying to contain the mischievous smile twitching on her lips.

'I wouldn't expect anything less coming from you, Ronnie.' Rex laughed, shaking his head in mock dismay.

Ronnie took a sip from her mug of Earl Grey tea.

'I look at Jackson and Pia and am amazed at how together

they are. They really seem to have the whole life–work balance sorted out. They're focused, responsible, sensible even. We were never like that at their age. Quite the opposite, in fact!'

'I'm not sure we're like that now. Perhaps Jackson has watched and learnt from his parents' mistakes. He's certainly got his head screwed on right and with Pia at his side they make a formidable team.'

'Exactly, he's lucky to have her. We're lucky to have her,' Ronnie added with emphasis, leaning across the table towards Rex. 'She really is the heart of Primrose Hall. I can't tell you how much I'm looking forward to Pia becoming an official member of the family.' She gave a small clap of delight. 'Honestly, I'm counting down the days.'

'I know you are, love,' Rex said with a tolerant smile. Sometimes he thought Ronnie was more excited about the upcoming event than the bride and groom. Seeing her so animated and enthusiastic made him happy, reminding him of the young and beautiful woman he'd married. She was still as alluring with her mass of silver curls that she piled high on her head, her intelligent eyes and sparkling wit, and while it was true that he didn't spend a lot of time mulling over the past, he wouldn't be human if he didn't feel an occasional pang of guilt that he had effectively crushed Ronnie's dreams of a happy marriage of her own.

Rex pulled out his phone from his pocket, scrolling through his messages, before scrabbling around to find his wallet, pulling out his payment card and handing it over to Ronnie.

'If you want to settle up the bill, love, I just need to make a quick phone call. A mate of mine from Spain wants me to put him touch with a mutual friend that he's lost touch with. I'll meet you down on the bench by the old town hall. I'll be ten minutes at the most.'

'You go ahead and do what you need to do, Rex.'

Ronnie had to smile. At one point in time, he might have left and not come back for days, or weeks even. At least these days she could be confident that he would be true to his word. Not 100 per cent, but pretty certain that he would be waiting at the designated time, with a smile on his face. As to that tiny inkling of doubt, born from her bitter experience all those years ago, well, it only added to that frisson of excitement, relief and happiness every time he turned up and fulfilled the promises he made her.

3

'I'm a princess! Wheee!' Little Rosie, her arms out wide, gave a twirl in the middle of the kitchen floor at Primrose Hall, showing off her bridesmaid dress, which had a flowing cream tulle skirt with a lace overlay and a satin tie around the middle.

'You really are,' said her mum, Katy, who was looking on proudly.

'I think the sizing is just right.' Pia was relieved that Rosie had grown since the last fitting and that the dress now sat ideally. 'Stand still for a moment and we can see if we need to make any changes.'

'Noooo! This is my dress.' Rosie hugged her arms around her chest as though she might never take the gown off again. 'I don't want it changed,' she said, looking pleadingly at her mum.

Pia grinned.

'Don't worry, we won't be changing it completely, we just need to make sure it fits you properly, but actually...' Pia managed to catch hold of Rosie before she danced off again, running her hand around the seams of the dress. 'I think it's perfect.'

'I am princess perfect,' sang Rosie, clearly very relieved, standing on tiptoes and pirouetting around the room. 'Ooh, are there cakes?' The little girl spotted the selection of goodies piled high on the table and rushed towards them, which provoked an immediate reaction from Katy and Pia.

'Wait! Let's take that dress off and hang it up. We don't want chocolate down it, do we? And then we can all sit up and have some afternoon tea.'

With Rosie back in normal clothes and appeased by the promise of cake, she sat up on the window bench seat overlooking the garden, occupied by a colouring book and crayons, while her little brother Pip sat alongside her, delving into the plastic box of delights that Pia kept for any visiting children.

Ruby, Pia's sister-in-law, had arrived with her three-month-old baby, Freddie, and her best friend Abbey was also there with little Willow, who was only a couple of months older. Pia thrived on the energy and love that the babies and children brought to the hall and felt privileged that she was a doting auntie to Freddie and a besotted godmother to Willow.

While Pia made the tea, she listened in interestedly to the chatter about breastfeeding, sleep patterns and dirty nappies which made her smile as it was all entirely alien to her, and she marvelled at how quickly both Ruby and Abbey had adapted to their new roles. Pia couldn't imagine being a mother. It was worry enough caring for their two fur babies who she absolutely adored, so she could only imagine the emotions and responsibility involved in caring for a real one.

That wasn't to say she hadn't thought about having children with Jackson. She'd probably spent far too long imagining what their offspring might look like, who they would take after and what names they might give them. Despite Jackson's protestations that he didn't like children, everyone knew it was an act. You only had to see how he was with Rosie, showing a genuine interest in the little girl ever since they'd struck up a bond at the inaugural Christmas carols evening. He'd asked Rosie to come up with some names for the newly acquired donkey and Shetland pony and she had immediately risen to the challenge, plumping for Twinkle and Little Star, which suited the cheeky animals perfectly.

Definitely, thought Pia, her thoughts drifting. Jackson would make a great dad, but she couldn't be distracted by those kinds of thoughts. For the time being, they had enough on their plate with running the hall and preparing for the biggest event on the calendar, their own wedding.

For now, Pia was happy to pick up tips from Ruby and Abbey, making herself available as chief babysitter when required, enjoying being an over-indulgent auntie by spoiling the babies with all sorts of gorgeous outfits and toys, and being an excellent provider of hugs whenever she was able to. Now, with the pot of tea on the table and her visitors helping themselves to the sandwiches, biscuits and cakes that she'd made earlier, Pia took advantage of the opportunity to have a cuddle with Willow.

'Oh, don't you look the part,' said Katy, laughing, seeing Pia rocking from side to side with Willow on her hip. 'I wouldn't get too close to these two though,' she said, gesturing at Ruby and Abbey, 'or else you'll be pregnant before you know it. There's definitely something in the water around these parts.'

The women laughed and Pia, struck by a pang of self-consciousness, shook her head firmly.

'Definitely not. Jackson and I are happy as we are. Although...' Pia inhaled a trace of Willow's baby scent and something stirred deep within her. Her precious goddaughter filled her arms completely, and the little girl's eyes looked up at her, wide and curious. 'I could just spend hours staring at her. She's beautiful. How on earth do you ever get anything done?' she asked her friends.

'I don't,' Ruby laughed. 'It's as much as I can do to get us up, fed, dressed and out of the house some days.'

Abbey nodded her whole-hearted agreement.

'Everyone tells me these moments will pass in a flash so I try to make the most of them while I can, and to hell with the house-work. Luckily, Connor is a complete star and as soon as he gets home from work, he's very hands-on with Freddie and usually takes care of dinner as well,' said Ruby.

Pia had always known her brother would make a great dad. He was kind and capable, and if there was a problem he would invariably try to find a solution to it, in much the same way as their own father had. Connor idolised Freddie and seeing her brother bonding with his son made Pia's heart warm. It was bittersweet knowing how much her mum and dad would have loved to meet their grandchild, but she knew how proud they would be.

'Come and sit down,' urged Abbey. 'I'll put Willow in her car seat. She's due a nap. Let's get these arrangements confirmed.'

With both Willow and Freddie settled in their seats and looking as though they might fall asleep at any moment, Pia sat down at the table with her friends, topping up the cups of tea.

'So,' said Abbey, with a mischievous grin on her face. 'We need to get this hen night sorted. I've been chatting with Ruby and Katy, and we think we've come up with the best plan. So, we're thinking of starting with cocktails, followed by supper, then Magic Mike, and possibly an overnight stay in London.'

Pia's heart sank with every word. She'd been grateful that

Abbey, her matron of honour, had been full of enthusiasm for organising her pre-wedding celebrations, but Pia had been thinking of something much more low key. Pia was experienced in organising big events as part of her job, but even she was surprised at how the arrangements for her marriage to Jackson had taken on a life of their own. She couldn't back out now even if she wanted to...

'Oh, Pia, your face!' Abbey burst into laughter, unable to keep up the pretence any longer. 'You don't fancy Magic Mike then?'

'No, I do not! In any possible sense. Really, I don't want a big fuss. I'm thinking something like this would be fine. Afternoon tea in a nice hotel or something?'

'This is your hen do, Pia, not an old dears' day out. We've got to do something a bit lively, don't you think?'

'Okay, fine, but no male dancers, please. I couldn't bear it.'

'That's a shame,' said Ruby wistfully.

'Honestly, that's all I was coming for,' said Katy.

'I suppose it is Pia's hen do,' said Abbey reluctantly.

'Exactly!' Pia laughed.

'You have to realise we're all married women now with children. We don't get out much. We need to find our thrills where we can.'

'Okay. Well, let's do something local. Maybe we could go to The Three Feathers; they have live music on some dates through the month. We could take over the back bar, that might be fun.'

'Okay, well, leave it to me and I'll make a few enquiries. How many of us will there be?'

Pia rolled off the names that immediately came to mind.

'Well, there's us four, Rhi, Lizzie, Ronnie, Sophie, Ivy, Diane, and I'll have a chat with Wendy to see if she might want to come along.'

Wendy had been her neighbour at Meadow Cottages where

she grew up with Connor. She'd been a good friend to her parents initially and a huge source of support to Pia when she'd been caring for her dad, and then her mum. In some ways, Wendy was like a second mother to Pia, but in recent years, when Wendy suffered poor health and a series of falls, the roles had been reversed and Pia stepped up to help out in whatever way she could, doing Wendy's shopping, and any other jobs that might have needed doing. Most importantly she walked Bertie, Wendy's precious Dalmatian, every day. Not that it had been any hardship for Pia. She loved those times when she could slip Bertie's lead on and head over to Primrose Woods where they would walk amongst the trees and she would stop to chat to other dog owners and their charges. Sometimes she would take a moment to sit on one of the benches by the lake and watch as Bertie splashed about happily at the water's edge. They'd formed a close bond and it was a huge source of relief to Wendy knowing that Bertie was still getting his much-needed exercise each day. When Wendy was taken into hospital after a particularly bad fall and it became clear that she wouldn't be able to return home, Pia immediately offered to take in Bertie, even though she was about to move out of her childhood home herself. In a serendipitous turn of events, Pia, soon after, found the job at Primrose Hall and with it a home for both herself and Bertie.

Now, Pia gave some further thought to the hen night. If Wendy didn't fancy a night out on the tiles, then perhaps Pia would arrange a nice afternoon tea, just the two of them, which, despite her friends' protestations that she needed to live more dangerously, Pia knew they would both enjoy immensely.

'So there should be between ten and twelve of us, I reckon,' said Pia, 'which is a proper party right there.'

'Can I come to the party?' piped up Rosie, who was never shy in coming forward.

'Sorry, Rosie, but this is a grown-ups' party. We'll be going to the pub and they don't allow children in, I'm afraid,' said her mum.

'The real party will take place at the wedding, though,' Pia was quick to reassure the little girl. 'There'll be lots of opportunities for dancing and we can even ask the band to play some of your favourite songs if you like.'

'Yes! Princess songs!'

'Absolutely,' said Pia, not having the first idea what they might be, but making a mental note to have a chat with the band to see if they might be able to throw one or two into their set.

Just as Pia was topping up the pot with some hot water, the back door opened and in wandered Ronnie and Rex, who always cut such a glamorous pair. She turned and greeted them with a knowing smile.

'I'm guessing it was a successful shopping trip,' laughed Pia, catching sight of Rex swaying under the weight of all the carrier bags he was carrying as he staggered into the room. His antics elicited a look of incredulity from Ronnie.

'Take no notice of him. I was very restrained if you must know. We got some black patent leather shoes for Rex, and some other small bits and bobs, and had a lovely lunch. It was a good morning, wasn't it, Rex?'

'It really was,' Rex said with a crafty wink in Pia's direction.

'Come and join us for some tea and cake?' Pia offered, gesturing to the table, which still had plenty of treats on offer.

'Thanks, love, but I'm ready for my afternoon nap. Ronnie's worn me out walking round all those shops.'

'What about you, Ronnie? You'll have some cake?'

'We've been chatting about Pia's hen night,' Ruby ventured.

With Rex taking the opportunity to slip off, Ronnie accepted the invitation and joined the others at the table.

'Well, I'm sure that will be a lot of fun. I never had one. They weren't really a thing back in my day. The whole wedding industry has moved on big time since we were young. We had to make do with a few curled sandwiches and a couple of drinks at the local pubs. Although truthfully, it was more than a couple of drinks.' Ronnie laughed, shaking her head at the memory. 'Rex was pie-eyed even before we got to the ceremony.'

'How long have you been married?' Katy asked, resting her chin on her clasped hands, fascinated by Ronnie's charisma and flamboyance.

'Rex and me? Ha! No, we're not married. Not now. We didn't last very long at all. About five years, I think, before it imploded around us. Both of us were free spirits; we both wanted to do our own thing and were too stubborn to compromise. Then... well, Rex won't mind me saying, but he liked the booze, and all his money went on that and chasing the next big deal, wherever that took him. He broke my heart. And poor Jackson was caught in the crossfire.' Ronnie gave a nonchalant shrug. 'Now, for some reason, fate has brought us together again.'

'Well, you were obviously meant to be together. Even if you did spend all those years apart. Some things are written in the stars,' said Ruby, who'd been hanging on to Ronnie's every word.

'That's what I tell Rex, although he likes to say that he's just been unlucky. He escaped me once, but couldn't manage it a second time.' Pia loved to hear Ronnie's distinctive laughter ringing out around the kitchen.

'We haven't finalised the details for the hen night,' said Abbey, 'but the date is fixed, so pop it in your diary, won't you?'

'Really?' Ronnie looked from Abbey to Pia. 'Does that mean I'm invited? I thought it was for you youngsters only.'

'Absolutely, you're invited. It wouldn't be the same without you, Ronnie,' Pia said.

'In that case, I'd be delighted. Fancy getting to my age and never having been to a hen night. There really is a first time for everything! Ooh, I'm just wondering... will there be naked men?'

'No!' said Pia emphatically as her friends fell into peals of laughter around her.

4

'Well, this is lovely,' sighed Sophie, looking all around her as she took a seat at the table shown to them by the waiter in the window of the tapas restaurant. Tom sat down opposite her and fixed her with that smile, the one that reached his dark brown eyes and made her tummy flip. She peered out through the old sash windows along the length of the cobbled alleyway off the high street, marvelling at the pretty sight of the shops lit up with strings of white fairy lights. Inside, the aromas of garlic, tomatoes and onions wafted around them, stirring Sophie's appetite. It was her first time here, although she'd heard nothing but good reports about the food.

After ordering drinks, a glass of fizz for Sophie and a low-alcohol beer for Tom, they chatted as they always did, without any awkwardness, jumping from one subject to another as the conversation led them. It was one of the things that she'd liked about Tom when she'd first met him, over Christmas lunch at Primrose Hall, an impromptu invitation from Pia on the day. She'd been seated next to him at the table, and they'd laughed and chatted as if they'd known each other for years, no doubt helped by the free-flowing wine and with zero expectation of ever seeing each other again. When she did run into him again, a few months later, when he took over the running of the Sunday craft fairs at the stables at Primrose Hall, where Sophie had a regular pitch selling the silver jewellery she made in her spare time, she was surprised at how easy it had been to pick up where they'd left off, quickly re-establishing the connection they'd made. That connection had turned into an easy friendship, which had seen them enjoying convivial nights in the pub, sometimes just the two of them, sometimes with the other traders, walks over at Primrose Woods and impromptu suppers at Sophie's cosy cottage.

On discovering they had both recently come out of long-term relationships and were enjoying their newfound single status with no inclination on either of their parts to change the status quo, it had given them something else to bond over. It had also removed the pressure of them ever being anything other than good friends. Which had been all well and good until Sophie found herself thinking about Tom much more regularly than someone might normally think about a friend, and recognising how she looked forward to seeing him again with increasing anticipation. She wasn't to know that Tom had been struggling with his own feelings, not wanting to voice them for fear of jeopardising their close friendship. It was over the following weeks as they opened up to each other and showed their vulnerability that the pair of them were able to admit that their feelings for each other had grown in a way that neither of them had expected. It had been a delightful revelation to them both. They'd agreed that they would take things slowly and see how things evolved as they continued to get to know each other better.

Now, observing Tom from across the table, Sophie couldn't help a smile from spreading across her face. For her, it was so much more than simply enjoying their conversations; it was the sensation of being totally relaxed and at ease in his company, as though she didn't need to try too hard. She could simply be herself, and spending time with Tom always lifted her spirits. The fact that his broad shoulders, mussed-up brown hair and dark sparkling eyes made him very easy on the eye only served as a bonus.

'Should we have a toast?' Tom asked a little later when the waiter poured glasses of wine for them both.

'Definitely! What are we drinking to? Apart from us, of course. And the fact that it's a Wednesday?'

'Well, actually, I do have a bit of news that I suppose is worth celebrating.'

'That sounds intriguing. What is it?' Sophie leant forward in her seat, resting her arms on the table, her hands clasped in anticipation.

'I've been offered a job in pharmaceutical sales management. You know, like a proper job,' he said, his mouth twisting in a self-deprecating smile.

'Really? That's great. I didn't realise... I thought...' A myriad thoughts rushed through Sophie's mind. She'd always got the impression from Tom that he didn't want to go back to his previous high-powered career. He'd given it up before she'd met him, when he discovered the truth about his parentage, and had taken some time out to come to terms with his newfound reality. As well as turning his back on his job, he'd broken up with his long-term girlfriend, moving out of their home together to start over again. That's when he'd turned up in Rex's life, announcing the news that he was his long-lost son, which had been some-thing of a shock to Rex, and then to Jackson too when he discov-ered he had a half-brother he never knew existed.

Tom had navigated that difficult period by simplifying some

other areas of his life. He'd taken on a variety of odd jobs including working at an estate agents assisting with the viewings, doing some shifts at a builders' merchants and then helping out at Primrose Hall with the craft Sundays. Practical work that he didn't need to think too hard about. He enjoyed the physicality of those roles and the fact that it took his mind off everything else that might be going on in his world, but the financial rewards fell far short of his previous career. Tom took on further responsibility at the hall when Jackson was out of action due to his motorcycle accident earlier in the summer, but he'd always known that it would be a short-term arrangement and with Jackson's recovery well on the way, it was only a matter of time before his services there would no longer be required.

'I think it's probably about time.' Tom shrugged, looking thoughtful. 'I've known for a while now that I would need to find something more permanent and secure. I've had a great time, effectively being my own boss these last few months, but I don't want to be stuck in my poky flat for much longer. I want to get back on the property ladder, put down some roots. And that means joining the corporate rat race again.'

'Right,' said Sophie, matching Tom's smile, but inside a pang of concern flared in her chest. What would it mean for their fledgling relationship? They'd been enjoying spending time with each other and, of course, she got to see him every fortnight at the craft fairs. Was he intending to give up his role there as well? 'Congratulations! Here's to your brilliant new career!' she said, raising a glass to him, pushing her doubts to one side.

'Well, not quite a new career.' He chinked his glass up against hers. 'But a new start in the old career. Probably a bit overdue too.'

'And I just know you'll make a huge success of it.'

She was saying all the right things, but selfishly Sophie could only think about what it would mean for them as a couple. She'd taken for granted him being around the corner. It meant that they could arrange to meet spontaneously after work for a walk or a drink.

'Where will you be based?' she asked, as casually as she could muster.

'The head office is in Manchester, but like before I'll be pretty much on the road for most of the time.'

'So lots of travelling then?'

'Yep' – he gave a nonchalant shrug – 'but I'm used to that.'

'And what about the craft fairs? Will you still be looking after those?' she couldn't stop herself from asking.

'I'll certainly see out the rest of the season, but it would make sense for someone else to take over the reins next year. Although I've not had that conversation yet with Jackson. I was waiting until I get the formal offer through so...' Tom made an action of zipping his lips closed. 'I'm sure he'll be fine about it.'

'Well, I'm pleased for you, Tom, but I'll miss you at the Sunday craft fairs and I know the other traders will too.'

Hadn't he told her once that if he were to get another nine-to-five job, he would still want to carry on working at the stables on a Sunday? That they were such a tight-knit community that he couldn't imagine a time when he wouldn't want to be a part of it?

'You're bound to miss us all too,' she said lightly.

'Of course. Some more than others, especially,' he said, reaching a hand across the table to take hers. 'You know how much I've enjoyed those Sundays. I've made some great friends and we've had some good times together, but you know things don't stay the same for ever.' He quirked an eyebrow. 'But listen, you won't be able to get rid of me that easily. I'll be staying in touch with everyone and turning up at the pub for the socials.'

'I'm pleased to hear it.'

Staying in touch. That sounded far too casual for Sophie's liking. She couldn't help thinking how Tom's new job was bound to impact on their relationship. He'd be working long hours, travelling up and down the country and knowing Tom and his strong work ethic, his focus would quite rightly shift on to his new role. Who knew what opportunities would open up to him, the places he would go and the people he might meet? Already Sophie's head was taunting her with images of late-night business meetings and glamorous work colleagues. She gave an imperceptible shake of her head to rid herself of the ridiculous thoughts.

'I couldn't have taken this step last year. My head was too full of everything else that was going on. I'm in a much better place now. I've found my family and I feel good about that. They're not going anywhere and I'm never going to lose that connection with them, but I'm ready to move on in other areas of my life now. I feel as though I've found myself again.' He took a sip from his glass of wine, looking thoughtful, his dark eyes, glistening with excitement, lingering on hers from over the top of his glass. Had she been just another part of Tom's recovery process, a friend to see him through a few difficult months, a summer that they would look back on fondly, that had been an enjoyable distraction, but only ever destined to last a few months? In all his new plans there was no mention of her and how she might fit into them.

Perhaps this was Tom's subtle way of telling her that he would be moving on... without her.

5

It was a bitterly cold November evening and the bonfire built by Jackson, Tom, Mateo and Frank, from a huge amount of kindling, wood, branches and twigs, all collected from the grounds of the hall, was now ablaze, its orange crackling flames reaching up into the dark night sky over Primrose Hall. The glow from the fire and the flickering and snapping of the flames was mesmerising and the scent of wood smoke mingled with the tempting aromas of hot dogs and candy floss from the food stalls. A big crowd of visitors had gathered to watch the fireworks and people stood in huddles with their friends and families, chatting and laughing, enjoying the sights and soaking up the atmosphere.

Last year Pia had been concerned about going ahead with the event. She'd been worried that the fireworks would scare the local wildlife, not to mention Little Star and Twinkle, and Bertie too, but Jackson had gone out of his way to reassure her and had managed to source some silent fireworks. Pia had been doubtful about how or if they would work, so she had made sure that the animals were safely housed, and arranged for someone to sit with them in case they were spooked, but she needn't have worried.

The display had turned out to be as spectacular as any fireworks she had ever seen but without the accompanying loud screeches and bangs. The feedback from their visitors had been just as positive and so it had meant that she'd been able to look forward to this year's event with much more enthusiasm.

Now, as she snuggled up against Jackson, they watched the display above them, gasping at the sight of colourful flashes zigzagging across the sky and rainbow trails raining down over their heads. Children stood with sparklers, waving them in the air, their little faces filled with delight at seeing the twinkling lights tracing patterns in front of them. Earlier, Jackson had judged the guy competition and this year's entries had far surpassed last year's in quantity and in creativity. Pia suspected that many of the parents had given a helping hand to the creations, but it didn't matter because they were all brilliant and had provided a great deal of conversation and laughter to the assembled visitors. All the money raised from the entry fees would go to a local charity that Jackson supported, a drop-in centre for disadvantaged and troubled teens, a cause close to his heart.

'Hello, sweetheart.' Rex came up on the other side and slipped an arm around her waist. 'The pair of you have put on another great evening.'

'It is, right? I'm really pleased with the turnout, which is even better than last year. You couldn't persuade Ronnie to come over?'

'No, she insists it's because she wants to look after Bertie and Teddy back at the ranch, but she's absolutely in her element, in the warm, with her glass of red wine, watching the fireworks through the windows.'

'I think she's probably got the right idea,' said Pia, shivering. 'It's freezing out here!'

'I wouldn't have missed it for the world.' Rex rubbed his gloveless hands together. 'I bumped into some of my old mates earlier. I think a lot of them thought I'd popped my clogs,' he said wryly.

'Well, I'm glad you proved them wrong, and you're still here to put them straight.'

Pia spotted Rhi and Luke standing in the crowd, their arms wrapped around each other, and gave them a wave.

* * *

'Hey!' Rhi waved through the crowds at Pia, who was standing between two of the Moody men, Rex and Jackson. Even at a distance, in the half-light, the familial resemblance was obvious.

'They're looking well,' Rhi whispered to Luke, who nodded, his main focus taken by the fireworks currently lighting up the sky.

Rhi enjoyed coming up to the hall because there was always such an electric atmosphere, and invariably she would bump into people from the pub or some friends. Already they'd stopped to chat to Katy and Brad, and their children, and Lizzie and Bill too. She'd seen her friend Abbey as well with her husband Sam, and little Willow, who was wrapped up in a cute pink snowsuit, her wide eyes and little red nose just visible beneath all her layers.

'We're so lucky to have this on our doorstep. It always reminds me of that first Christmas when we came for the carols. Do you remember?'

Luke turned to look at her and his deep blue eyes were even more intensely blue, offset against the dark November sky.

'I do. That was when we first properly started going out together, right?'

'Yes! And I can remember being worried that you were

moving away to start a new job and thinking I might lose you. I wanted to spend every single moment with you in case I never saw you again.'

Their attention was distracted by a fizzing whoosh of colour that exploded in the air, before Luke pulled Rhi into his arms and kissed her on the forehead.

'I would never have let that happen. I was already completely smitten by that stage.'

Rhi could hardly believe so much had happened in such a short space of time. She'd met Luke at work but at the time she'd been romantically involved with Jason, one of the senior managers, not realising he was actually engaged to someone else. As she soon discovered, to her shock, he'd been intending to marry Abbey only a few weeks later. The revelation had caused both women, who were unknown to each other at the time, a great deal of heartbreak and upset, but out of that trauma and their shared anger towards Jason, an unlikely bond had been formed. It wasn't long before they were congratulating themselves on having a lucky escape from their slimeball 'ex', and soon Jason was all but forgotten and the new friendship between Rhi and Abbey had continued to grow.

At the same time, Rhi had grown close to Luke, who had always been a funny, sometimes annoying presence at work. When she walked out on her job, not wanting to see Jason ever again, Luke had kept in touch and provided a sympathetic ear when she was at her lowest point. His blond-haired, blue-eyed charm, combined with a genuine kindness and decency, soon won Rhi over.

'When was that, two years ago?'

'Luke!' She elbowed him in the ribs. 'Yes! Two years ago. You can't have forgotten?'

'Nah, never,' he said, fixing her with those deep blue eyes

which held the power to make her forgive him anything. 'It's just... wow... two years, eh?'

'I know. Sometimes it feels as though I've known you forever and then other times it's like it all happened yesterday.'

'Right, two years, though.' Luke nodded, as though he could hardly believe it himself. 'We should celebrate. Let's go out to that nice Italian in town next weekend.'

'How lovely,' she said, looking forward to it already. Her gaze drifted up into the night sky, goosebumps from the cold chill in the air and the beauty of the surroundings, sending a ripple of anticipation down her spine. Luke pulled her firmly into his embrace and cupped her face in his gloved hands.

'I love you, Rhi, you do know that?'

She would never tire of hearing those words from Luke, but standing here in a magical spot that held such special memories, they sounded even more enticing.

'I love you too, Luke.'

Back in the warmth of the kitchen at Primrose Hall, the aromas of jacket potatoes, fried onions and hot dogs wafted in the air. Ronnie saw to drinks for everyone, insisting they all tried her special hot chocolate, which was made to order, the smooth silky chocolate concoction offered with a variety of scrummy extras including whipped cream, marshmallows with flaked chocolate on top and even a slug of Baileys for those who wanted it.

'What a fantastic evening,' Tom beamed.

'I loved it,' agreed Sophie. 'I'd never heard of silent fireworks before, but what a great idea, and you would never know the difference just watching them.'

'What I like is seeing all the kids having fun,' Jackson said, going across to the drinks fridge to pull out a bottle of white wine, placing it on the table. 'When I was a kid, fireworks night was a big thing. They used to have a bonfire over at the rec and me and my mates would make a guy, nothing like the ones we saw tonight, and we would drag them round the village hoping to cadge a few quid off the villagers. Trouble is, they were all a bit suspicious of us louts.'

'That's hardly surprising, you were a right little troublemaker then,' said Ronnie, shaking her head indulgently.

'Yeah, but look at him now. He's not done too badly for himself, has he?'

Jackson gave a nonchalant shrug, the half-smile on his lips suggesting that he appreciated Pia's support.

'I really hope that our annual bonfire night celebrations might have a similar resonance to some of those kids that turned up tonight,' said Jackson. 'That it might give them something to look back on fondly and to look forward to next year, somewhere they can meet up with their mates and something they can get involved in, through the guy competition.'

'I think you could be on to something there,' said Rex. 'Everyone seemed to have a whale of a time tonight, especially the youngsters.'

Ronnie placed the hot dishes from the oven onto the table and urged everyone to get stuck in. There was coleslaw, salads and chunks of fresh bread to accompany the sausages and burgers, and after being out in the cold night air they were all ravenous, so they quickly filled their plates with the delicious food.

'Ah, you do realise what today is, don't you?' Ronnie asked, finally sitting down to join the others.

'Err... is that a trick question, Ronnie?'

'No, I mean obviously it's bonfire night, but it was also this day last year that Tom came to the hall for the first time. Do you remember?'

'Oh, God,' said Pia, 'how can I forget?' She grimaced exaggeratedly, before breaking into laughter. Sophie looked between Tom, Jackson and Pia for clarification.

'It was emotionally tense at the time. It was our first ever bonfire night event and, like tonight, it had been a real success. We came back to the house and Tom was here, unexpectedly, and I suppose it was the first time that we'd all come together as a family.' Pia gestured to Rex, Ronnie and Jackson. 'It should have been a wonderful time, but there was a bit of a misunderstanding and...'

'What Pia is trying to say is that I threw my toys out of the pram and nearly decked my brother who I'd only just met, so we got off to a really good start, didn't we, Tom?' said Jackson.

Tom nodded and grinned, and in that moment, the family resemblance between the three Moody men had never been more apparent.

'It was a baptism of fire, that's for sure. Dad invited me along, but I have to admit I was taken aback, and I guess a little intimidated too, to discover that my little brother had his own country estate. Can you imagine? I thought, hell, I'm never going to be able to invite my family back to my little flat. Thank goodness for Pia and Ronnie, though,' Tom explained to Sophie. 'Somehow they managed to smooth things out between us and, well, look at us now.'

'I know, it's great, isn't it,' said Rex, looking around the table at his family. 'Who would have thought it, eh? For years, I made the mistake of thinking that life was out there somewhere, that I had to chase after it, when all the time it was here with the people that I love.' He cast a glance in Ronnie's direction.

'Rex Moody, you're getting soft in your old age!'

'Very likely,' he said, chuckling.

Jackson went round and filled up the wine glasses.

'So here's to family and friends, and to us all being here for a bonfire feast next year and for years to come, too!'

Pia felt the hairs prickle on her arms as she joined in the toast. The events at the hall which had proven so popular with their visitors were family occasions too, invariably culminating in everyone sitting around the kitchen table after all the guests had gone home, swapping stories about the people they'd met and the conversations they had.

'Now, Tom, you'll be around tomorrow, won't you?'

'Yep, I was going to help with the big clear-up before getting started on the set-up for the workshops at the weekend.'

'Good,' said Jackson, 'because there was something I wanted to talk to you about.'

'Fine,' said Tom, nodding keenly, aware of the slightest hint of trepidation inside. He supposed tomorrow would be a good as time as any. It would be the ideal opportunity, in fact, because there was some news he needed to share with Jackson too.

6

'And this is something you really want to do?' Tom cringed inwardly, hearing the note of disbelief in Jackson's voice.

The brothers were over in the refurbished stables at Primrose Hall where the Sunday craft fairs were held, rearranging the chairs and tables in readiness for the weekend.

'Yes,' said Tom with as much conviction as he could muster.

It was the second time in the space of less than a week that he had delivered his news and received a less than enthusiastic response.

'Well, to be fair, I didn't see this coming.' Jackson raked a hand through his chestnut hair, biting on the edge of his lip. 'Obviously I'm not going to stand in the way of you following your dreams, but I can't say that I'm not disappointed.'

Tom gave a wry smile. Had he imagined a note of sarcasm in his brother's words? After all, they both knew that while Tom's job sounded a good proposition with a great salary, company car, pension and bonus, it was hardly the stuff of dreams.

'I feel I'm ready to get back out there and do what I'm experienced and trained to do. It's definitely time. I want to find somewhere else to live, somewhere bigger, with outdoor space where I can put down some roots.'

Jackson had never seen Tom's place. Probably because Tom never invited anyone round there. His small flat was always intended as a short-term rental, a stop gap after moving out of the house he'd shared with Anna, his ex. It suited his needs initially, it was simply a place to put down his head of a night, but he'd outgrown it long ago. Funny to think that Sophie's response to his news had been lukewarm as well when she was the catalyst behind his decision to go back into the corporate world.

Spending time with her these last few months had been an eye-opener. He hadn't been looking for a romantic connection, but somehow she'd managed to get beneath his skin so that he spent far too much time thinking about her, anticipating when they might be able to meet again. He'd realised he was ready to put the past behind him and take a chance on this new connection to see where it took them. He enjoyed the suppers he'd shared with Sophie at her cottage in Wishwell, but he was in no position to repay the favour and he felt bad about that. They'd gone out to restaurants instead, but he missed not having a place of his own where he could entertain friends. He wanted to be in a position where he could offer some kind of future to Sophie, but that would only happen if he had a decent job to fund his lifestyle.

'So what does this mean for the hall, and in particular the stables?'

'I don't start the new job until January so obviously I'm on board to help with all the events leading up to Christmas. As far as the stables are concerned, whilst I love all the traders and being a part of those Sundays, it probably makes more sense for me to hand the reins to someone else. I don't want to be in a position where I'm letting you down. It's feasible that I might need to be at the other end of the country for a 9 a.m. start on a Monday morning which would mean me travelling on a Sunday. Besides, the stables are in good shape now, so it won't be difficult to bring someone else in to take over that role.'

'You've got it all worked out.' Jackson pressed his lips together.

'Well, we both knew it was only ever meant as a short-term arrangement, so now is probably as good a time as any to move on.'

Tom had been glad to take up the position at the stables. It fitted in well with his other commitments and he quickly became a central part of the team, his presence proving indispensable when Jackson had his motorcycle accident in the summer. Worryingly, in the first twenty-four hours, it had been touch and go as to whether Jackson would pull through, so it was a huge relief that the surgeons were able to stabilise his fractured pelvis. With Jackson's favourite event on the calendar, the classic car show, happening the following weekend, the accident couldn't have come at a worse time, but Tom stepped up to fill Jackson's shoes and, along with Pia, put on a fantastic summer show that surpassed even the previous year's events.

Unfortunately, Jackson had to undergo further surgery and intensive physiotherapy, which was still ongoing, but if you didn't know, or didn't notice the slight limp to his gait, then you would never guess that he'd been in a bad accident. Only the occasional stab of pain or his inability to stand on his feet for long hours at a time, which was a huge source of frustration to him, indicated that there was anything wrong. Jackson was back in his domain, overseeing his estate on a daily basis, managing the latest project or preparing for the next event at the hall. Tom was surplus to requirements and while he was grateful to Jackson for offering him work when he'd needed it, he didn't want to rely on his ongoing charity.

Now as the pair of them moved tables and chairs around the barn in preparation for the craft workshops at the weekend, Tom got the distinct impression that Jackson wasn't best pleased, and for the life of him, Tom couldn't work out why. He honestly thought he would have been relieved to get Tom off the payroll now that Jackson was back working almost full time.

'Obviously I can help out on the occasional weekend if you need me,' he suggested. 'I mean, I won't be leaving you in the lurch. Will I?'

Tom noticed the few moments of hesitation from Jackson.

'No. Not at all. You need to do what's right for you.' Jackson turned his back to move some more furniture. 'We managed before, and we'll manage again. I had thought you enjoyed working here, though,' he threw out as an aside.

'I did. I do! You know that. I've loved every moment, but... hey, Jackson.' When he didn't turn round to face his brother, Tom caught up with him and grabbed his arm. 'I didn't think this would be such an issue. I thought...' Jackson shrugged away his touch.

Was it too much to hope that his brother might be pleased for him? Tom shook off the worm of annoyance that spread in his gut. Jackson was a control freak, used to doing things on his terms, for people falling into line with his plans and getting his own way. Surely though he could appreciate and understand why Tom needed to make decisions to secure his own future.

Tom bit on his lip. He couldn't help wondering if Jackson would have welcomed him into his life quite so readily if Rex hadn't been on the scene. Certainly Ronnie and Pia had been instrumental in persuading Jackson to keep an open mind about his new half-brother and to give their relationship time to build, especially when Jackson was suspicious of Tom's intentions.

It had been a faltering start to their relationship but despite the obstacles, they had found some common ground in the following months. They discovered they shared a love of the great outdoors, and also enjoyed regular competitive games of squash. Tom took pleasure in being objectively the better player, although Jackson was on a mission to lessen the gap in Tom's winning streak. They could rib each other, were still debating who was the better-looking brother and could enjoy a heart-to-heart over a pint of beer. They might not have spent their formative years together, but Tom had dared to hope that they were making up for lost time and building a bond.

Hell, Jackson had even asked Tom to be his best man at his upcoming wedding. Surely the brothers' relationship wasn't so shaky that it might be threatened by Tom calling the shots for once. Was their relationship only valid when Tom played a supporting role to Jackson?

Now he suppressed a sigh.

'Anyway, what was that thing you wanted to talk to me about?'

'Oh, that.' Jackson batted it away with a shrug. 'That's really not important now.'

But Tom had come to know Jackson well enough by now to know that it was probably more important than his brother was letting on.

7

'What's the matter?'

Pia had been preparing a mushroom risotto when Jackson wandered into the kitchen from the office. The dogs, curled up in their basket beside the Aga, gave small wags of their tails to acknowledge his arrival, but they were far too snuggly to leave their beds at this time of day. Jackson made himself a gin and tonic and poured Pia a glass of white wine, but she'd known instinctively that something was troubling him. Jackson's moods preceded him. It was always a bit of a joke between the others at the hall that they knew how Jackson was feeling before he'd even entered a room or uttered a word. Right now, Pia could tell from the set of his jaw and the heavy sighs coming from his direction that he wasn't in the best frame of mind.

'It's Tom. He's only gone and found himself a full-time job. Pharmaceutical sales apparently.' Jackson shook his head as though it was a complete mystery to him. 'We won't be able to rely on his help at the hall next year.'

'Really?' Pia's brow furrowed as she turned to look at Jackson.

'He didn't mention anything to me. He'll still be looking after the stables, though?'

'No. He'll carry on for the rest of the season, but he thinks it's for the best' – those words were emphasised by air quotes from Jackson – 'that he steps down from his role so that he doesn't have to let us down further along the line.'

'That's a shame. I can see why you're so disappointed.' Although Pia suspected Jackson had taken Tom's news as a personal snub. 'We've come to depend on him up at the stables and the changes he's implemented, setting up the workshops, well, he's kind of made it his own. The traders will miss him, that's for sure, and then there's Sophie as well. I wonder what she thinks about all this.' Pia was thinking aloud. 'I don't suppose it was an easy decision for him, but he must have good reasons for finding something more permanent.'

Now it was Pia's turn to give a shake of her head. To be honest, she was struggling to understand his decision too. Tom was a key member of the team, especially so in recent months and she'd thought, or rather hoped, that he might stay on as a permanent member of staff.

'Who knows? I can't see why he would want to rejoin the corporate rat race. It doesn't make sense to me. I just wish he'd come and told me when he was thinking about it rather than presenting it as a done deal.'

Pia wandered over to Jackson and rubbed a consoling hand over his back.

'I'm guessing he wasn't interested in your offer then? Of bringing him on board on a full-time basis?'

'Well, I never asked him. Not when he told me about the new job. There didn't seem any point.'

Pia went back across to the stove and added some more stock

to the pan, stirring all the while, a waft of delicious aromas meeting her nostrils.

Jackson's disappointment was palpable. She knew how much he'd come to rely on Tom's help over recent months, but it was more than just practical and physical help Tom provided. He'd also been a sounding board for Jackson's ideas, someone he'd been able to confide in. Jackson was an intensely private person who rarely opened up to anyone other than Pia. When Rex had suffered his heart attack earlier in the year, it was Tom who had instinctively rushed out to France to be with their dad and Ronnie, to help support them through Rex's treatment and to take care of their travel arrangements home. Jackson had wanted to jump on the first flight out there himself, but he was confined to a hospital bed with a broken pelvis at the time, and although he didn't seem to think that should thwart him in any way, Pia managed to persuade him that he needed to concentrate his energies on his own recovery. Knowing that Tom was there to step into his shoes had been such a relief to Jackson.

'Maybe it's just a financial decision,' said Pia, trying to placate Jackson. 'I guess working all those casual jobs doesn't add up to the same as a proper full-time job.'

'No,' said Jackson, dismissing that idea out of hand immediately. 'If it had been about the money, he would have said something. Jeez...' He ran a hand through his wayward chestnut hair, making it even messier, if that was possible. 'I suppose I should have expected something like this.'

'Something like what?' Pia asked, looking up from where she was serving spoonfuls of creamy risotto into bowls. She took them over and placed them down on the table.

'Family. Letting you down.'

'Don't be like that. It's not personal, I'm sure.' She grated fresh parmesan onto the top of the bowls, followed by a twist of black pepper. 'It's the best thing to have ever happened around here, you reconnecting with your dad and finding out you have a brother in Tom, but I suppose it's only natural that he has his own life to lead.' Her mouth twisted and her brow furrowed as she shook her head at him, reading his expression. 'You're lucky, Jackson. What I wouldn't do to have my mum and dad still here, sharing meals around the kitchen table, chatting and laughing together.'

Jackson gave her a sideways glance, widening his eyes, before turning his attention to the food in front of him.

'Especially after the year we've had,' Pia went on. 'Almost losing your dad and your terrible accident too. It could so easily have been a different outcome for you both. You have to make the most of the time you do have with your family because you can't take any of it for granted. Having Tom in your life is a bonus. The brother you never knew about. You should do everything to hang on to that.'

Jackson fixed her with an expression that she was familiar with, one that told her he wasn't really listening to what she had to say. He'd already made his mind up on the matter.

'Okay, I get all that,' he said dismissively, and she chastised him with a look. 'But my experience of family is very different to yours, as you well know. Don't get me wrong, I'm grateful that we're all back together, I'm not a completely heartless bastard, but they're my family. I'm allowed to moan about them. And sorry, but I do feel as though Tom has let me down. I went out of my way to find work for him and to try and make him feel part of the family and now he just throws it back in my face.'

Pia suppressed a heavy sigh, taking a moment to think so that she didn't snap at Jackson or say something she might regret. He'd had a troubled relationship with his parents and still bore the scars from his teenage years when both his mum and dad separately abandoned him, his dad absent from his life for years and Ronnie for months at a time when they both went off to pursue their own needs and desires. Free spirits, that's how Ronnie always described herself and Rex, but there had definitely been a fall-out as far as Jackson was concerned. Even though he'd gone on to make a big success of his life professionally, obtaining huge material rewards, he still struggled with his emotions when it came to dealing with Rex and Ronnie. There was a part of him, Pia suspected, that was vulnerable to the idea that he might still be abandoned by his own parents, even at his advanced age. Tom arriving on the scene had stirred all sorts of feelings for Jackson: antipathy initially, followed by suspicion and then begrudging acceptance before a growing bond had developed that neither of the brothers had really expected.

'You're taking this personally when I'm sure Tom would never have intended it that way. He's got his own life to lead, his own career path to follow, but that doesn't mean it has to impact on your personal relationship.'

'We'll see.' Jackson didn't sound convinced and Pia hoped that this wouldn't drive a wedge between the brothers. You didn't get to achieve Jackson's level of success without being single-minded, making things happen by sheer determination and will. While those traits were admirable in a business setting, they didn't transfer so readily into his personal relationships. However much he might think he knew what was best for other people, Jackson couldn't always influence his friends and family to act in the way he might want them to.

'Trust me.' Pia pushed her bowl to one side and reached out a hand to Jackson's arm. 'It will all work out for the best. And it's not as though you're going to lose touch with Tom. He'll be around just as much as he is now.' She paused for a moment, looking into his dark eyes. 'Sometimes I think you expect too much of people.'

'And what's wrong with that?'

'Only that it leaves you open to disappointment. You have to accept other people's foibles, their decisions and choices. We all have our funny ways, some more than others,' she said, with a pointed look in his direction.

Jackson scrunched his mouth and shook his head, a smile reaching the corners of his lips.

'When did you get to be so wise?'

Pia smiled and shrugged.

Wise, probably not, but sensible, yes. It wouldn't be the first time she'd been described that way and she was never certain it was intended as a compliment.

'And I can always look after the stables again,' she added. 'You know how much I enjoyed doing it before. I'm down there most Sundays anyway.'

'Yes, but it's one thing popping down as and when, because you want to catch up with everyone, but it's another proposition having the responsibility of doing that job every fortnight. Especially as we'll be married by then.' He ran a finger along her jawline. 'We'll be wanting to do old married couple stuff on a Sunday afternoon.'

Pia's laughter rang out.

'Like what?'

'Like having a sumptuous roast dinner with...'

'With the family?'

'If we have to,' said Jackson, with a roll of his eyes. 'But I was thinking just the two of us, Sunday lunch, a couple of glasses of red wine, an old film on the telly and an afternoon nap on the sofas with the dogs.'

'Just like we do pretty much every Sunday now then?' she teased him.

'Yeah, but obviously as a married couple it will take on much more significance.'

'Well, I hope you haven't got plans to turn into a pipe and slippers type as soon as we're married.' Pia giggled, but it wouldn't be the first time that she'd wondered how things might change once they were wed. Theirs had been the definition of a whirlwind romance. In the space of eighteen months, she'd taken on a job at Primrose Hall, moved into the guest accommodation, rekindled her romance with Jackson, been upgraded to the master suite, set up several new events at the hall, adopted another fur baby, navigated the interesting family dynamics at the hall, nursed Jackson after his accident, and got engaged. Their wedding at the end of the year was the culmination of a hectic and busy period. Neither of them had had time to draw breath and sometimes it seemed as though events had run away with them.

Life with Jackson was anything but dull, but then it had always been that way. It was one of the things that had first attracted her to him when she was a young girl. Jackson had a reputation for being a wild child, for burning up the local country lanes on his motorbike, for rarely turning up at school and for setting teenage girls' hearts alight. She'd been swept away by his charisma and swagger, relishing those moments sitting astride the back of his bike, the wind lifting her hair, making her feel vibrant and alive, and so entirely in love with her bad boy. She wasn't to know then that he would suddenly leave the village, following a motorcycle accident which resulted in the death of one of his best friends. He told none of this to Pia, gave no explanation as to why he left without so much as a goodbye. She was heartbroken and carried that hurt and anger for years, not realising when she turned up for the job at Primrose Hall that the new owner was none other than her teenage boyfriend. A smile spread across her lips. It was funny to think how far they'd come. She'd been reluctant to have anything to do with Jackson again, but she was right out of options, needing a job and a place to live urgently, and when he offered her both of those things, she'd been in no position to say no. Now, they were on the cusp of making a lifelong commitment to each other and Pia only hoped that there would be no further big surprises along the way.

In many ways, he was still that same wayward teenager, doing his own thing, carving his own path, and while he had let down some of his defences, certainly for her, that vulnerable, misunderstood young man wasn't far beneath the surface. His sensitivity was palpable even if she suspected that others might not view him in the same light, and that fact tugged on her heart.

'See, you've done it again.' Jackson interrupted her musings. 'You've made me feel better without even trying to. As long as we've got each other, then all the other stuff, well, it doesn't really matter.' He tipped up her chin and she leant forward, his mouth a magnetic draw, placing a kiss there.

Accepting Jackson's marriage proposal had been the easiest decision she'd ever made; in fact, she hadn't thought twice. She'd answered instinctively, joyfully, and only afterwards wondered if it was the right decision, for them both. She was under no illusions that being married to her mercurial, maverick husband-to-be would be easy. It would be an adventure, filled with challenges, but it was one, she hoped, she was more than ready for.

8

Sophie had been looking out for Tom all morning, her eyes on the double doors to the stables as people came in and out. The traders were setting up their units for what promised to be an especially busy Sunday, as people's attentions turned towards Christmas and gift buying. She always felt a delicious sense of anticipation as she unpacked her jewellery and placed the pieces on her display stands.

After all the nights and weekends she'd spent alone in her makeshift studio at the back of her house perfecting her craft, working on items that would never see the light of day because of imperfections, or designs that simply didn't work out, she felt a huge sense of accomplishment seeing her finished products all together. Selling her wares including silver necklaces, bangles, earrings and bracelets at the stables made all those hours working long into the evenings worthwhile. She'd recently set up an online store as well and had sold a handful of items, which she was hoping would only increase as she widened her range of goods on offer. As much as that was incredibly satisfying, nothing could beat the feeling of meeting her buyers face to face at the

stables, some of whom were now repeat customers. It was interesting to hear which of her items they particularly liked and who
they intended them for, their mum, or a friend, or a much-loved
aunt. It stirred her creativity and helped her to decide which
items to add to the new collections.

Another huge source of inspiration was the beautiful
surroundings of Primrose Woods. She only needed to look out of
the windows at the stables to drink in the breathtaking scenery:
the redwoods, the oak and monkey puzzle trees standing tall in
the distance and the lush green lawns and meadows surrounding
the hall and stables. On every visit Sophie would spot something
new, a different bush that had come into bloom, or pretty wild-
flowers shooting up in a palette of colours. Now, the colours had
turned into burnished bronzes and golds, the woods covered in a
carpet of crunchy leaves.

'Hey, how are you?' Sophie turned at the sound of Tom's
distinctive voice, something lifting inside of her as she snagged
eyes on him. He was tall and broad, and with his chestnut hair
that curled on his collar and brown sparkling eyes, undeniably
handsome. Ordinarily, away from the busy comings and goings in
the stables, she would have stepped in for a hug and a kiss, but
Sophie was aware that Tom was preoccupied with the preparations for the day's events, and besides, she suddenly felt self-
conscious in his presence.

'Good,' she said, pressing on a smile. 'Well, if I'm being
honest, I'm pretty nervous, but I'm sure it will be fine.' She
grimaced, hearing the note of hysteria to her own voice.

'You'll be fine.' Tom graced her with that warm grin of his and
then wrapped her in the hug that she had so badly needed,
breathing out a huge sigh of relief in the comfort of his arms. If
only she could stay there all afternoon. It wasn't that she was
embarrassed by the show of affection, the other traders knew that

she and Tom were in a romantic relationship, but she didn't want to distract Tom any more than was entirely necessary. He had enough on his plate today and she couldn't help wondering how he might be feeling knowing that he would soon be saying goodbye to this role at the stables. Ever since he'd told her about his new job, she'd been playing it over in her mind, wondering how it would impact upon their relationship. She wasn't naive enough to think that it wouldn't change things. It was bound to. Tom would be putting all his energies into his new job, would meet new people and might decide he was ready to make those permanent changes to his life that he'd spoken about. With or without her, she didn't yet know. She reluctantly extracted herself from his embrace.

'I really hope so,' she said with a helpless shrug. 'I hope I don't get asked any technical questions.'

'Listen, people will be attending the workshop because they're interested in your jewellery and want to learn more about your work processes. Once you get started and relax into it, the time will just fly by.'

This had been one of the new ideas that Tom had instigated at the stables, running a workshop to showcase the skills and talents of the different craftspeople. At first, Sophie had been reluctant to take part, not certain that anyone would be interested in her particular way of working. Everything she'd learned about jewellery making had been self-taught from online videos and books and a great deal of trial and error. She knew only a few of the technical terms and processes, but Tom had reassured her that it was precisely that that people would be interested in learning about.

She simply had to pretend that she was at home in her small studio working on a hammered silver bangle while giving a running commentary at the same time as she transformed the piece into the finished product. It was a step out of her comfort zone, but then wasn't that what she had been determined to do from the start of the year? She'd spent far too long in a relationship and job that had made her miserable and she'd wanted to make up for lost time. Being part of the Primrose Stables family had been a huge help in building her confidence and making new friends. She'd enjoyed the camaraderie amongst her fellow traders, providing her with a sense of belonging, and knowing she would be seeing Tom there added an extra frisson to the day. It wouldn't be the same without him, that was for sure.

After giving herself a stern talking to, she walked to the front of the room, took a few deep breaths and plastered on a smile, taking her place behind the workbench. Tom stood at the back of the room and gave her a reassuring wink as she began the session, before he slipped out to see to his other duties. He'd been right, and as soon as Sophie started working, explaining to the small gathered audience what she was doing, holding their attention as she went through her processes, all her earlier worries were forgotten and she relaxed into the demonstration, quickly realising that everyone was genuinely interested in what she had to say. The time passed faster than she could have anticipated and there were plenty of questions from people wanting to know how she got started, which items she liked to work on the most and which were her best sellers. The workshop was an interactive experience all the way through and she felt a huge sense of relief and accomplishment when she got to the end, and almost a sense of disappointment that it was over.

Afterwards, when she returned to her unit in the stables, she was thrilled to discover that the interest in her session had translated into lots more visitors to her stall, where she handed out her business cards. The session definitely gave a boost to her sales that day as she sold more items than she was expecting to, including some bangles similar to the one she'd made in the workshop, along with some necklaces and earrings.

After the rush had died down, Tom came across and whispered in her ear.

'See, I told you you'd smash it! Well done!'

He laid a light hand on her waist and she couldn't help a flush of pride seep around her body. Mostly, she was pleased with herself, that she'd managed to overcome her fear of public speaking and do something that she would never have even contemplated a year ago. She didn't need anyone's validation, but there was no denying that Tom's support and encouragement made her feel ten foot tall.

'Hey, Tom. What a great turnout today. This was such a good idea of yours. I'm not sure why we didn't do it sooner.'

Tom and Sophie's moment was interrupted by the arrival of Pia, who had a big grin on her face.

'Yep. I hoped it would be popular and it's great to be proved right.' He narrowed his eyes and gave a devilish smile, which from anyone else might have been misconstrued as arrogance, but Tom had an inherent charisma that drew people towards him.

'Honestly, Tom, I'm not sure what we'll do without you when...' Pia stopped herself, a hand flying to her mouth as she gave an apologetic shrug to Tom.

'It's fine,' he reassured her. 'Sophie knows, although I've not yet mentioned anything to the other traders,' he said, lowering his voice.

'Thank goodness,' said Pia. 'Me and my big mouth, eh? It's good news though about Tom's new job, isn't it?'

'Yes,' Sophie agreed as enthusiastically as she could muster. She could never admit that she thought it was the worst possible news. The other traders were bound to be disappointed too when they learned that Tom would be leaving, although not as much as her, she suspected.

'I hope I haven't left you with a headache. Jackson seemed a bit put out when I told him. I'm sure there'll be plenty of candidates to fill the role?' Tom offered hopefully.

Pia gave a wry smile.

'Oh, don't worry about him.' She waved a hand dismissively. 'We're just sorry to see you go, that's all. After Christmas we can look around to find your replacement, although that will be no easy task. I've told Jackson that I'm more than happy to step in again, but he's keen that we keep Sundays free for the both of us. I can see his point. Living and working together is great but it can be all-consuming, so it makes sense to create some boundaries. Especially as a married couple!'

Sophie smiled at Pia's enthusiasm and positivity. It was what she remembered from the first time she met Pia, when she turned up for her first session at the stables, full of trepidation and doubt. It was only Pia's warm and friendly welcome that had encouraged her to stay.

'I'll certainly miss being part of the team,' Tom added, 'but look, I'm not disappearing off the scene entirely.' He glanced from Pia to Sophie. 'I can always cover the occasional weekend if you need me to.'

Sophie saw her Sundays at the stables as sacred, and if it were up to her, she wouldn't want them to change in any way, but Tom's decision to move on only served to remind her that the lovely bubble she'd existed in these last few months could be so easily burst. She should have anticipated it. After all, she'd known that Tom had been job hunting, but she'd been under the misapprehension that those special times at the stables were as important to Tom as they had been to her. Clearly she'd been wrong.

'Well, that's good to know,' said Pia, chuckling. 'You're one of the Moody clan now, so you can't entirely escape us even if you wanted to.'

And while that might possibly be true as far as his family was concerned, Sophie realised, as his new girlfriend, she had no such guarantees.

9

The Three Feathers was abuzz with chatter, laughter and the satisfying sound of clinking glasses. The aromas of home-cooked Sunday meals wafted in the air; steak and ale pies, chicken cobbler and roasts of all descriptions including tender Scotch beef with crispy roast potatoes, mixed vegetables, creamy cauliflower cheese and humongous Yorkshire puddings, stirring Sophie's appetite. Usually, after the Sunday craft fairs, she and Tom would linger at the pub after the other traders had gone home to their families, and they would inevitably end up ordering some delicious pub grub, enjoying the time spent together. They'd made no firm arrangements for tonight and she didn't like to make any assumptions. Now, as she waited at the bar to be served, she looked across at him, sitting at their usual long table in the snug, deep in conversation with Mike, one of the traders from the stables.

'Sophie, how are you? What can I get you?'

Rhi appeared with a friendly smile on her face, and Sophie's mood lifted. She was always pleased to see Rhi, who worked part-time behind the bar, alongside running her own business, and had made a point of befriending Sophie when she first moved into the village and started visiting the pub. They quickly discovered that they had mutual friends in Abbey and Pia, so they were soon running into each other at local events and became part of the same social circle.

'I'm good, thank you! I'll have a lime and soda, please. We've been up at Primrose Stables today.'

'Oh, that's right, you had the workshops on, didn't you? I would have come along, but I've been working here all day. How did it go?'

'Really well. We had a good turnout and my session went better than I could have expected after I got over my nerves. I sold a few pieces too.'

'Ooh, I bet you were fab. Let me know when the next session is on and I'll make sure to come along.'

'Thanks, Rhi. I will do.'

There were no further plans for any other workshops yet and Sophie had to wonder if the idea would fall by the wayside if Tom wouldn't be around to arrange them.

'How's life with you then?' she asked Rhi.

'Busy! I've picked up a couple of additional customers this week, working on some marketing and social media campaigns, so I've been putting in some late nights. Most of it has come through word of mouth so I must be doing something right.'

'That sounds great. You'll be able to give up the evening job soon then.' Sophie whispered the words behind her hands in case of listening ears.

'You know, I probably could, but I'd never want to stop working here. I did that once before when we moved away for a few months and I missed it too much. It gives me some sanity coming here, especially when I spend so much time sitting at my computer, working from home. It gives me the social outlet that I need. It means I get the best of both worlds.'

'I get that completely. It's a similar situation with me and my job. The nine-to-five in an office pays the bills, but I'm glad to have my jewellery-making sideline because that's what I enjoy. I look forward to getting home from work and disappearing into the studio. The hours fly by and I get completely lost in whatever I'm working on. Everyone should have something of their own, something that makes their heart happy.'

Rhi laughed.

'Ah, well, that would probably be Luke for me! Although we're a bit like ships passing in the night right now. He's really busy too. He's recently been promoted, so he's doing a lot of extra travelling around the country, but at least it makes Friday night pretty special when we get to see each other again.'

Sophie had met Luke a couple of times and was struck by what a great couple they made. With his shock of blond hair, piercing blue eyes and easy, affable manner, contrasting with Rhi's dark curls and sparky personality, they made such a striking pair. It was clear to see from the way they constantly interrupted each other, teasing and joking, their eyes sparkling with affection, that they were totally besotted with one another.

'And I'm guessing it's a certain Moody brother who makes your heart swell,' teased Rhi, who flashed a glance over in Tom's direction.

'Hmmm,' sighed Sophie, nodding, a knowing smile spreading across her lips. Sometimes she wished Tom didn't have such an effect on her. She hated the way her body and mind reacted instinctively to his presence, the thought of him and how she couldn't rationalise her feelings. She'd been determined to hold a part of herself back so that she could remain in control of her emotions, but she realised it was already too late for that. Somehow, at some point, she'd fallen for him, without even intending to. Just then, Tom, probably aware of two sets of eyes observing him, looked over, his gaze lighting up when he saw Sophie. He lifted his eyebrows and gestured to the empty space next to him.

'I should probably go and join them. See you later, Rhi.'

All the traders were on a high, revelling in the success of the day, sharing their experiences of their own workshops and the feedback they'd received. Their animated chatter greeted Sophie and the general consensus was that it had been a successful day with everyone agreeing that they would be keen to do it again.

'So, when's the next one?' Cecily, whose unit always smelled sublime from the colourful soaps and bath bombs that she made, piped up.

'Let me look at the calendar and I'll have a chat with Pia, see what we can get organised. I'm sure we can get something lined up for early next season.'

Sophie nodded as Tom glanced in her direction, knowing that it would be someone else supervising the day then. From a purely personal point of view, it wouldn't be the same for Sophie without Tom being there, even if the popularity of the craft days, and now the workshops too, might continue to grow with someone new at the helm.

It was only later when the other traders had left for home and the pair of them had decided to stay for something to eat that Sophie felt that she was able to speak honestly.

'So, you didn't mention to the others you were leaving then?'

'No.' Tom looked up from his plate of roast chicken with all the trimmings. 'It didn't seem the right time. I didn't want my news to overshadow the success of the day. There's no hurry, I can let them know next time.'

Sophie wondered if Tom was holding back in case he had a

change of mind over his decision, but perhaps that was wishful thinking on her part.

'Well, they're not going to like it when they do find out. I nearly did a Pia and let it slip when I was chatting to Katy. I promise now though that my lips are sealed, although I must admit I've never been very good at keeping secrets.' She injected a touch of humour to her words, but Tom grimaced.

'To be honest, I'm not expecting it to be received with a fanfare if Jackson's reaction was anything to go by.' He quirked an eyebrow and she dropped her gaze, pushing her food around her plate.

'Oh, did he not take it well then?'

'You know Jackson, he's not great at hiding his feelings.' Tom gave a tight smile. 'Was it too much to expect that he might be pleased for me?' He shrugged. 'I didn't think so, but clearly he's more concerned with what's good for him and the hall, and not necessarily for me.'

'I'm sorry he made you feel that way.' Sophie felt a pang of guilt and placed a hand over his on the table. She hadn't been overjoyed to hear Tom's news either, but she hoped she'd managed to cover it up well. At least better than Jackson had.

'As Pia says, Jackson will get over it,' Sophie tried to reassure Tom. 'Perhaps he was just disappointed that you're moving on. The pair of you make a great team working together.'

Tom laid down his knife and fork and pushed his plate away.

'We do, but you have to remember there's a huge disparity in our circumstances. Jackson has the whopping big house in the country, a thriving business, a classic car collection to rival some museums, and a wedding to look forward to. While I have…' Tom twisted his mouth in thought. 'A poky one-bedroomed flat and a handful of casual jobs? Not that I'm bitter,' he said, his eyes lifting skywards. 'It's just seeing everything Jackson's achieved has made me realise I want some of that! Obviously, not on the same scale, I mean, I'm not completely delusional. I'm not expecting to bag a stately home of my own, but a house, a decent job, a future with someone I love, it's not too much to ask, is it?' His gaze briefly flittered over Sophie's face before his attention drifted around the pub. Sophie understood where he was coming from. Tom didn't resent Jackson his success, but it was natural that he would look to his brother and compare his own situation. He was only human, after all.

'Well, I'm pleased for you if that makes you feel any better?'

Tom fixed his gaze on hers, the intensity of his dark brown eyes making her toes curl.

'Are you... really? I got the impression you may have thought it was a bad idea too when I first told you, or perhaps I was just being over-sensitive?'

She swallowed down a sigh. So she had done a rotten job at hiding her true emotions, and now she chided herself for putting her own feelings before Tom's. It had been a knee-jerk reaction to some news she hadn't been expecting.

'I'm sorry, Tom. I was being selfish. Thinking what it would mean for me and not you. Going to the stables is the highlight of my fortnight and you're a big part of that. I'll miss seeing you there.'

'Really? If you're trying to make me feel better, it's working.'

'Honestly, I do understand why you've made this decision, and the job sounds like a brilliant opportunity. I am really pleased for you, I promise.'

'Okay,' he said, with that lazy smile of his that shone a light in his eyes. 'I'll forgive you, but just this once, you understand?'

Sophie was mightily relieved. Tom would never know just

how much his support and encouragement had helped her on those Sundays. If she had to do it without him, then she would, but she knew it wouldn't be the same without him there, that was for sure.

10

On a crisp autumnal day, Jackson steered the jeep around the local country lanes while Pia peered out of the passenger door window and breathed in the scenery, appreciating the muted hues of the hedgerows laden with haws and berries. They were only ten minutes away from home when Jackson turned off the main road. There was a faded old sign by the roadside on which, if you peered closely at the peeling paintwork, you could just make out the words Rosewood Farm. Pia knew it of old, having driven through these lanes with her parents on a regular basis over the years, every time they took the trip into town. Sometimes they would call into the farm and pick up fresh milk and eggs, but that was many years ago now and the farm had fallen into disrepair a long time since. Pia didn't know the full story but there had been rumours of a falling out between the two brothers who had inherited it, a rift that couldn't or wouldn't be resolved, which brought about a sad end to the business and the subsequent crumbling of the farm buildings. As they made their way along the lane, Jackson turned off into a side track and took the approach slowly, navigating the holes and bumps carefully until he pulled up outside a terrace of three cottages.

'What do you think?' Jackson said, turning to her, an expectant smile on her face.

'Blimey, I think if I gave one big blow they might all fall down.'

Pia climbed out of the car and stood to examine the cottages more closely as Jackson came to join her. Up close, it was clear to see that the buildings were in a much worse state of disrepair than Pia had first thought.

'Are they all empty?'

'The two on the right are, but the one on the left is where Mr Adams lives. He used to own the farm many moons ago but then he moved into the cottage with his wife. She died about two years ago. She ran it as a smallholding with chickens and goats and sheep, but of course it became too much for Mr Adams to deal with when she died. He told me all this when I came to visit the other week. He's moving into a care home in a few weeks, the one Abbey manages. I think he's quite looking forward to it.'

'So what are your plans for the cottages?'

'We'll completely gut them and basically start all over again. They'll need repointing, new roofs, a total strip out inside, new electrics, bathrooms and kitchens. There are a few original features which I hope to retain, but effectively it will be a complete refurb.'

Pia could hear the enthusiasm in Jackson's voice and she was in no doubt that he would do a fabulous job in restoring the buildings. You only had to look at the before and after photos of Primrose Hall to appreciate his attention to detail and skill set.

'What, and then sell them?'

'No, simply add them to the property portfolio. I was thinking we could let them out on short- or long-term rentals, preferably to young local people who are struggling to find affordable accommodation, or even maybe as holiday lets. To be honest, this was the project I wanted to hand over to Tom. He would have been great at managing this with all his experience from the builders' merchants, but...' He gave a shrug. 'It doesn't matter. This is small fry compared to what we did up at the hall. We can manage it between us. How are you with a brick hod?' he said, dazzling her with a sidewards grin.

Pia laughed.

'Well, I'm sure I could learn,' she said doubtfully.

Jackson wrapped an arm around Pia's shoulder, pulling her into his side.

'I'm only kidding. We'll employ the different trades. We'll just need to manage the project and make sure the right contractors are here on the right days and that all the supplies are ordered and arrive in time. It's good for you to see the site and to know what we're trying to achieve. When we get back to the hall, I can show you the drawings. Come on, let's go and say hello to Mr Adams.'

They walked through the picket gate that was hanging off its hinges and rapped on the old-fashioned knocker. They might have thought the place was empty if hadn't been for the muffled sound of voices coming from the front of the house, and Pia could just make out a television flickering through the grubby net curtains. Jackson leant forward and tapped on the window, trying to peer inside.

'Mr Adams! It's Jackson Moody from Primrose Hall.'

There was an awful lot of shuffling noises and then a 'You'll have to wait' before finally the door was opened. Mr Adams, hanging on to his walking frame, peered out at them through watery eyes, his expression disgruntled.

'What do you want?'

'Hello again, Mr Adams. It's Jackson Moody,' he repeated, unsure whether the elderly man recognised him or not. 'I was here last week to talk about the cottages. I just wanted another chat, if that's okay with you. This is Pia, my fiancée.'

'Hmmm,' he muttered, sounding none too pleased to be interrupted.

'Actually, I just wanted to show Pia around the cottages as she'll be working on them with me. Hopefully my solicitor will have been in touch with the agent and we can finalise the contract in the next couple of days.'

'Pah, I don't know about that. Look, I'm going to have to go and sit down,' he said, doing a three-point turn with his walker. 'My old legs can't hang about here. You can come in if you were thinking of staying but I shan't be able to make you a cup of tea.' Mr Adams shuffled back down the hallway, grumbling. Pia followed tentatively, looking over her shoulder at Jackson, who encouraged her onwards with a nod of his head.

'Look, I could always make a cuppa if you fancy one, Mr Adams?' Pia asked, hoping she wasn't overstepping the mark. The last thing she wanted was to offend him.

'That might not be a bad idea,' he said, dropping down with a thump into the armchair just inside the door of the front room. 'I could do with one, now you come to mention it. The mugs and tea are in the cupboard above the kettle. I have carers coming in three times a day. They get me up and ready for the day, do me some breakfast, then they're back at lunch, and again in the evening. I don't like the idea of strangers coming in to do the things I should be doing for myself, but I'm not sure where I'd be without them.'

'How do you take your tea, Mr Adams?'

'Make it strong for me, will you, love, and one sugar. Oh, and call me Harry.'

Pia wandered off into the kitchen and easily found the tea-making equipment as she heard Jackson talking to Harry. The place was clean enough but there was a whiff of neglect and tiredness wafting in the air. She peered out of the window into the long and narrow gardens behind and what looked to be paddocks beyond. It was wild and overgrown, but she knew that once Jackson got the landscapers in it would be quickly transformed to show off its true potential. There was no denying that Jackson had great vision, and his determination and desire to do his best work in every project he took on was unquestionable, so she could easily imagine how the cottages would be converted into beautiful, sustainable contemporary homes. Standing in the small kitchen, she gave a thought to all the previous tenants who had made this place their home. Harry and his late wife in bygone years when the home would have been filled with love and laughter, the aromas of home cooking wafting in the air. Now, there was a stillness and sadness about the place that seeped out through the walls.

She found the fridge and pulled out a pint of milk, giving it a sniff before adding a splash to each of the mugs. It was all part of the natural course of life, she supposed. Her own family home, the setting for so many happy times and memories, had seemed sad and forgotten when she closed the door on it for the very last time. Nothing stayed the same forever and she hoped Harry would at least leave here with a raft of happy memories.

'I've told them I'm not going until I'm good and ready. I don't know that I really want to go into a home. I can't have that much longer left so I might as well spend my days out here. I'll get by somehow.'

Pia flashed Jackson a look as she came into the room with the tray of teas, and she noticed the tell-tale furrow of concern on his forehead.

'This sale is more trouble than it's worth. I've already turned down a couple of offers. I might be an old man, but I'm not bloody daft.'

'I would never presume you are and I'm sorry if I've got hold of the wrong end of the stick, but I had thought after our conversation last week that we had agreed in principle a deal. I'm not here to cause you any upset or to put any pressure on you. You must do exactly what you want to do. We'll have our tea and then be on our way. What I will do is give you my card and then if your circumstances change you can contact me.' Jackson delved into his pocket and pulled out a business card, handing it over to Harry.

'Primrose Hall, eh?' His lips suppressed a smile. 'I've already got one of these. Put it up on the mantelpiece for me, love,' he said, addressing Pia. 'I remember the hall from when I was a lad. I think there was a story about family difficulties, the wife running away. It stood empty and run-down for years.'

'I don't know if you've seen it recently, Harry, but Jackson has completely refurbished the hall. It's a beautiful building now and we're very lucky to live there. We run events like a classic car show and a Christmas carols concert in the grounds. Everyone says what a marvellous job we've done. We're getting married there in December.'

Harry peered more closely at Pia.

'Are you from around these parts?'

'Yes! I lived with my family up at Meadow Cottages, all my life. I must admit I've not really travelled very far, but then I've never wanted to. I love this area and I can't ever imagine wanting to live anywhere else.'

'I know Meadow Cottages well.' He nodded sagely. 'You and me alike, love. I didn't travel very far,' he said with a wry smile. 'My brother and I couldn't agree on what to do with the farm and in the end we split it up. He took the main farm buildings and I had these cottages. He ran the business into the ground and then disappeared off somewhere. We never spoke a word again. I heard that he died a few years ago.'

'That's very sad that you weren't able to resolve your differences,' Pia offered.

Harry gave a shrug.

'These things happen, eh? We never really hit it off. We were young, pig-headed. Both believing our way was the best way. He did his thing and I did mine. I was lucky, I had my Vera and all the time she was at my side I was happy. We had a little small-holding here, grew our own vegetables out the back and kept some animals, while I worked as a farm labourer on some other farms. Course, we had these cottages too. We rented them out to other labourers, who became our friends. It brought in a bit of extra cash, but mostly we were relieved that we had decent neighbours. We had lots of happy times here, but then... well, I'm the only one left now.'

'At least you have some lovely memories to cherish. Do you have any family nearby?'

'No, we didn't have any children. Vera never much fancied them and they never came along so we always thought that was the way it was meant to be. Our animals became our family.'

'I know exactly what you mean,' said Pia, laughing. 'We've got animals up at the hall. A donkey called Twinkle, a rascal of a Shetland pony called Little Star, and then a couple of dogs, Bertie the Dalmatian and Teddy, a little scruffy bitsa. They really do become like family members.'

'Anyway,' said Jackson, standing up with his empty mug. 'We have taken up far too much of your time as it. We'll leave you in peace. Sorry for the confusion and you've got my card if anything should change.'

Pia and Harry both looked up at Jackson, their disappointment evident in their expressions.

'Surely you don't have to rush away just yet?' Harry turned his wrist over to look at his watch, before giving a resigned chuckle. 'I forget, you people have busy lives. Places to go and people to see.'

'Well, we're not in that much of a hurry. We could stay for a while, couldn't we, Jackson?'

Jackson gave a nonchalant shrug.

'Of course. I just didn't want to take up any more of your time than was strictly necessary.' Jackson looked from his mug to theirs.

'We could have another cuppa if you wanted one?' Pia suggested.

'Oh, let's do that. I think there could be a packet of chocolate digestives in the cupboard too.'

11

This time it was Jackson who rounded up the empty mugs and wandered out to the kitchen to make some more teas. All the time, he could hear Pia and Harry chatting away as though they were old friends. Pia had a natural affinity with people, always knowing the right thing to say and connecting with them in an instinctive way, as she was doing right now with Harry, his warm chuckle reaching the kitchen. Jackson smiled as he found a spoon and stirred the teas before wandering back to the living room where Harry was explaining about his living arrangements.

'Everyone says I need to move into somewhere a bit safer. Have you seen the staircase here? It's very steep and narrow, but then I think I've managed all these years, I'm sure I can do a few more. I have got a room with my name on it at the care home over on the other side of the valley. I've put down a holding deposit and I've heard I can move in when I want, but now, well, I'm not sure that I want to. Do you know it?'

'Do you mean Rushgrove Lodge?' Pia asked keenly. 'I do know it! My best friend Abbey is the manager. And my old neighbour from Meadow Cottages, Wendy Peterson, moved in about eighteen months ago. She's settled in really well. She was in a similar position to you, living in a home that she loved, but unable to manage like she once had. She wasn't keen on moving somewhere new, but honestly, she says it was the best decision she ever made. They have so much going on at the lodge, weekly whist drives, visiting speakers, and it's always someone's birthday so lots of celebrations. The thing Wendy likes is that she can join in with as much or as little as she wants to. If she prefers to be by herself then she can stay in her room and watch some telly or read her book.'

'Hmm, well, it might suit some people, but I don't think I'd like it. Those places are full of doddery old snowy tops.'

Pia bit back a smile as she glanced across at Jackson, whose gaze deliberately avoided hers.

'You might be surprised, Harry. Whenever I visit Wendy at the lodge, I'm struck by how lively it is up there. There's always a lot of chatter and laughter, if you want to join in with that, of course. And if you were to move in, it doesn't mean that you won't still be able to get out and about. I often take Wendy into town or bring her up to the hall so she can see Bertie, our Dalmatian. He belonged to her originally, you see, but it got to the point where she couldn't really look after him any more. I used to walk him for her every day and although he's a big softie, he's such a playful goofy dog that I was always worried that he might accidentally knock her over. When I promised that I would take Bertie with me when I moved, it was a great weight off her mind. Of course, none of us could have known then that we would have ended up at Primrose Hall. We both landed on our feet.'

'And I for one am very glad that you did,' said Jackson from the armchair over the other side of the room. 'The hall would be very quiet without Pia and the dogs about the place,' he told Harry.

'There'd be less muddy pawprints too,' Pia said with a wry smile.

'I've had some good offers on this place,' Harry said, 'but then I know exactly what it's worth. I'm sitting on a little gold mine here. The cottages might be run down but it will only take some hot-shot builder to come along, do a quick renovation and then sell them off to the highest bidders.'

'I think Jackson was intending to keep them and let them out to local people, or maybe even use one of them as a short-term holiday let. He's...'

Pia went to carry on but Jackson silenced her with a small shake of his head.

'It's not all about the money, though.' Harry pushed himself up in his seat, becoming animated. 'It's about my sitting tenants, Humphrey, Marvin and Jack. I'm not signing on the dotted line until I know they've got somewhere to go.'

Pia exchanged a puzzled look with Jackson, who gave an imperceptible shrug of his shoulders. He clearly hadn't heard this snippet of information before either. Pia couldn't think where these tenants might be living. The other two cottages, with their broken and boarded-up windows, looked as though they'd been sitting empty for some time. She couldn't imagine anyone living in those conditions.

'Oh right... Do they...?' Pia ventured, not wanting to be too nosy, but Harry carried on regardless.

'They'll want to stay together. I couldn't split them up even if I wanted to because my Vera will be up there waving her fist at me. She adored those boys and I made a promise to her that I would take care of them, as long as I was able to.'

'Oh, I see,' said Pia, not really seeing at all. 'Have you got something in mind for Humphrey... Martin and John?'

'Humphrey, Marvin and Jack,' Harry corrected her. 'They

were Vera's uncles. Her father died when she was a girl so they stepped up and took her under their wing. They always looked out for her, and Humphrey even gave her away at our wedding. As they got older, the tables were turned and she was the one to take care of them.'

'So...' Pia's voice trailed away and her brow crumpled in confusion. No, she still couldn't make sense of it.

'When we got the alpacas, Vera insisted we name them after her much-missed uncles.'

'Ah...' Pia laughed. 'Alpacas! I thought you were talking about actual people. It's good to get that cleared up! How lovely!' Pia gave a small yelp of delight. 'I've always wanted some alpacas. Where are they then?'

'They're in the paddock out the back. After Vera went, I did my best to look after them, it gave me something to do each day, but I struggle to get down there now with these useless legs of mine. I've got a young lass who comes in to see them each day, Molly, she's training to be a veterinary nurse, but I know that situation can't last for ever.'

'Would it be possible to go and see them?'

'Course you can, darling!' Harry was delighted by Pia's interest in the animals. 'If you go out the kitchen door and walk along the garden path you'll come to a gate that leads to the paddock. The fawn one is Humphrey, he's in charge, and Marvin and Jack are the black ones. They'll be pleased to see you. They're always very curious about new visitors.'

Pia jumped out of her chair.

'Are you coming, Jackson?'

'Why don't you wander down and I'll stay and keep Harry company.'

In the garden, Pia was barely able to make out the stone path as it was overrun with weeds and long grass from the unmown lawns. There was a wooden shed to one side which was in a similar state of disrepair to the cottages, but it wasn't hard to imagine how lovely it might once have been when the row of terraced houses and the gardens were well tended. There were apple and plum trees acting as a border to the neighbours' garden and she could see where the vegetable patches had been, and she could visualise them brimming with the year's crops. It was such a peaceful spot with views onto the fields beyond. In some ways it reminded her of Meadow Cottages where she'd grown up and although it was in the middle of the countryside, she could picture it filled with life and vibrancy when the cottages had been occupied. She continued on her way and when the alpacas first came into view she gasped at the sight of them, a small trickle of anticipation running along her spine.

'Hello, boys,' she said softly as she eased her way into their field, carefully closing the gate behind her. She couldn't stop herself from smiling as the alpacas looked at her, their bodies held erect, their heads turned towards her with curiosity. They wandered over and she spoke to them all the time, not knowing how they might react to her presence. She didn't want to spook them. Each one of them had such a cute and inquisitive expression that she would have loved to throw her arms around their necks and give them a big hug. Instead, she stood still, but she needn't have worried because their inquisitiveness got the better of them and they came right up alongside her, making eye contact, which she took as an invitation to gently pet them.

'Aren't you beautiful,' she cooed, in her element in their company. Their fleeces were soft and silky beneath her fingers, and she could understand why Vera had adored these boys so much. It must have been a huge responsibility for Harry to fulfil his promise to his late wife. No wonder he was reluctant to leave his home, but this situation couldn't go on in the same way much longer. The alpacas appeared well looked after and had shelter and clean water, but what would happen if circumstances changed for the girl who was helping out with the animals? Even the thought of Harry wandering through the garden on his own to go and see the alpacas made Pia shudder. The ground was uneven under foot and there were all sorts of hazards that could send Harry toppling over. Whether Harry liked the idea or not, he needed to make some changes to his living arrangements, and soon.

On her way back from the paddock, Pia stopped to peer into one of the remaining windows of the other two cottages. She couldn't see very much through the dirt and grime, but what she could make out was that it was dark, dingy and damp inside. It was easy to imagine how Jackson might quickly transform the workers' cottages by completely gutting them and rebuilding the interiors, although it sounded as though he might not even be given the opportunity now.

Back inside the kitchen of Harry's home, Pia poured some hot water into the sink and started washing up the dirty mugs, just as Jackson wandered in from the other room.

'Hey!' She held a finger to her lips and took him by the arm and led him outside the back door, pulling it closed behind them so that Harry wouldn't hear. She held a hand to her chest.

'I've seen the alpacas and oh my goodness, they are adorable, but honestly there's no way Harry can look after them properly on his own. I was just thinking...'

'I know exactly what you'll be thinking,' said Jackson, with an indulgent smile. He placed a hand on her shoulder.

'The thing is, Jackson, we've got the space for them. They could have their own paddock at the hall and we've already got Twinkle and Little Star to look after so it wouldn't make a great difference to us in terms of our time and money. Think about it;

they would be a great addition to the hall. I know some places offer walks with alpacas as an attraction. Wouldn't that be fun? Think of it as a business opportunity.'

Jackson gave a wry smile and shrugged his shoulders.

'You've got it all worked out, haven't you? Well, I have no objection, but I'm not sure what Harry will have to say about the idea. As you've seen, he knows his own mind, and he might not be so easily persuaded. He also might think we're trying to sweeten him up so that he'll sign the contract with us. I don't want to be seen to be putting undue pressure on him.'

'Hmmm...' Pia nodded. 'From the way you were talking about it earlier, it sounded like a done deal.'

'I thought it was but I've been in business long enough to know that you can't take anything for granted, not until both parties have signed on the dotted line. It would have been a brilliant opportunity for us and a great add-on to the business interests at the hall, but if it doesn't work for Harry, then I'm not going to push it.'

'It's disappointing, but there'll be other opportunities,' Pia said, not entirely convincingly. 'But regardless of the deal, I think we could give those boys a good home, and surely that's exactly what Harry would want?'

'Well, I suppose it's worth a try,' said Jackson, 'but don't get your hopes up.' He opened the back door again and ushered Pia inside where they rejoined Harry in the living room. She took a deep breath, trying to gauge how Harry might react; the last thing she wanted to do was upset him. Unsure of the best way to approach the subject, she simply blurted it out.

'Harry, I've been to see the alpacas and honestly, I fell in love with them at first sight! They're such intelligent, friendly boys. I could quite easily have stayed there all day talking to them and petting them. Look, I know you don't know us terribly well, but we have room at Primrose Hall to re-home Humphrey, Marvin and Jack if you would like us to? We'd take really good care of them. Would you like to see some photos of Twinkle and Little Star?'

Before Harry had the chance to answer, Pia had pulled out her phone from her pocket and was scrolling through hundreds of photos, giving a running commentary.

'This is the hall,' she said, bringing up images of the restored seventeenth-century building looking resplendent on a summer's day. 'Jackson did a lot of the work himself on refurbishing the building.'

'Well, I had a good team around me as well,' Jackson added. 'I didn't do it all with my own bare hands.'

'Crikey,' said Harry, peering closer to look at the pictures. 'That does look different from the last time I saw it. Then it was all boarded up and the grounds were overgrown.'

'Yep. When I was a kid, me and my mates used to climb the fences and hangout over at the hall. With a few cans and some cigarettes, we would spend hours over there larking about. Even then in its run-down state I used to think how special it was. There was always a magical atmosphere about the place, as though it held a web of secrets inside. When I got the opportunity to buy it, it was as if it was always meant to be.'

Harry narrowed his eyes and observed Jackson closely as though he was seeing him in an entirely different light. It was rousing hearing the passion behind Jackson's words, his animation and enthusiasm for the hall and everything they'd achieved infectious.

'Now, this is Twinkle the donkey and Little Star the Shetland pony,' Pia went on. 'They are such great characters. Little Star is the instigator, she definitely leads Twinkle astray. They used to be escape artists and would jump their paddock, trampling over all the flower beds on their way, making a proper mess, which didn't go down well with Mateo, our gardener. Sometimes they would get as far as Primrose Woods and the rangers would have to bring them home in the trailers. Honestly, they were right little trouble-makers. We've stopped all their antics now though so they can't get out of the paddocks any more.'

Harry chuckled as Pia told her story.

'Oh, and this is Bertie the Dalmatian and Teddy, who's the newest member of the Primrose Hall family. We found him in the grounds caught up in the fencing on the boundary to the woods. He was in a terrible state; his fur was matted and he was absolutely filthy. He stunk to high heaven too. We took him to the local vets, and to cut a long story short it turned out that his owner didn't want him back again.' Pia shook her head in dismay. 'I mean, who would do that to a defenceless little dog? Anyway, we didn't need to think twice about it, did we, Jackson? We offered him a home with us.'

Jackson nodded, not quite remembering it in the same way. He'd come home from a work trip away to find that the little scruffy mutt was making himself very much at home in Bertie's bed, and while Pia tried to convince Jackson that it was a short-term solution while Teddy recovered from his ordeal, he knew that Pia had already made up her mind as to where the little dog's new home should be.

'We take in all the waifs and strays up at the hall,' said Jackson wryly. 'I think Pia is determined to turn it into a petting zoo.'

'Look, these are the renovated stables and the barn,' Pia went on, deliberately ignoring Jackson's comment. 'We hold events in the barn, like our writing festival. It's such a stunning space with a vaulted ceiling and oak beams, and the light floods in through the windows and doors. That's where we're having our wedding reception in December. And these are the stables where the craft days are held.'

Harry nodded politely as Pia showed him photo after photo.

'Come on, Pia,' Jackson urged her. 'I'm sure Harry doesn't want to see your entire portfolio of pictures.'

'Sorry!' she said with a grin. 'I do tend to get carried away once I get started.' She pulled up another picture of Twinkle and Little Star grazing happily in the field. 'You can't see it from the photo, but just on the other side of here is another paddock which is standing empty at the moment. It would be an ideal place for your boys if you wanted it, and they'd get lots of interaction from us and all the visitors to the hall. It also means you could keep an eye on them too if you stay in the area because you would always be welcome to come and visit.' She filled in the awkward silence by adding, 'We would obviously offer you the going rate for the alpacas.'

'Hmmm, I've told you, it's not about the money,' said Harry vehemently. 'I've got to do right by my Vera.'

'I understand that,' said Pia, placing a hand over his on the arm of the chair. 'I just wanted to put the offer out there in case you wanted to take us up on it.'

Harry fell quiet for a moment, seemingly lost in thought, but Pia couldn't help but notice the emotion held in his faraway look. She gave a squeeze of his hand.

'We should make a move now. Thanks for letting me see the alpacas. It really has made my day.' She grinned and stood up, looking across at Jackson, who jumped to his feet.

'Before you go.' Harry waved a hand in Jackson's direction. 'Remind me what your offer was on this place?'

'It was the full asking price. I know my solicitor has put the offer through to your agent and to your solicitor, but if there's any more information you'd like then just let me know. You'll find all my contact details on the card.'

'But of course, us having the alpacas doesn't depend on this business deal going through,' Pia jumped in. 'We'd love to have them come and live with us if you don't find anywhere more suitable for them.'

'Yes, well, I shall have to have a think about that,' said Harry gruffly.

'Of course,' said Pia, taking hold of his arms and planting a kiss on his cheek, which completely disarmed the old man. 'Whatever you think is for the best. Thanks for the tea and biscuits, Harry.'

12

Sophie and Tom walked the short distance from the pub to Sophie's cottage, where Tom was intending to call a taxi home after he'd stayed for the coffee she'd offered him. It was a relief to have cleared the air because she hated the idea of there being any bad feeling between them.

'Come on,' she said as she approached her front door, taking Tom by the hand. Although she'd been living here for over six months now, she still felt the same buzz of excitement returning home, seeing her little chocolate box cottage, as she had the very first time she'd clapped eyes on the house.

It was only small, a two up, two down, but as far as Sophie was concerned it was so much more than just her home. It had represented the start of a new phase in her life where she could rediscover who she was and start enjoying some independence and freedom. No longer did she have to tiptoe around Kyle, or navigate his whims and bad moods. She could do what she wanted, when she wanted, and that came as a big relief. For far too long, she'd suppressed her own needs and desires to placate a man who had never been worthy of her time and energies. It was a shame that it had taken her so long to realise it, but she didn't have time for regrets. She was all about looking forward and moving on, and getting to know Tom had proved to her that there were some decent, good men out there.

Inside, she switched on a side lamp, turned the fairy lights on in the fireplace and lit the two pillar candles that stood on the mantlepiece. Instantly, the room felt cosier and warmer.

'Let me pop the kettle on,' she said, wandering through to the kitchen.

Tom followed her and watched as she pulled out a couple of mugs from the cupboard and spooned coffee inside. It gave her a sense of normality and homeliness to entertain visitors, and of all her guests, and there really weren't too many of them, Tom was definitely her favourite.

'Here you are,' she said with a smile, handing over a mug.

'Thanks, Sophie.' He took the coffee and placed it down on the worktop, reaching out to her and pulling her into his embrace. She wrapped her arms around him and snuggled into his broad chest, where she felt safe and warm. He leant back to look into her eyes, running a hand through her glossy brown hair.

'You do know that this new job won't affect what we have together in any way.' His gaze roamed her face. 'We'll still get to see each other and I'm going to be making a point of getting to the traders' meet-ups whenever I can. You've no need to worry on that front.'

'No, I know,' she said brightly, not sharing his certainty. 'The thing is, despite all my talk about stepping out of my comfort zone, I'm not too good when unexpected change comes my way. Which I know is totally ridiculous and entirely unfair on you.' She felt her cheeks colour as he looked at her, his touch sending a tingle the length of her body. 'I've quite enjoyed this little bubble we've existed in. If it was down to me then things would stay the way they are, but I know that's not possible or even very healthy. Things have to move on. That's part of life.' His thumb traced a trail along her cheek as she spoke. 'I am really happy for you, though. I promise.'

'I believe you,' he said, seemingly distracted now. 'Thousands wouldn't.' A smile formed on his mouth as he closed his eyes and leant forward to press his lips against hers. Her mouth parted automatically and she pressed her body up against his, enjoying the sensations his kisses elicited. She soaked up the scent of him, his masculinity. She could quite easily have succumbed to the temptation of Tom's touch, but much to her disappointment, he pulled away and gestured to the coffees, although the look in his eyes suggested that he might have easily been persuaded otherwise. Judging by the smile lingering on his lips, he knew exactly how she was feeling too.

Sophie picked up her mug and led the way into the living room, where they both sat down on the small cosy sofa.

'Today was fun. Thanks for pushing me' – she stopped herself, rethinking her choice of words – 'persuading me to take part in the workshop. I wouldn't have done it without your encouragement, and it was so interesting chatting to the visitors. It's always pleasing to get positive feedback and it's given me lots of ideas for new items. I can't wait to get back into the workshop to get started.'

Tom smiled.

'I don't know why you're so surprised. You're very talented and your jewellery always looks fabulous on the displays.'

Tom was so supportive of her work, which was another reason why she valued their budding relationship. She felt she could be her natural self in his company and wasn't constantly holding her breath waiting for a barbed comment or a criticism of her pieces. Her ex, Kyle, had been mostly indifferent to her hobby, although at the time, it had been a great excuse for her to escape into the spare room to get away from him.

'Pia was making me laugh today. She was trying to wheedle from me and Katy the plans for her hen night, but we've all been sworn to secrecy. She's worried that there's going to be male strippers and Katy and I were really winding her up by neither confirming nor denying it.'

'And are there? Going to be naked men?'

'Is it a proper hen night without them?' Sophie quipped. 'Actually no, thank goodness. I think it's all going to be very civilised, although with plenty of good food and booze involved, and a few surprises along the way.'

'That sounds like a very fun evening, although it will probably get messy knowing that lot. You'll definitely have to blank out the next day for recovery. You've reminded me. I need to speak to Jackson to see what he wants to do for his stag night. Assuming of course he still wants me to be his best man!'

'Don't be daft! Who else would he have at his side on his wedding day, other than his brother? It's obvious that Jackson is very fond of you. I think he really appreciates everything you did for him during the summer, helping out at the hall when he was in hospital and then dashing across to France to support Rex and Ronnie, after your dad's heart attack. Pia's always telling me that. You're his right-hand man now, his confidant. Don't take his reaction about your job personally. It probably took him by surprise, like it did me, and he's needed some time to adjust to the change.'

'Perhaps you're right. Come here,' he said, reaching out an arm and pulling her into his embrace. Sophie shifted up the sofa, snuggling into his side, looking up into his gaze. She loved these times spent together and it was only natural that her thoughts might wander to imagine a situation where it might always be like this. That she and Tom could have some kind of permanent future together. Not that she would want to mention anything along those lines just yet. They were still finding out about each other, having fun together. The last thing they needed was the additional pressures that came from a committed relationship.

'So are you excited about starting your new job?'

Tom looked down at her and his brow furrowed.

'I'm not sure excited is the right word. I'm more relieved than anything else. It means I'll be able to start making some proper plans.' He dropped his head back, lifted his chin to the air and closed his eyes for a moment. 'You know it was you that gave me the push to actually get out there and find this job.'

'What?' She sat up and turned towards him, her surprise evident in her reaction. 'How come?'

'Well, spending some time with you here, sharing a drink and a meal, it's been great. Simple pleasures, I know, but it's brought home to me that I don't actually have a lot to offer you in terms of prospects,' he said, with a twiddle of his imaginary moustache.

'Aw, come on, don't say that.'

'But it's true. I live in a flat the size of a broom cupboard, not somewhere I would want to invite people back to or where I can entertain. There's no outdoor space and it's generally a bit of a dump. I'd love to have somewhere we could hang out together, where I could return the favour and cook a meal for you for a change.'

'But that's the thing, I don't mind, Tom,' she reassured him. 'In fact, I love having you round. You might have noticed that I'm a proper home bird, never happier than when I'm pottering here, either making my jewellery or whipping up something delicious in the kitchen.'

'Yeah, I get that, but even so it would be nice to have the

option. Besides, you haven't tried my vegetarian moussaka yet, or one of my deadly cocktails.'

'Well, I like the sound of those, I must admit, but you could always use the kitchen here if you wanted to. I know it's not the same, but...' Her words trailed away as his expression told her that she wasn't getting the point. She knew from experience that there was nothing worse than living somewhere that made you unhappy.

'It's not just where I'm living,' Tom said, as though reading her mind. 'It's everything else that goes with it. Anna and I had a great lifestyle together, exotic holidays, meals out, theatre trips, and we always made a big deal of birthdays and Christmases. I took all of that for granted at the time, and now I hate having to think twice about whether or not I can afford to do those kind of things.'

Sophie nodded, hearing the frustration in his words. She supposed it must be difficult to have a big change in your circumstances like that. She'd never earned a big salary, but she knew how to budget and economise, although the fact that she didn't really have expensive tastes probably helped her to manage her money effectively.

'It shouldn't be too much to ask to be in a position where I'm able to spoil you, Sophie.' His dark brown eyes locked onto hers. 'To whisk you away on a European city break or take off for two weeks in the sun.'

'Oh...' She paused to allow his words to sink in. A holiday? With Tom. Suddenly an image popped into her mind of her and Tom walking along a soft golden beach, the warm rays of the sun kissing her skin. She sighed dreamily. The idea of a holiday hadn't even crossed her mind, but now Tom mentioned it, the thought filled her with excitable anticipation. She couldn't remember the last time she'd got away. It must have been when she went with Kyle's family to a caravan park on the Welsh coast when it had rained for the entire five days.

'Honestly, Tom, it's never occurred to me that I'm missing out on any of those things. Although...' A smile appeared on her lips as she was transported to another place. 'Now you come to mention it, some sun wouldn't go amiss, but really though, I'm a girl of simple pleasures. Aren't we having a great time doing what we're doing? Walks over at Primrose Woods, going to the pub or having supper together.'

Could she really be held responsible for Tom's decision to change his job?

'I've never once looked to you and had any level of expectation of...' Her words trailed away. 'I like you as you are, spending time together. That's enough for me.'

Tom puffed out his cheeks and exhaled a sigh.

'I appreciate that, and don't get me wrong, I'm not saying I'm not enjoying what we have, but I'm looking to the future, Sophie. I know it's early days for us, but this new job is about me having the financial freedom to have more control over my life. To do the things that I want to do, the things we might want to do together.' He gave her fingers, threaded between his, a squeeze. 'You know, when I look at Jackson and Pia and the life they have, it makes me realise that I need to be more focused and forward looking.'

Sophie shook her head.

'You have to stop comparing yourself with Jackson. There aren't many people who live in a house like theirs. Jackson is a great guy, but so are you and from where I'm sitting I definitely know who is the more attractive and most charismatic brother.'

'You see, I always knew you were a deeply wise woman. Although I'm pleased you didn't mention my pitiful financial situation,' Tom said dryly.

Sophie supposed it was only natural that Tom might compare

himself unfavourably to Jackson. It was only a little more than a year ago that he even discovered he had a brother, coming on top of the news that the man he thought was his father wasn't related to him after all. It had been a turbulent and emotional time for Tom coming to terms with his new reality, letting go of all the old misconceptions he held about who he was and where he came from. He was incredibly pleased and grateful to have Rex and Jackson in his life, but Sophie sensed that he still sometimes felt insecure in those relationships and the feeling of being an outsider hadn't yet left him.

Tom shifted on the sofa to turn his body to face her, and she shuffled up to his side, pulling herself up to his chest so that she could wrap her arms around his broad frame and see into his always enticing brown eyes. He stroked a hand over her cheek.

'I can honestly say it's never even occurred to me to think about your financial situation. I'm not that sort of person. I've never had a lot of money myself, but I always think there's so many other more important things to worry about. Seeing my mum get ill when she was still quite young and having her move into a care home has really brought home to me what's important in life. I know how much she would give to have her independence back so I don't ever want to take for granted the simple pleasures like going for a walk over at Primrose Woods or popping into town for a coffee. It makes me realise how lucky I am. And if I can get to do those things with someone' – she lifted her chin, her lips pursed, and her gaze travelled around the room – 'oh, I don't know, someone attractive, funny and really good company, then that has to be a bonus.'

'Hey, keep those compliments coming. Look.' Tom glanced at his watch. 'This has been great, but I should call that taxi.' He stretched his arms over his head. 'Thanks for the pep talk, Sophie.'

'Do you have to go?' she blurted without really thinking. All she knew was that she didn't want this day to end. 'You've said yourself you're not in a hurry to get back to your flat. And tonight you could stay here, if that works with your plans.'

His gaze settled on hers and the look that passed between them simmered with a promise that re-ignited all those sensations Sophie had felt earlier wrapped in his arms.

'Well, you do know I make a mean fry-up: sausages, hash browns, mushrooms, eggs and beans, the full works. I could do an early morning dash to the supermarket if needed.' He narrowed his eyes at her and she thought nothing had ever sounded quite so tempting.

'In that case, you simply have to stay,' she said with a smile.

13

'That's the best news ever. I can't believe it!' Pia clapped her hands together excitedly and danced around the kitchen. The dogs leapt up from their beds and joined in with what they must have thought was a new game.

Jackson had just come off the phone to his solicitor and was telling Pia the news.

'Harry really wants to sell us the cottages and let us have the alpacas as well? That's amazing. I wonder what made him change his mind.'

Jackson pursed his lips and looked at her wide-eyed. He knew exactly what had swung the deal in their favour.

'Well, apparently the agreement is on the proviso that we home Humphrey, Marvin and Jack together and that we allow Harry regular visiting rights. Your name was mentioned in the drawing up of the contract.'

'Really? Well, of course! We would have done that anyway. I'll have to go and see Harry again to thank him and to reassure him that the alpacas will have the best home here. Can you imagine how excited little Rosie will be knowing that we'll be getting more animals? Honestly, they'll be such a great attraction for the visitors. Most of all, though, I'm pleased for Harry. It must be a great weight off his mind.'

Pia paused for breath and Jackson nodded, smiling.

'And you must be pleased that Harry's had a change of heart about the cottages because it looked as though we might have had to walk away from that opportunity entirely.'

'It's a good result all round. It will probably take a few weeks to get all the paperwork signed so I'll be looking to make a start on the rebuild in the new year.'

'What's this then?' said Rex, who'd caught the tail end of the conversation. He came bowling along the passageway into the kitchen, with his usual distinctive gait, a wide smile on his face.

'You know those cottages I told you about at Rosewood Farm? Well, it looks as though we've agreed on the purchase. I'm going down to my solicitors in the morning to get the paperwork moving.'

'Well, that is good news. Congratulations, boy. There's a certain thrill in closing a deal. I know I was always chasing after the next big one, but invariably it never quite materialised in the way I'd hoped. You're a much better businessman than I ever was, Jackson.' Rex chuckled. 'What will you do with the cottages?'

'We'll give them a complete overhaul. Take everything out and start over again. They'll need damp proofing, repointing, new electrics, kitchen and bathrooms. Then we'll do some land-scaping, tidy up a bit outside and then they should be done. I'll hang on to them a while, offer them as rental properties locally.'

Jackson made it sound so straightforward and Pia admired how he had the skills and know-how to approach a project of that size. He wasn't at all fazed by the amount of work involved. He had the type of brain that could visualise a project and see how the finished product would look. Invariably, problems would crop up in the same way as they always did, but Jackson took those things in his stride, being an adept problem solver.

'Well, that deserves a glass of something to celebrate, I reckon,' said Rex, who was always ready to mark an occasion.

'Good idea,' said Jackson, heading for the fridge and pulling out a bottle of champagne, plus a bottle of alcohol-free fizz for Rex. 'Where's Ronnie? Will she be joining us?'

'Maybe a little later. She's headed to the van. There's some sorting out she needs to do.'

'Honestly, only Ronnie, eh? She's got a wonderful room here, all the space in the world, but she can't stay away from that old jalopy. It's like her comfort blanket.'

'I know,' said Rex, with a fond smile. 'It's... what do they call it? Her "happy place" where she can really be herself and fully relax and unwind. I'm not sure she'd ever get rid of the van now, even though our last trip in it wasn't the best. She has a spiritual attachment to those four wheels, more so now after it got us home safely from France after my funny turn.' Rex was keeping shtum about the real reason why Ronnie kept disappearing off to the van; she was grabbing any available moment to add some rows to the wedding blanket she was crocheting as their present.

Jackson eased the corks out of the bottles with a satisfying pop and poured the enticing fizz into three glasses before handing one to Pia and Rex.

'Well, here's to Rosewood Farm Cottages and their successful refurbishment.'

They all took a sip of the bubbles and clinked glasses, enjoying the moment of celebration.

'But we haven't told you the best thing yet, Rex.' Pia beamed, hardly able to contain her excitement. 'Harry Adams, who is selling the cottages, has some alpacas and wanted to find a good home for them before signing the contract, so we are shortly going to be welcoming Humphrey, Marvin and Jack to the family. Can you believe it? I've met them and honestly, they are the most gorgeous animals ever with really soft coats and funny expressions. You can't help but fall in love with them. It's the way they look at you, as though asking a question of you.'

'Well, the animal family is certainly growing around here then,' said Rex, chuckling.

'Oh, yes,' said Jackson, with a roll of his eyes. 'We'll have to start charging an entrance fee to the zoo soon.'

'Jackson, you love the animals as much as I do, you just like to grumble about them, but the alpacas are going to be such a great addition to the hall and they're going to be a hit with all our visitors. I honestly can't wait until they arrive.'

'Sounds to me as though you're more excited about the alpacas than you are about the cottages,' said Rex, with a grin on his face.

'Definitely. Jackson can take care of the cottages and I'll look after our new four-legged friends. That's what makes us a great team,' she said, smiling.

'Absolutely. If it hadn't been for Pia then I'm not certain Harry would have agreed on the sale, so you'll definitely have to be involved with any future negotiations. You're obviously a lucky charm.' Jackson winked at her, with that familiar half-smile on his lips, a gesture that always felt to her like a virtual hug.

Just then their attentions were distracted by the sound of an approaching car outside. Pia peered through the side window but she didn't recognise the silver hatchback or the figure inside.

'It's probably a delivery; let me go and see,' she said, dashing off.

Rex took a seat at the oak table while Jackson filled bowls with cashew nuts and crisps, to accompany the fizz, and then took a seat with his dad. Moments later, Pia was back.

'Look who's here!'

'Luke!' Jackson jumped out of his seat. 'How great to see you. How are you doing?'

'Good, thank you.' Luke's gaze ran over their drinks and nibbles, and immediately apologised. 'I'm really sorry to intrude and I won't keep you long, I promise, but I was passing and thought if I didn't stop and ask you, then I might never get round to it.'

'Absolutely no problem at all. We didn't have plans. Look, why don't you join us for a drink? We've just opened a bottle.'

'No, I won't, thanks. As I say, I don't want to take up too much of your time; and besides, I'm driving.'

'Just half a glass, maybe?' Pia suggested. 'Or we've even got some alcohol-free, if you prefer. We're celebrating a business deal and it would be great if you could join us.' Pia went across and picked the bottles out of the cooler.

'Go on then. You've twisted my arm, but I will go alcohol-free, thanks,' said Luke with a smile, taking the seat at the table Jackson offered him. 'How are you doing now, Jackson? You're looking well.'

'Good, thanks. I haven't got full mobility back in my left leg, but I'm getting there. The physio's ongoing so I'm hoping to be pretty much back to normal by the time our wedding rolls round as I'm told I'll need to be throwing some shapes on the dance floor.'

Pia rolled her eyes indulgently. Jackson was a reluctant dancer and all her previous attempts at persuading him to bop around the kitchen had been met with a firm refusal, but she'd told him that there could be no wheedling out of it on their wedding day. He would have to glide her around the floor of the barn in a romantic waltz for their first dance of the night whether he liked it or not.

'Well, that will be a sight not to be missed and it's not too long to go now. Rhi and I are looking forward to it, sharing your big day with you. Actually, the reason for my visit is in a way loosely connected, I suppose.' Luke took a breath and looked from Jackson to Pia as though bracing himself for whatever it was he had to say. 'I have a favour to ask of you. And I hope you don't think it's too cheeky.'

'Ask away,' said Jackson, expansively.

'Well, Rhi and I will be coming along to the Carols by Candlelight evening again. We've been to them all since they started a couple of years ago. The first one was when Rhi and I had only just got together. We always talk about that night because we mark it as the proper start of our relationship. Rhi loves Christmas and she was swept away by the romance of the occasion, seeing the lights and the huge twinkling Christmas trees, and huddling up together listening to the carol singers against the backdrop of the hall. All our friends were there as well, which made it extra special. Anyway, I've been thinking about this for some time now, but I've decided I'm going to propose to Rhi and I thought what better place and time than at the Carols by Candlelight evening. I know that it would be really special for Rhi. Only if that's okay with you both, of course.'

Pia swooned, flapping a hand against her chest.

'That will be so romantic.'

'I hope so,' said Luke with a sheepish smile. 'I'm not going to take anything for granted, but I was hoping I might be able to put aside a bottle of champagne with some glasses so that if or when she says yes we can celebrate with a toast.'

'Absolutely,' said Jackson. 'We can organise that for you no problem, and if there's anything else we can do to help make the moment even more special then you know you only have to ask.'

'Cheers, Jackson and Pia. Now I've run it past you, I can begin to make some proper plans, which is nerve-racking. I do hope she says yes or else I'm going to look pretty daft, not to mention heartbroken.'

'Absolutely no chance.' Pia was quick to reassure Luke. 'Rhi is going to be thrilled. Do you think she has any idea that you're planning to propose?'

'I don't think so. I hope it's going to come as a complete surprise. We'll see,' he said, laughing.

'It's bound to be. I can remember every detail of Jackson proposing to me as though it was yesterday and that was at last year's Christmas event. Honestly, I had no idea what he had in mind. We were relaxing in the hot tub at the end of the evening, beneath the stars, and Jackson produced a ring from out of nowhere.' She closed her eyes briefly, transported back to that time. 'I was totally speechless.'

'And as you can imagine, that's a pretty rare occurrence,' quipped Jackson.

'Well, you know what we must do? We'll have to have someone nearby to capture the moment on camera. And maybe, I don't know' – Pia looked from Luke to Jackson – 'I really don't want to interfere, but we could always help with the set-up if you wanted us to. We could put the proposal up in lights – can you imagine how amazing that would look? – arrange flowers or...'

'Pia! It's Luke's proposal. I'm sure he has in mind exactly the way he wants to deliver it. But yes, we can be around to help in whatever way you want us to. Just ask.'

'Congratulations, young man,' said Rex, who'd been observing the interaction with a great deal of interest.

'Thanks,' said Luke, beaming. 'I'll be in touch if I think of anything else. Well, I suppose I ought to go and source a ring now. I'm guessing diamonds are the way to go?'

'Yes, or you could go for rubies or sapphires, which would

both suit Rhi's colouring, or...' She was stopped in her tracks by a warning look from Jackson. 'Although you can't really go wrong with diamonds,' added Pia, which seemed to be the answer Luke was looking for.

Later, after Luke had left, Jackson topped up their glasses and Pia took another sip, the bubbles matching her excitable mood after all the good news of the day.

'I love Rhi and Luke, they make such a gorgeous couple and I'm going to make sure I'm exactly in the right spot so that I can see her reaction when he proposes. It will make the evening all the more special. Like reliving our proposal from last year. It's such a romantic gesture from Luke!'

'Yeah, but not quite as romantic as my proposal in the hot tub though?' Jackson furrowed his brow, a look of mischief in his eyes.

'Oh, absolutely not! Nothing could ever beat that, my darling!'

It had been a perfectly clear December night with the stars sparkling in the sky complementing the lights in the trees and on the buildings. Jackson had arranged champagne too and it had been so romantic and intimate. They'd enjoyed the bubbles in their glasses while luxuriating in the warm bubbles of the hot tub as they discussed the success of the evening, recounting the conversations they'd had with their friends. They might have sat there all night enjoying the moment of peace and satisfaction, against a twinkling night sky, but Jackson had taken Pia's breath away when he proposed, totally unexpectedly. Now, as she retold the story to Rex, one he had heard several times before, she could conjure up all those feelings she'd felt in that special moment: disbelief, wonder and excitement. There was no doubt she had been swept away by the romance of the occasion.

Now, with the big day fast approaching, she presumed it was only natural to have some last-minute nerves. Sometimes she woke in the middle of the night, her heart thumping, an indistinct anxiety taunting her as she tossed and turned. Was she doing the right thing in marrying Jackson? Might it cause a subtle shift in their relationship and affect the running of the hall, or was she worrying unnecessarily? What would her mum be advising her to do if she was still around? Every girl needed their mum's support in the run-up to her wedding and it was at moments like these that Pia missed her being here hugely. She suppressed a sigh and focused her attention back in the room.

'I'm not sure how I proposed to Ronnie,' Rex was saying, his face scrunched up as he tried to recall the moment. 'Or if I even did? It's certainly not very memorable, although you can rest assured Ronnie will remember.' He gave that distinctive throaty chuckle. 'I probably won't ask her about it because she'll only tell me! And I know I will have been sadly lacking.'

'Yes, but what's important is that you're back together now, Rex.' It might have taken them a couple of decades, but they'd reached a point where they both appreciated and respected each other. 'You're both happy and enjoying each other's company, and it doesn't get any better than that.' Pia took another sip of her champagne, thinking how fortunate Rex and Ronnie were to have found each other again in their later years, her mind flittering to where she and Jackson might be in twenty, thirty, forty years' time. It was hard enough to look beyond the wedding, let alone decades ahead.

All she did know was that today had been a particularly auspicious day and she wouldn't allow any niggly doubts to spoil the mood. Hadn't she been long convinced that there was something magical in the air around Primrose Hall? She had to keep believing that it was true.

14

_____

'One of these days, you're going to have to let me beat you. Just for my self-confidence. I always had myself down as a half-decent squash player, but in all my games with you, I think I've only beaten you, what is it, about three times?'

'Twice actually,' said Tom, correcting Jackson with a smile. Well, to his way of thinking, there weren't many areas where he could top Jackson's skills, so if he could continue to thrash him at their preferred choice of racket sport, then he was going to make the most of it.

The brothers had just left the sports centre after their regular and energetic game of squash and were heading for their cars.

'Worse than I thought then,' said Jackson with a wry smile. 'I really need to up my game. Are we going to grab a beer?'

'Sure thing,' said Tom.

He was relieved that Jackson didn't seem to be harbouring any ill-feeling over his decision to leave his job at the stables. Maybe Sophie was right and Jackson had just been taken by surprise at Tom's news to go back into the corporate world. Perhaps now that he'd had time to consider what it meant, he'd realised it was no big deal and they would quickly be able to find someone else to fill the vacancy. Tom wasn't sure. Although the bond between him and his brother was growing all the time, he still found it hard to judge Jackson's moods or his true feelings. He found himself trying to second-guess how Jackson might react to any given situation and wondering if he might upset him inadvertently.

The alternative, and more likely, scenario, was that Tom was far too sensitive. He could see that and was attempting to be less so, but when you'd been lied to by the people closest to you, your mum especially, then it was inevitable that it made you wary of other people and their intentions. The ripples caused by the discovery about his true parentage continued to impact his life and the people around him. It would take some time to truly come to terms with how he fitted in this new world.

One of the positives that came from finding you had a brother you never knew about was sharing a beer with him in the local pub. He felt a certain amount of pride walking into a bar and seeing heads turn, knowing that people were seeing the likeness between them. They took their pints and sat in the window seat of The Three Feathers, which overlooked the village green.

'So how are things?' Jackson asked.

'Yes, good. I was pleased with how the workshops went at the weekend. Everyone seemed to enjoy the sessions and the feedback from the visitors was positive. I'm hoping they're something you might want to think about continuing on a semi-regular basis, perhaps a couple of times a year?'

'Absolutely. Pia and I were saying the same thing, and now you've implemented the idea I'm sure whoever takes over will be able to pick it up and run with it.' Jackson took another mouthful of his beer. 'Look, I wanted you to know that I'm really pleased for you with regards to the new job. I probably didn't say that when you told me and I should have done. It sounds like a great career move for you.'

'Cheers, Jackson. I appreciate it.' Even if his unexpected words might have wrong-footed Tom, Jackson had obviously done some thinking since their last interaction. Perhaps he was finding it as tricky to navigate this new relationship as Tom was. 'Yeah, it means I'll be able to make some proper plans. Mainly, I want to get on the property ladder again. I feel I've been living like a student these last couple of years.'

'I can understand that.' Jackson nodded. 'Where do you think you might end up? Will you move closer to work?'

'No, that's one thing I am certain on. Now I've found my family – you and Pia, Rex and Ronnie – I want to stay nearby so that I can see you guys on a regular basis. Dad's not getting any younger so I don't want to be that far away that I can only get to see him a couple of times a year. I want to be around to play a proper part in all your lives, to help out and provide support when I can. Basically, what I'm saying is that you're stuck with me now whether you like it or not.'

'Well, I'm pleased to hear it. It's been good having you around. I'd hate for us to lose touch when we've only just got to know each other. Family is important, right? Even if they can drive you mad at times.'

'Yeah, exactly.' Tom laughed, slightly taken aback by Jackson's rare display of sentimentality. 'And of course Sophie is here too so there's another incentive to stay.'

'Great. It's going well for you two then?'

'Yep.' Tom took a moment to think about that, an image of Sophie popping into his head, the sound of her laughter ringing in his ears, a smile involuntarily spreading across his face. 'She's a great girl. We get on well and it's so easy being with her. We seem to gel and I suppose I want to be in a position where we can make some plans together for the future, if we decide that's what we want.'

Despite Sophie's assurances that she liked Tom for who he was and that she wasn't bothered about material considerations, Tom was more pragmatic. She might feel that way now, but how would she feel a year, two years down the line if they wanted to move their relationship on to another level? What if they wanted to find a place together or start a family? Those things took some serious money. Perhaps now was too soon to be thinking along those lines for their relationship, but they were definitely goals he wanted to achieve some time in the future.

'Actually, I saw Sophie the other night and she was talking about Pia's hen do, how the girls were winding her up over what they had planned for her, but it got me thinking that we probably need to make some plans for the stag. Have you got any special requests?'

'Something low key probably. I'd be happy coming down here for a few pints with a few friends.'

'You only get married once...' Tom gave a small grimace. 'Well, hopefully, at least... so maybe we could mark it with some kind of activity, like paintballing or clay-pigeon shooting, and then go for a few drinks after.'

Jackson mulled the suggestion over in his mind for a moment.

'You know what would be fun? Quad biking or kart racing. I think everyone would be up for that.'

Tom raised his eyebrows at Jackson.

'Are you kidding me? After what happened to you in the summer? Pia would never forgive me if I organised something where you might end up doing yourself another injury. I know it's your stag do, Jackson, but I've got to make sure you get home safely so that you're in one piece for the wedding. Let me have a think about it and see what I can come up with.'

'Fair enough,' said Jackson with a wry chuckle. 'You might have a point there.'

Tom wanted to give Jackson a memorable and fun stag night, one where they could all let off some steam and share a few drinks, but he was also mindful that he had a duty to Pia, his soon-to-be sister-in-law, to ensure Jackson didn't come to any harm, so two- or four-wheeled activities were definitely off the cards. He'd give it some thought. He was just pleased that he and Jackson were on good terms once again because he took his responsibilities as best man, and perhaps even more importantly, as a big brother, very seriously indeed.

15

'Here's two of my favourite girls! How lovely to see you both! There's a special seat over there by the window. It's the best view in the house. Why don't you wander over and I'll be across to take your order in a moment.'

Pia and Sophie had arrived at the Tree Tops Café to a characteristically warm and friendly welcome from Lizzie. It was a beautiful spot offering panoramic views of the landscape and the café had a first-class reputation for its homemade quiches, soups and sandwiches, along with a wide and scrumptious selection of cakes. This place would always hold a special place in Pia's heart because it was where she first learnt about the job at Primrose Hall, her eye taken by a hand-written advertisement on a postcard in the display box at the front of the café. She often thought where she might be now if she hadn't noticed the job vacancy that day and hadn't rushed off an email to the address given. The advertisement had given away few details, only that it was a live-in job as a personal assistant involving admin work and animal care, and while she didn't have a lot of experience on either front, she thought there would no harm in taking a punt, never believing for one moment that anything would actually come of it. Had she known that Jackson Moody, her teenage crush, was behind the unknown email address and was also the new owner of the refurbished Primrose Hall, then she would never have applied for the job in the first place. There were so many coincidences and a synchronicity that led Pia to reconnecting with Jackson. When she'd accepted the job at Primrose Hall, albeit somewhat reluctantly, she'd only ever viewed it as a short-term solution to her urgent need to find a job and somewhere to live for her and Bertie.

Now, Pia sat down at the table and let out a satisfied sigh as she always did as her gaze took in the sight of the huge redwood trees around them.

Who could have known then that eighteen months later she would be preparing for her wedding to that boy, now a man, who had once broken her heart? She still had to pinch herself that she had found a whole new family and community, a home, a menagerie and the love of her life, all within the grounds of Primrose Hall. There had definitely been something of that magic working in the air around that time and Pia liked to think it was her mum and dad looking out for her, giving her a gentle nudge in the right direction.

'So how have you been?' Sophie asked, breaking into Pia's thoughts.

'Good, yes, really good! Busy, as usual. We've got some new animals coming to join us at the hall soon.'

Just then Lizzie arrived with her notepad and wide smile.

'What are you girls having?'

'I'll go for a cappuccino and a toasted teacake, please.'

'And I'll have a latte and a Chelsea bun,' added Sophie with a smile.

'Anyway, tell me about these animals,' she asked when Lizzie had gone to see to their order. 'It sounds very intriguing.'

'Ah, yes! Well, Jackson's secured a deal to buy some old cottages. He's going to do them up like he did with the hall, but Harry, the man selling them, was dragging his feet because he had his three alpacas who had belonged to his late wife to consider. He didn't want to sign on the dotted line until he knew the animals had a home to go to. Jackson had taken me along to show me the cottages and it looked as though the deal might fall through, but of course once I found out about the alpacas I knew we simply had to have them, regardless of the cottages. Honestly, Sophie, they are gorgeous and they are going to fit in perfectly over at the hall. You'll have to come and see them as soon as they arrive.'

'Jackson really is the consummate businessman, isn't he?'

'Yeah, he is.' Pia paused, noticing the knowing smile hovering on Sophie's lips, the light in her eyes. 'What do you mean exactly?'

'Well, taking you along, knowing that you would be able to persuade the guy to sign the deal with a promise to look after his alpacas; it's genius!'

'But Jackson didn't know...' Pia's words trailed away as she clearly considered that idea. Was that why Jackson had taken her along in the first place? Had he known about the situation with the animals and anticipated that Pia would jump in to offer the animals a home? 'Oh my God, I wonder if he did. It didn't even occur to me... the...'

She saw the smile spread across Sophie's lips, the nod of her head. Was Pia a fool not to have even considered the possibility? At that moment Lizzie reappeared with their order and placed their coffees and cakes on the tables.

'How are you, Pia? How's life at the hall?'

'Yes, good,' she said, putting all thoughts of Jackson's dodgy business dealings to one side. 'We're just gearing up for the last few events of the year, and then the wedding will be here. It's come round so quickly!'

'We're looking forward to it. We'll be there for the Christmas carols, we wouldn't miss that now, and then to have the wedding the following week, well, it's going to make the festivities extra special. Rosie is so excited to be your bridesmaid, I really think she might go pop. We can't wait to see her in her dress; oh, and you in your dress as well, obviously,' said Lizzie, laughing.

'It's fine,' said Pia with a grin. 'I know exactly who's going to be the star of the show that day: little Princess Rosie.'

Despite Pia's best plans to keep the preparations low key, the build-up for the wedding had taken on a force of its own. She supposed it was only natural that the people around her would be excited for her, but the constant chatter about the big day was doing nothing for her nerves. To think that in the matter of a few weeks she would be Mrs Moody or Lady of the Manor, as Jackson liked to tease her, only added to her trepidation.

'Anyway, tell me your news,' Pia said, conscious that once they got on to the subject of weddings, they might never get off it. 'How's Bill?'

'He's absolutely dandy, revelling in being a granddad. He absolutely adores little Willow, but then we all do! She's such a little cutie.'

'I know, isn't she just? Abbey brought her round the other day and Ruby came with little Freddie too. We had such a lovely time with lots of cuddles, which played havoc with my hormones, I can tell you! Being an auntie and a godmother has to be the best.'

'I can tell you being a grandmother is pretty decent too!' said Lizzie, chuckling.

When Lizzie left to see to another customer, Pia turned her

attention to Sophie, whose vibrant chestnut hair fell loosely onto her shoulders, offsetting the healthy glow radiating from her skin. Pia reached across the table and squeezed Sophie's hands.

'You're looking great, Sophie! How are things going?'

'Good!' A smile spread across her lips as though she was hugging a big secret to herself. 'I don't want to jinx anything, but I can honestly say I'm happier than I've been in years. The job's going well, I'm settled in my little cottage in Wishwell and I'm enjoying being able to do what I want, when I want, without having to answer to a bad-tempered boyfriend.'

'Well, the new lifestyle certainly suits you.'

'I feel so much better in myself. When you've been in a toxic relationship like I was with Kyle, it impacts on every aspect of your life. Your job, your health, your friendships. When I look back, I realise what a bad way I was in, but when you're in the middle of something like that it's difficult to think clearly or to see a way out. It makes me shudder to think that I could still be in that relationship if it hadn't been for my friends, you and Greta especially, helping me to find a new path.'

'That's kind of you to say, but you'd already taken those big steps on your own before I'd even met you. But what I do know is that you're unrecognisable from the girl I met on that first day at the stables. Then you were shy, fearful and almost invisible beneath your dark clothes. It's been lovely seeing you come out of your shell and being the person you were always destined to be. That might sound corny but it's true! And I'm really glad that we've become good friends through this time.'

'Me too. It's been a revelation to me, putting the effort into my female friendships. When I was with Kyle, I lost touch with my friends because he never liked me seeing them. He would give me a hard time if I even suggested doing something without him, so in the end it became easier not to. I should have taken that as a red flag, but I was blind to his controlling behaviour. Meeting you and Greta, Abbey and Rhi, Katy, it's just brought home to me how much I appreciate having you all in my life. I'll certainly not make the same mistake again. My girlfriends will always come first now before any man!'

'Really?' Pia took a sip from her cappuccino before taking a bite from her buttery, delicious teacake, dabbing at her mouth with a napkin. 'I had thought that Tom might be playing a part in this newfound happiness of yours.' Pia's eyes were wide and filled with curiosity.

'Okay, so he might have something to do with it too,' Sophie said lightly. 'It's funny because I swore off men, after Kyle, and told myself I'd be better off single, and then when I least wanted to, or expected to, I met Tom and that's thrown all my best-laid plans up in the air.'

'And is it such a problem?'

'Not really. I suppose I'm just worried about getting hurt again. I like Tom, he's such a sweetheart and we get on well together, but I guess I'm wary, having had my fingers burnt before. It's almost like it's too easy and I'm trying to find reasons why it shouldn't work. We both told each other we weren't looking for anything serious and so I think the way we feel about each other has taken us both by surprise.'

'Well, I can give a great character reference for Tom if that helps? I've not known him long either but he's one of the kindest, sweetest men I've ever met. He would do anything for anyone and we wouldn't have coped without him when Jackson was in hospital and when Rex had his heart attack over in France. He took care of all the arrangements. He's slotted into the family really well, as though he's always been part of the clan, and has even managed to win Jackson round, which is no mean feat.'

'He is lovely,' said Sophie, sighing. 'I'm conscious that he's been through quite a difficult time with everything that's happened and I really don't want to put any additional pressure on him, so I'm happy just to carry on the way we are and see where things take us.' Sophie shrugged. It scared her to admit how strong her feelings were for Tom. In truth, she realised she'd fallen in love with him weeks ago, when she could no longer put down her stirrings of longings and desire as a passing infatuation. Not when she spent all her time thinking about him, wondering when she might see him next and imagining a future they might have together. 'I think finding this new job is a big step for him. He sees it as a way of getting his life back on track.'

'Sounds like a good move for him, although we were disappointed because Jackson and I had hoped Tom would stay working for the hall. It's perfectly understandable though that he would want to pursue his own interests.'

'I think it's more about the money. He had a very good career before and a great lifestyle too, so when he turned his back on all that, his living arrangements changed quite significantly. Now, he's ready to get back on the property ladder so I think that's what's behind the decision. He did say something about...' She tried to recall Tom's words. 'Something to the effect that he didn't have much to offer me materially, that he'd like to plan some holidays and decent nights outs for us, to be able to treat me, which is a lovely thought, but those things aren't really important to me.' It made Sophie feel special enough that Tom would even think that way. 'I just like spending time with him, that's enough for me.'

'But not for Tom by the sounds of things.' Pia nodded her head as though one of life's mysteries had been revealed to her. 'He's obviously thinking to the future, which has to be a good sign, right?'

'Yes, I guess so,' said Sophie, although she still couldn't be certain that he was thinking long-term future as far as she was concerned, or just until something better presented itself.

'Just think, if you and Tom do end up together, then we might become related to each other one day. Sisters-in-law. How fantastic would that be?'

Sophie laughed.

'Now you really are getting ahead of yourself, but I must admit I love being involved with the Primrose Hall community so I would never want to lose that connection. As for me and Tom, well, we'll have to see how it goes.'

Pia and Sophie finished their coffees and cakes, soaking up the atmosphere of the busy, vibrant café, their gazes continually drifting outside to the eye-catching scenery. Pia put down her mug decisively and turned to Sophie.

'You've got me thinking. I'm wondering if Jackson did know about Harry's alpacas all along and took me with him knowing I wouldn't be able to resist some defenceless animals that needed a home. Do you think he would do something like that?'

'Absolutely, he would,' said Sophie, laughing. 'That's got Jackson's signature all over it. I'm sure there's no ill intent there. He just knows the right way to seal a deal.'

Pia widened her eyes and shook her head, hardly daring to believe it.

'Honestly, I'm going to have words with that man and if he has done that, then... Well, I'm not sure what I'll do.'

'Call off the marriage, I reckon. Or else you'll have to let that old man down and send those poor helpless animals to a rescue centre instead. That will show Jackson,' said Sophie, teasingly.

'Hmmm, well, I would never do that, but I'll get the truth out of Jackson, don't you worry.'

'Well, I'd like to be a fly on the wall when you have that

conversation. Come on,' said Sophie, still laughing, 'we should get going.'

On their way out, Lizzie came across to say goodbye, enveloping them both in a hug.

'See you soon. Thinking about it, the next time will be at your hen do, Pia. Katy and I are really looking forward to it. Sounds as though it will be a fun night and we can't wait to see all those bronzed, lean, dancing men up close.' Lizzie flapped a hand over her heart dramatically. 'It will be a proper treat.'

'Oh my God,' exclaimed Pia fiercely. 'I hope you're kidding me. I've told Abbey I don't want anything like that. If she—'

'It's fine, Pia,' said Lizzie, holding up her palms to prevent her friend from having a full-on meltdown in the middle of the café, and giving her another hug. 'I was joking. There'll be no hunky men, or at least I don't think there will be.' She gave a far too nonchalant shrug, her gaze lifting to the ceiling. 'Although every hen night should contain a few surprises, don't you think?'

16

'Hello, Harry, it's only me! Pia. I was here the other day with Jackson Moody.'

Pia had arrived at Rosewood Farm Cottage on a cold November morning and was calling through the letterbox as she didn't want to alarm Harry unnecessarily. As before, she heard movement from within the house and waited for several moments until he reached the door.

'Oh, hello, love!' His face brightened to see her. 'Come along in. I was just going to have a cuppa. Pop the kettle on, would you, and we can have a natter. I shall have to go and sit down.'

Pia appreciated just how much of an effort it was for Harry to do the simplest of tasks, getting out of his chair: walking along the hallway or making himself a drink or something to eat. It brought Pia out in a cold sweat to think how he managed the stairs, and she wondered if he didn't get lonely spending so much time on his own. The cottage really was out in the middle of nowhere and she suspected the only people he got to see were his carers, who were only able to stay for short periods of time.

With the drinks made, Pia went and sat down beside Harry.

'I just wanted to come and say a big thank you for agreeing the contract with Jackson and, most importantly' – Pia gave Harry a gentle squeeze of his arm – 'for handing over the care of your precious alpacas to us. I know how much they mean to you and I wanted to reassure you that we will take the best care of them. We have their paddock ready and we're looking forward to welcoming them to the hall.'

'Good, I'm pleased. You know, I wouldn't have left here without knowing that the boys had a good home to go to. I didn't want them separated. Every time I look at them, I'm reminded of my Vera. She would have wanted me to do the right thing by them.'

'And you have done, Harry. Remember that you are always welcome to come to the hall to see how the alpacas are doing. I can pick you up, or Abbey from Rushgrove Lodge often brings Wendy along to see her dog, Bertie, so we'll definitely be able to get something organised.'

'That gives me a great deal of peace of mind. Thanks, love. If it hadn't been for you then I might never have agreed to leaving this place. They would have had to carry me out in a box.'

'I honestly think the move to Rushgrove Lodge will give you a new lease of life. There's lots of people around and so many activities that you can get involved in, if you want to, of course. Do you have a moving date yet?'

'Well, my room's booked so I can go when I'm ready. I know the contracts on this place won't be sorted for a while yet, but I'm not worried about that. Now our solicitors have got the wheels turning it will run its natural course. There's a few bits I need to get sorted here, decide what I'm going to take with me and what can go to the charity shop.'

He looked around him and Pia followed his gaze. More than a

few bits, she thought; more like a lifetime's worth of possessions and memories.

'If I can help at all then you only need ask.'

'That's kind of you, Pia, but I'm sure I'll manage.'

Harry sounded chipper, but Pia knew it couldn't be easy for him.

'It must be quite a wrench to leave your home, the place where you spent so many happy times with your wife.'

Harry pondered on that for a moment, nodding his head.

'It can't be any worse than when I lost my Vera. This is just a house. We had some lovely times here, happy times, but it's not the same without her by my side. She made this place a home and now, well, it's an empty shell. The heart of it is gone and I think it makes it worse being here on my own. I think it's probably the right time for me to move on.'

'I understand that, Harry. It's not an easy transition, but I'm certain once you get to Rushgrove Lodge you'll settle in quickly. Besides, I think you probably deserve a bit of looking after, having your meals made for you and having people on hand if you should need them.'

Harry picked up his mug with both hands and lifted it to his lips. Pia wasn't sure if his eyes were rheumy or if they were filled with emotion from talking about his late wife. Either way, her heart went out to him.

'Let us know when you'd like us to take Humphrey, Marvin and Jack and I'll arrange to send a trailer down to come and collect them.'

'Well, as far as I'm concerned, the sooner the better. I worry about them down there on their own in case they fall ill or injure themselves and we miss it somehow, or else they might get their heads stuck through the wire fencing. It wouldn't be the first time. I'm grateful to Molly for all her help, but it's not the same as having someone there all the time to keep an eye on them.'

'Well, you've no need to worry any more. The alpacas will soon adjust to their new lodgings and they'll have plenty of people checking on them every day.'

'I'm sure they will,' he said, chuckling. 'They'll be living in the lap of luxury. Really though, I'm very grateful to you and Jackson. You've given me some peace of mind.'

'I'm so pleased you feel that way, Harry, but there's no need to thank us. We should be the ones thanking you. Look, I'll get the transport organised in the next couple of days and will let you know when we intend to collect them. I'll make sure to come down at the same time and I'll pop in to see you so that you'll know what's going on.'

'Right, well, I can start making some proper plans now, get my stuff packed up, the bits I want to take with me, and then move into the lodge. My room's lovely, it's got everything I need, a bed and an armchair, and there's room for me to take some of my own furniture too. All these photos I shall have to take, but really there won't be much else I need. My room's on the ground floor with some double doors onto the garden, and they get lots of wildlife over there apparently, so I'll be able to sit and watch the birds and squirrels. It's got to beat this view.'

Pia had to agree, taking a glance around the room. Although there was plenty of countryside surrounding the cottages, from Harry's vantage point from the armchair in his front room, looking out through some grubby net curtains, you could barely see anything at all, only a snapshot of the greying sky.

In comparison, Rushgrove Lodge was a bright and airy building with modern artwork on the walls and full-height windows in the communal rooms overlooking the central atrium where there were birdbaths, water features and colourful flower beds. The main lounge was spacious, but still managed to be cosy and welcoming with comfy armchairs where you could sit and chat to friends, or else find a quiet corner to simply contemplate the view outside. Pia suspected that Harry would really benefit from the change of scene.

'You know, we're getting married next month at Primrose Hall. I was thinking about what you told me about your wedding, and how Vera's uncle Humphrey gave her away. It's funny to think that Humphrey, Marvin and Jack will be there to see us on our big day too and I reckon that has to be a lucky omen! I'm definitely going to have some photos taken with the alpacas in my wedding dress so that I can show you. I might even get them some new harnesses in a colour to complement the flowers in my bouquet. Although I think Jackson might say that's taking things a step too far. Not that I'll take any notice of him. He's always going off on some wild flight of fancy so why shouldn't I?'

Harry chuckled, charmed by Pia's bubbly personality.

'Well, I hope it's true, that the boys will be lucky for you. One thing I can tell you is that if you're half as happy in your marriage to Jackson as my Vera and I were together, then you're in for some special times ahead.'

Harry took off his glasses and rubbed at his eye with the knuckle of his index finger before replacing his spectacles and looking at Pia closer.

'I like you,' he said. 'You're a sweet girl and Jackson's a lucky man to be marrying you, although I'm certain he knows that. Make sure he treats you properly.'

'He will do, don't you worry about that.' She certainly wasn't worried. If people knew the real Jackson, if they could see the kind, caring and gentle man that she knew and loved, then they would have no concerns about his integrity. 'Jackson's a real softie beneath that sometimes gruff exterior,' she explained.

'I'm sure he is, love, and I'm pleased to do business with him. What is it they say though? "Behind every successful man is a good woman," and Jackson wouldn't be half as good without you at his side, you know that? Still, I'm very happy that you'll both be taking over custody of these old cottages.' His gaze travelled to the far cobwebbed corners of the room. 'Like me, they're in desperate need of a bit of an overhaul,' he said, with a twinkle in his eye.

17

Rex rolled into the kitchen where Ronnie and Pia were sitting at the kitchen table looking at floral table decorations on the laptop. Pia had decided on a frosty blue and white scheme for the flowers featuring roses, anemones and silver brunia, with a nod to the Christmas season with some pinecones, berries and mistletoe. With Ronnie at her side, she could exchange ideas and gain a different perspective, but most of all she appreciated the moral support when her enthusiasm wobbled or if she got stuck on a decision. It was bittersweet, of course, because it should have been her mum at her side, holding her hand and imparting advice. She would have been excited for her and would have relished every moment of the preparations, helping to choose the outfits, picking out the flowers and selecting the menus, but she would have been a steadying influence too. Pia missed the reassurance that her mum could have provided. *Did she like Jackson?* Pia could never marry someone that her parents didn't approve of. *Was it too soon to be thinking about marrying when she'd only been with Jackson for little over a year? Did she think Jackson really loved her for who she was and didn't just consider it to be a good business decision to make Pia his wife?*

These were hardly questions she could ask Ronnie, but Pia shook her head, chastising herself. She was being ridiculous even entertaining such thoughts.

It made her sad that her parents weren't here to see how much she'd achieved since she'd moved out of Meadow Cottages in both her personal and professional life. Like her, they would never have quite believed that she was living in a manor house only a few miles away from home, with her teenage love, Jackson Moody. It was a shame they never got to meet him, even as a teenager, but Pia had kept her relationship with Jackson a secret because his bad-boy reputation was well known throughout the village. If her parents had discovered the truth, then they would definitely have tried to put a stop to the relationship.

Now, she allowed herself a smile. How things had changed. If her parents had met Jackson today, of course they would have approved. He was a successful businessman, a renowned public speaker, and a philanthropist, and they couldn't fail to be charmed by his good looks and everything that he'd achieved. They would be impressed by his wealth, obviously, but most of all, her mum would have been delighted simply by the fact that Jackson had fallen in love with their daughter and cared for her just as much as her parents had done.

They would have been thrilled too to be grandparents to little Freddie. They would have spoilt him rotten and been on hand for all the babysitting duties, but sadly it was never meant to be. Pia often recognised that pang of regret in her stomach that they had been taken far too soon, missing out on so much of their children's and grandchildren's lives. She always allowed herself that moment of reflection when the memories of her parents came flooding into her mind along with the what-ifs, but neither her mum nor her dad would want her to be unhappy. They would be urging her to live her very best life. She felt a pressure to make the most of every moment, especially after everything that had happened this year with Jackson's accident and Rex's health scare, a timely reminder that life was short and you couldn't take anything for granted.

Mind you, seeing Rex now, looking smart in a pair of brown and white pinstriped trousers, with a white collarless shirt and black waistcoat, that familiar wide grin on his face, you would never believe that he had been seriously ill just a few months ago.

'Well, you're looking very dapper, Rex,' Ronnie said, her gaze sweeping up and down. 'Where are you off to?'

'I'm going into town. There are some jobs I need to see to. I might stay for some lunch too, so I'll probably be back about mid-afternoon.'

'Well, that sounds like fun. Why don't I come with you? I think we're pretty much done here, aren't we, Pia? We can make a day of it.'

'No!' Rex held up a hand to refute that idea, before softening his response. 'It's all right, Ronnie. You stay here with Pia. The stuff I have to do will be pretty boring. I don't want you to have to traipse around the shops after me.'

'Oh, I see,' said Ronnie. The disappointment in her voice was tangible even if Rex hadn't already noticed the truculent curl to her lip. 'Are you meeting someone then?'

'No. Who would I be meeting? I'm going to have a mooch about on my own.'

'Hmmm, well, I'm not sure why I can't come with you, but if you don't want me to then there isn't much I can do about that.'

Rex chuckled, shaking his head at Pia.

'Don't be like that, Ronnie. You don't know what I might be up to. I could be buying your birthday present for all you know.'

'Rex!' The dismay on Ronnie's face was clear to see. 'My birthday was two months ago!'

'Ah, yes,' he said, laughing. 'Well, perhaps I'm getting ahead of myself and buying for next year. Or' – he tapped the side of his nose with his forefinger – 'have you thought that I might be doing some Christmas shopping?'

'Oh, Christmas!' Ronnie sounded marginally appeased. 'I keep forgetting about that. I'm so focused on the wedding, I can't really think of anything else, although I did buy most of my presents weeks ago and have wrapped them too.' She looked at Rex through narrowed eyes. 'I'm not sure I actually believe you, Rex. You forget that I know you of old and I always have a sixth sense when you're up to something.'

'Honestly, Ronnie, what do you take me for?' Rex said expansively, doing nothing to allay her fears. 'One of these days you're going to have to start trusting me.'

Pia didn't like to take sides so she stayed quiet, but she couldn't help wondering if Ronnie was right and maybe Rex was up to something. He was being evasive, as though he was hugging a secret to himself, and tight-lipped too, but perhaps it was just a special Christmas present he had in store for Ronnie after all.

'Right, well, I shall leave you two good ladies to it. Come here, Ronnie,' he said, holding out a hand to her and lifting her to her feet. 'Do you want me to get you anything while I'm in town?'

He wrapped his arms around her waist, pulling her into his chest, and Pia noticed how Ronnie instantly relaxed in his embrace, a smile spreading across her face, her previous concerns forgotten in an instant. She dropped her head against his chest, revelling in the moment.

Pia recognised the effect it had upon Ronnie because it was the exact same way Jackson made her feel when he held her.

Warm, safe and protected, as though nothing could touch her all the time she was wrapped in his embrace.

'You don't think he's got a doctor's or hospital appointment that he's not telling me about?' asked Ronnie once Rex had gone on his way.

'No, he would have said.' Pia got up and flicked the kettle on. 'Besides, you always go with him to those and I thought he didn't have to go back for another three months? In any case, did you see him? He was positively beaming with good health.'

'That's true. There was a definite spring in his step. Maybe he's got something else on the go then,' said Ronnie.

Pia shot her a glance, knowing exactly where Ronnie's mind was going.

'Don't be daft. Everyone can see how fond he is of you. Honestly, the pair of you are like a couple of teenagers when you get together.'

'Hmm, I don't doubt that he's fond of me, but is that enough? What would happen if his head was turned by something or someone else? He'd be off without so much as a backwards glance.' Ronnie shook her head, obviously perturbed by the idea. 'I know,' she said, putting a finger in the air, as though solving a crime. 'He's probably having a few beers with his pals. He knows I don't like him drinking, it's not good for his health, so that's why he'll be keeping it quiet.'

'You worry too much.' Pia brought over two mugs of tea and placed them on the table. She also opened the cake tin, which was filled with cherry and sultana scones, gathered some plates and knives from the cupboard and put out small ramekins of creamy butter and jam. 'What you have to remember is that Rex is a lot like Jackson. They're independent and free-spirited, and need time to themselves when they can pursue their own interests. To be honest with you, I adore Jackson with every bone in my body, but he can be very intense, as you know, so I've come to make the most of those times when he's occupied with something else. It gives me the space to do the things I enjoy, like reading or baking or pottering about the house, without him getting under my feet.' Pia laughed.

'Yes, I suppose you're right. It's funny how Rex has always had the power to tie me up in knots. He did when I was a young woman and he's still doing it these days. Mind you, he's not going to change now and I'm not sure I'd even want him to.'

Pia flashed Ronnie a supportive smile, as they both tucked into the tempting-looking scones. The dogs padded about the kitchen, mooching around beneath the table in the hope of uncovering some stray crumbs. Pia felt privileged that Ronnie confided in her, that they could have a good-natured moan about the Moody men, knowing exactly that the other would understand, without making a comment or passing judgement.

'Oh, did I mention, I told Harry at Rosewood Farm Cottages that I would have some photos taken in my wedding dress with the alpacas. His wife Vera, who he was devoted to, had been very close to her uncles, so when they got the alpacas she decided she wanted to name them after her closest relations. Her uncle Humphrey actually gave her away at her wedding so I thought it would be fitting for me and Jackson to have a photo, in all our wedding finery, with the alpacas. Like a link to the past really.'

'What a lovely idea,' agreed Ronnie. 'I can't wait to meet these new members of the family. I've heard so much about them and they sound like proper characters. Oh, and you'll have to have some photos done with the rest of the animals too.' She took another bite from her scone, which was topped with apricot jam. 'We didn't have any professional photos taken on our wedding day. We couldn't afford it so Rex lined up one of his mates to take some snaps for us, but predictably the pair of them were pretty pie-eyed by the time they made it to the registry office. I think his friend remembered halfway through the day what he was supposed to be doing so there's a couple of photos of us in the pub, but they're all a bit blurry. I suppose like the rest of us were,' she said, laughing.

'Well, our wedding will be the ideal opportunity for you and Rex to have some decent photos taken together, when you're all dressed up to the nines.'

'It would be nice to have a framed photograph of us both, something we can put on the side, that's if I can ever decide on what to wear.'

'Oh, Ronnie,' chided Pia, looking at her exasperatedly. 'I thought that was all sorted? What about that floaty deep pink dress you showed me?'

'Yes, well, that's one of the contenders. But there's also that embroidered pale green dress that I bought online which reminds me of a summer meadow. I really love it, but maybe it's not suitable for a chilly December day. Then when we were in town the other day, Rex pointed out a vintage long gown that would be perfect for a winter wedding. I keep wondering if I should go back for it.'

'No!' Pia was quick to dissuade Ronnie. 'The pink dress will be ideal. There's no need to buy another one. Look, why don't we have a try-on this afternoon, with shoes and accessories, then we can make a final decision, once and for all.'

'We could do,' said Ronnie, her face lighting up. 'Although I suspect, even with a third dress, I might not be able to make up my mind until the day of the wedding. It will all depend on the weather and on my mood; and besides,' she said with a devilish grin, 'I like to keep people guessing.'

18

'You do realise I could get very used to this?' Sophie woke up to the sight of Tom, half dressed in boxer shorts and T-shirt, wandering into her bedroom with a mug of tea in his hand. She couldn't help her gaze running the length of his body, taking in his well-built upper body and his muscular thighs. She watched, with a smile on her face, as he placed the drink down on her beside cabinet and then went across to draw the curtains, before returning to her side, perching on the edge of the bed, depositing a kiss on her lips.

'Well, you know I aim to please,' he said, with a quirk of his eyebrow. 'Do you fancy any breakfast?'

'I might just have a slice of toast when I get up. Are you going to bring your tea back to bed?' she said hopefully, patting the space beside her.

'Now, while that is a very tempting thought, you have to get to work. And so do I come to that.'

'You're a spoilsport, do you know that? So where are you working today?'

Sophie couldn't keep up with Tom's schedule at the moment.

Some days he worked at the builders' merchant, others he was at the estate agents and a couple of days a week he helped Jackson and Pia with whichever events or projects they were working on.

'Over at Primrose Hall. Apparently Pia wants me to give her a hand with a special delivery as Jackson is up in London today. It's his first public speaking engagement since the accident.' He paused for a moment. 'Thinking about it, she was quite vague on what we'll be doing, so who knows what she's got in store for me.'

'Do you think you'll miss working at the hall when you start your new job?'

'Definitely. Of all the casual jobs I've had, working at the hall has been the most satisfying. By a long chalk. No two days are ever the same and the fact that it's usually quite physical and in the great outdoors too is a bonus. There's something therapeutic about working in the elements. You can forget anything that might be troubling you and just concentrate on the job in hand. They are such a good crowd up there too and, let's face it, there's not many jobs where you get a home-cooked breakfast in a country kitchen, or cakes fresh from the oven. And really I can't imagine a more picturesque workplace.'

'It will be quite a change then to go back to a stuffy corporate environment.'

'It will.' Tom nodded. There was no denying it and he knew Sophie, despite her assertions to the contrary, didn't think it was the right move for him, but he really didn't have any choice. He ran a hand through his already mussed-up hair and plastered on a smile. 'Think about it, though; in a few months' time I'll hopefully have my own place, somewhere a bit bigger, somewhere I can entertain you for a change. Won't that be fun?'

'Yeah.' She gave a nonchalant shrug. 'But until then you're more than welcome to stay round here on the nights we see each other.'

'I appreciate that.' He locked eyes with her, running a finger along her cheek. He'd enjoyed staying over much more than he might admit to Sophie. Going to sleep with her, feeling her limbs entangled with his during the night, waking up to see her gorgeous brown hair fanned out on the pillow... He knew there was no other place he would rather be sleeping. But he was conscious of not taking advantage of Sophie's good nature and hospitality. This was very much Sophie's home and he didn't want to overstay his welcome.

Sophie stretched her arms high over her head. 'Well, if I really can't tempt you back into bed then I suppose I ought to get up and get ready for work,' she sighed regretfully.

'Sorry, as much as I'd love to, I really shouldn't lead you astray; and besides, Pia will be expecting me soon.'

'Honestly, Tom,' she said, giggling. 'You can lead me astray anytime you'd like to.'

* * *

On his drive from Wishwell over to Primrose Hall, Tom couldn't stop the smile from spreading across his face, recalling Sophie's words. There'd been nothing he would have liked more than to stay round at Sophie's today, taking their time over a leisurely breakfast, going out for a long walk over at Primrose Woods, before snuggling up on the small sofa to watch a film, but he was as conscientious when doing his freelance work as he was in his permanent roles and didn't like to let anyone down. Especially not Pia and Jackson.

'Morning!' A little later, Pia greeted him fondly at the kitchen door of Primrose Hall, having heard his car arrive outside. 'Do you want to come in for a coffee before we get started?'

'I've just had one, thanks.' Tom rubbed his hands together

against the sharp nip in the air. 'What have we got planned for today then?'

'Well, this is probably your most exciting assignment yet, Tom! We're going to collect the alpacas!' Pia gave a squee of delight and clapped her hands together excitedly.

'Err... sorry, did you say alpacas?'

'I did! Have we not told you about them? Hop in the car, we're going across to Primrose Woods first. Sam is lending us the trailer and then we'll go over to Rosewood Farm Cottages to collect the boys and I'll explain everything.'

Tom shouldn't have been surprised. He'd become used to expecting the unexpected, but herding alpacas was something he'd never imagined would be on his job list.

'Here we are.' A little later, after a short detour to the country park, Pia brought the car to a halt outside Harry's house and turned off the ignition. She peered out of the windscreen to take in the view, hoping that the threatened rain, from the grey clouds overhead, would hold off until they'd managed to get the alpacas safely on the trailer. 'So these are the cottages. I know they look pretty run down now, but can you imagine how picturesque they were at one time?'

Tom climbed out of the car and appraised the row of cottages, his gaze running along the roofline, taking in the buckled guttering, the broken windows and the crumbling brick and woodwork.

'Wow! And Jackson's actually bought these?'

'Yep.' Pia held up her crossed fingers to him. 'The paperwork is going through at the moment. Jackson's going to give them the full Moody treatment with a complete renovation. The same as he did at the hall, but obviously on a smaller scale. He'll be in his element, getting stuck in and getting his hands dirty.'

'He's planning on doing the work himself?'

'Well, supposedly, although how he'll find the time, I don't know. He's got a full diary already for early next year. All those engagements that we had to cancel when he had his accident have been rescheduled for then, but he tells me he's going to project manage it, alongside me apparently.' She gave a shrug. She didn't have the first idea what that entailed, but her time at Primrose Hall had taught her that she was much more capable than she might have given herself credit for eighteen months ago, and that she could learn on the job and discover new skills. 'I think he was hoping...' Pia stopped herself. It probably wouldn't help to mention that Jackson had wanted Tom to take the lead in the new property-developing business, not when Tom had already made clear his career plans. 'Well, he's hoping that the refurb shouldn't take too long.'

'Great. And what's he going to do, sell them on for a quick profit?'

'No, he's planning on keeping them to add to his rental portfolio. He wants to give first refusal on the renovated cottages to local people who might otherwise find it hard to find somewhere in the area to live.'

Tom nodded, taking in the scene. He had to admire Jackson and his vision. There he was wondering how to get out of his poky rented little flat while his little brother Jackson was buying up properties for a renovation project. That he was then going to use for a good cause. Tom felt a mix of emotions: awe, pride and, he supposed, a touch of jealousy, too. He would defy anyone in his position not to feel the same way. Sibling rivalry, he guessed. Not that he would ever admit to such feelings. He just had to swallow them up and put on a brave face.

'That's amazing and very noble of Jackson to be thinking along those lines. I'm still a bit confused though. Where do the alpacas come in?'

Pia explained about Harry and his beloved animals and how providing them with a new home had been part of the agreement.

'Oh, God,' said Tom, laughing. 'Only Jackson could get three alpacas thrown in when doing a business deal.'

'Come on, let me introduce you.'

Tom had thought Pia was going to introduce him to Harry, but instead she led him past the cottage, through the gardens to a fence overlooking a field where he soon spotted the alpacas mooching about the paddock.

'Why don't you go and say hello while I go and have a word with Harry? I'll just let him know that we're going to get the boys loaded on to the trailer.'

'Right. Great. I will do.' Tom liked to take the initiative and get stuck into any task he was given. He was nothing if not a diligent worker and liked to think he could get on with most people. He just hoped his easily approachable manner might extend to dealing with alpacas too.

'Hey!' Tom called over the fence, raising a hand, as though that might be the correct way to address a group of alpacas. He clicked his tongue, hoping to beckon them in his direction, which only made them stop and stare at him in curiosity. It was only then that Tom realised he didn't know the first thing about these animals. They might look cute and furry, but would they spit at him if he got too close? Were they aggressive? Could he be putting himself in danger by stepping into their territory? He didn't think so, but he wasn't entirely sure and he decided now wasn't the time to find out for certain. He would wait until Pia returned, and thankfully he didn't have to wait too long.

'Tom, this is Harry. He's come to say goodbye to his boys, although really it's only farewell because he'll be coming over to the hall soon to see the alpacas in their new home.'

Tom turned to see Pia assisting an elderly man as he shuffled along the path, holding on to Pia with one arm and clutching a walking stick in the other hand. His breathing was heavy and laboured. Tom stepped forward to greet him.

'Good to meet you, Harry.'

'Ah, hello.' The older man peered at Tom. 'You must be related to Jackson, I'm guessing. You're a dead ringer for him.'

'Brothers,' said Tom with a smile. He wasn't sure he would ever get used to introducing himself as Jackson's brother. It was a real novelty, and it gave him a kick knowing that other people could see the family resemblance.

'There're some harnesses in the shelter. The boys are used to wearing them. They shouldn't give you any trouble getting onto the trailer, they're very friendly, gentle lads. I shall miss them, but it's the right time for them to go. It's a fresh start for us all, eh?'

With the help of Pia and Tom, Harry was able to get right up to the fence where he spent a moment saying his goodbyes to his precious animals, patting Humphrey, Marvin and Jack each in turn.

'Well, boys, behave yourselves. I don't want to hear any bad reports about your behaviour from Pia here.' Harry's tone was jolly enough, but Pia could detect a quiver to his voice. 'Right, that's it. I should get back indoors or else I'll freeze to death out here. Look after them for me.'

'You can rest assured we will.' Pia gave a shiver to ward off the nip to the air, and snuggled up closer to Harry, who looked as if he was also feeling the cold, as his eyes were brimming with water.

While Pia accompanied Harry back to the house, and with the old man's assurance that the alpacas were friendly, Tom wandered into the field and went in search of the harnesses.

'Hey, look at you, you're a natural!' Ten minutes later, Pia was back with a smile on her face seeing Tom walking Marvin down the side of the house into the trailer.

'Well, I am a man of many talents,' he said, grinning. 'You will have to start calling me the alpaca whisperer. I intend to add it to my CV.'

Later that day, with Humphrey, Marvin and Jack carefully and safely transported to the hall and the trailer returned to Primrose Woods, Tom and Pia retreated to the kitchen where Pia made coffees and sandwiches. They sat in the window seat overlooking the gardens, the glimpse of sun through the trees suggesting a warmth that belied the freezing temperature outside. Pia didn't mind; she loved this time of year, especially when she was snuggled up inside with the heat from the Aga radiating a comforting glow all around them.

'So what have we got on the agenda for this afternoon?' Tom asked. 'There are no more animals we're bringing home to Primrose Hall? A few reindeer to add to the menagerie, perhaps?'

Pia laughed.

'You're not a million miles off there. Sam's bringing over the Christmas trees, five of them in total. One for the front of the house, one outside the barn, one in the stables and two for inside the house.'

'Blimey, you don't do things by halves around here, do you?'

'I know it might seem a bit excessive, but a big house takes a lot of Christmas decorations, and the barn and the stables will need to be at their best for all the upcoming celebrations. It's not only for us but for the whole community. I want to create a magical winter wonderland effect for the Christmas carols, and for the wedding, of course.'

'Well, if last year's display was anything to go by then I know you'll pull it off.'

'I meant to say, I do hope you and Sophie will be joining us for Christmas lunch this year?'

'Cheers, Pia, that would be great, if you don't mind. I'll have a word with Sophie, but I'm sure she'll be delighted to come along. She hasn't stopped talking about last Christmas yet. It was the first time we met, of course.'

'I know,' said Pia, definitely taking all the credit for introducing the pair.

'Well, I didn't like to presume, but I was secretly hoping for an invitation,' Tom said, with a twinkle in his eye.

'No invitation required. You're family now and it simply wouldn't be the same without you. There'll always be a place for you and Sophie at our Christmas table.'

'Cheers, Pia.' It might be something that a lot of people would take for granted, spending Christmas Day with their family, but for many years it had only been Tom and his mum, and although she'd tried her best, he'd always had a sense that he was missing out on something. Now, having found his extended dysfunctional family, he knew exactly what he'd been missing out on. The noise, the chaos, the energy and most of all the laughter. Nothing could beat that feeling of belonging, of being amongst people who truly cared for you, and with Sophie at his side, this time as his girlfriend and not as a stranger, this year's festivities promised to be the best yet. Tom rubbed his hands together gleefully. 'I reckon the Christmas celebrations start right here!'

19

'Well, you two have certainly been busy today.' Pia perked up hearing the familiar voice, seeing Jackson walk through the door after his day in London. Suited and booted, she thought how handsome he looked in his Italian grey flannel suit and open-collared white shirt, his broad but lean physique and dark hair lending him a rakish quality, as though he'd just stepped from a fashion shoot in the pages of a magazine.

'How did your day go?' she asked, greeting him with a hug once the dogs had got their effusive welcome out of the way.

'Good, it went well, although I'm completely knackered now. I need to up my visits to the gym as my stamina is next to non-existent at the moment.'

'Well, maybe you're doing too much too soon, Jackson.' Pia slipped a hand around his waist, planting a kiss on his cheek. 'You're still recovering from the accident and you're bound to get tired, especially being on your feet all day.'

Jackson shook his head but Pia couldn't help noticing the weariness etched across his features.

'We were just going to open a bottle of wine. Do you fancy a glass or would you prefer a cup of tea?'

'Wine sounds good,' he said, placing his jacket over the back of a chair, going over to greet Tom, with a brotherly hug. 'Yeah, it's frustrating. I think I'm pretty much back to normal but then a day in the city completely wipes me out. It feels as though I'm going backwards.'

'It's part of your recovery, Jackson. I know it's taking longer than you would have hoped, but you'll get there. In the meantime, you'll have to go at your own pace. People will understand if you can't do as much as you did before.'

Jackson swept away Pia's comment with a roll of his eyes. Impatience was Jackson's middle name and she knew he hated showing any sign of weakness or letting people down in any way.

'She's right,' said Tom, with a sympathetic smile. 'You need to take it slowly.'

Jackson took the glass of wine that Pia had poured and joined Tom at the table, sinking into a chair and taking a welcome sip from his drink.

'Thanks for your help today, Tom.'

'No problem. It's been an interesting day at the office! First off, herding alpacas onto a trailer and then manhandling Christmas trees into place.'

'There's never a dull moment here, that's for sure,' said Jackson, chuckling. 'What did you think to the cottages?'

'Great! There's a huge amount of potential there and they're going to look first class when the work is done.'

'Yeah, I'm excited to get going on them, but that won't be until after Christmas now. I hope the weather will be kind to us so that we can turn them over in a relatively short space of time.'

Jackson took the wine glass to his lips, closed his eyes and savoured the white wine, and it was as if Pia could see the tensions of the day escape from his body. He turned to Tom.

'This was the project I had in mind for you to manage, obviously before I realised about your new job.'

'Really?' Tom flashed Jackson a questioning look, recognising a pang of regret in his chest. Even the fact that Jackson had faith that he was capable of handling the project meant a lot to Tom. His time working behind the counter at the builders' merchant had given him a wide range of experience and contacts within the trade, and his hands-on skills would be put to good use overseeing a job of that size from the beginning to the end. He couldn't help thinking it was a missed opportunity, an experience that probably wouldn't come his way again. 'You know I would have jumped at it if I hadn't committed to this other job. Sorry, Jackson,' he said, with a shrug, 'but thanks for thinking of me.'

'No need to apologise at all,' Jackson told him. 'I totally get it. Besides, I've brought another project manager in. She's a bit green, but I think with some careful managing, she should be up to the job.'

'Oh, God!' Pia said, realising Jackson was talking about her. 'I'll do my best, but I'm not relishing the idea of dealing with all those contractors. I know from what you've told me how difficult they can be.'

'They wouldn't dare mess you about, Pia. Especially in your new role as Lady of the Manor,' said Jackson. 'I'll make sure of that.'

'Right,' she said, unconvinced. 'I shall have to get myself a high-vis vest and a hard hat then,' she said, laughing.

Tom laughed too, trying to hide his disappointment that he might well be missing out. It wasn't the first time he'd experienced those feelings. There'd been several times when he'd wondered if he'd done the right thing in accepting the new job.

He couldn't deny it was a great opportunity with an attractive remuneration package, but he wouldn't have the same level of freedom, flexibility and satisfaction he'd enjoyed these last few months. Not that he would admit any such thing to Sophie or Jackson, who he knew would jump on any signs of doubt from Tom's side, to persuade him to stay. The truth was, if money was no object, he would gladly continue working on a freelance basis at Primrose Hall, as part of the team. He'd never been happier, but what would happen once the overhaul on the cottages was complete? There could be no guarantee that there would be further work and his income could quite easily dry up.

'I'll just finish my wine and then I should be making a move,' said Tom.

'Won't you stay for some supper?' Pia offered.

'That's kind of you, but I need to get back.' He was conscious of not intruding on their evening. They probably had a lot to talk about and he didn't want to overstay his welcome even if the thought of going back to his own four walls was deeply depressing. He knew that if he contacted Sophie she would tell him to come straight round, but again he didn't want to take advantage of her good nature. Instead, he would head to a quiet village pub, have a soft drink and something to eat, and then go home, straight to bed.

After Tom had left, Pia diced a chicken breast and then browned it in a pan, before adding some mushrooms, peppers, tender-stem broccoli, baby sweetcorn and sugar-snap peas, allowing the vegetables to cook. The noodles, sherry and plum and soy sauce would be added later, along with some prawns, for a quick and delicious dinner. Both Pia and Jackson enjoyed cooking and this time of the day, catching up on each other's news, while either one of them prepared the supper and enjoyed a glass of wine together, was a time they both valued.

'So you weren't able to persuade Tom to take on the management of the cottages then when you took him round there?'

'I didn't realise I was meant to,' she said, turning to Jackson and looking at him questioningly.

'Well, I suppose I was hoping it might have happened organically once he'd seen the cottages. I know you two are close and I thought if anyone could persuade him to stay working for us then it would be you.'

'Oh, come on, you get on with him just as well.'

'Yeah, but you have a different kind of relationship. He's my brother, my new brother, my big brother, and I'm only still working out what that means and how to be around him. It's kind of weird.'

'Really? It doesn't seem that way.' Jackson's show of vulnerability touched her. 'The pair of you have really hit it off and from where I'm standing it seems pretty natural too, as though you don't have to try too hard. Anyone would think that you had grown up together. Not that that would have been any guarantee that you would still get on as adults. But you do. And that's great and, you know, I'm sure the weirdness thing will pass,' she said with a cheeky smile.

'Maybe, although to be fair, I'm not sure if it's Tom who's weird or me.'

'I think it's probably a family trait,' joshed Pia. 'For Tom though, I think he's looking for financial security, that's what's behind this career move. It's not a reflection on his relationship with you.'

'You could be right. It's a shame because I know I could have left him to look after that project and he would have delivered a first-class job. Still, we'll manage somehow,' he said, fixing Pia with a grin. He got up from his chair and sauntered across to her at the stove, placing his hands on her waist. 'After all, we're the dream team, aren't we?' He spoke into her ear, sending a tingle along her spine. She glanced up at him and smiled, before shrugging off his touch.

'I think this is about ready.' She put the final touches to the stir-fry before spooning it into bowls and then taking the dishes across to the table where they both sat down.

'Actually,' she said, resting her chin on her clasped hands, 'on the subject of me doing your persuading for you, I need to ask you something.' She cast him a wide-eyed look. 'Did you know about Harry's alpacas before you took me to the cottages that day?'

'What?' Jackson's brow furrowed and his lips pursed. 'What on earth do you mean?' He dropped his head to one side and Pia couldn't help thinking that he might be overdoing the amateur dramatics.

'Exactly what I said. Did you know Harry was holding back on signing the contract until he'd found a home for the animals?'

'Oh, Pia.' He shrugged away her concerns with a wave of his hand, tucking in hungrily to his dinner. 'I can't remember the exact sequence of events. You know how busy I am. Sometimes the days merge into one another.' He looked at her through narrowed eyes, but she couldn't help noticing the small upwards quirk of his mouth.

'You did, Jackson! I knew it! That's terrible, taking advantage of an elderly, vulnerable man and making me an accomplice. I really can't believe you would do something like that. Why didn't you tell me? Honestly, it just makes me wonder what kind of man I'm marrying?' Her words were filled with exasperation more than anger, but Jackson's underhandedness niggled at her.

'Don't be like that, Pia,' he said, reaching out a hand to grab hold of hers, fixing her with a look that would normally make her heart melt, but she wasn't certain she was in the mood for forgiveness now. 'There's no way you can say we took advantage of Harry. He needed a buyer for the cottages and a home for the alpacas, and now he has both. You know there could be no better home for them than at Primrose Hall?'

Pia shook her head; she could hardly disagree with that.

'He achieved the full asking price for the site and an additional sum for the alpacas so he was more than happy. He's got the outcome he wanted and needed, and so have we. This way it means that Harry can still get to see the animals when he wants to.'

'Hmm, I suppose,' said Pia, 'but you should have told me. I don't like dishonesty even if it is done with the best intentions. I feel bad for Harry, as though I've tricked him.'

'There's no need. Harry might come across as a charming, helpless old gentleman, but you have to remember he was a farmer and a businessman. He's a wily character and knows exactly what's he doing. He certainly wouldn't have signed on the dotted line if he had any doubts. I had a chat with him and his solicitor the next day and he sounded relieved, more than anything, to get everything sorted.'

'Okay, okay,' she sighed, running a fork through her noodles. 'I will forgive you this once, but next time you must tell me what you're scheming.' She scolded him with a look.

'But you're my secret weapon, the better half of the team. The person everyone loves. Including me. Me most especially.'

It was impossible to stay cross with Jackson for long and soon they were tucking into their dinner companionably. Pia's gaze drifted across to the smaller of the two Christmas trees, which was in place in front of the double doors to the garden, ready to be decorated, the scent of pine detectible in the air.

'Honestly, where has this year gone? It's flown by. Can you believe that we're actually getting married this month?'

'It can't come a day too soon,' Jackson said, his gaze running over her face. 'After my accident and Dad's heart attack it seemed that events were conspiring against us. It's what kept me going through the darkest hours, knowing that at the end of it we would have our wedding to look forward to.'

Pia put down her knife and fork and pushed her bowl away.

'Sometimes when I stop to think about it all, it makes my head spin. When I accepted your job offer, I thought it would see me through a couple of months until I found something better. I was already planning my escape.' She chuckled. 'I could never have imagined that I would end up staying, finding a family, a home and a husband in the process.'

'Well, I'm very glad you didn't escape. Mind you, I wouldn't have allowed it, that wasn't part of the master plan at all,' he said, narrowing his eyes and furrowing his forehead. 'I'm so looking forward to making you my wife, Pia.'

She supposed there was a part of her that felt it was too good to be true, a gnawing fear that everything might come crashing down around her and that the happiness she'd found could be snatched away at the last moment. She couldn't allow those niggly doubts to overwhelm her though. She'd made some big and bold decisions ever since moving out of the family home at Meadow Cottages, surprising herself with her own resilience and determination. This was simply another decision on her life path, admittedly the biggest one of them all.

Being married to Jackson was going to be an adventure, but one she was more than ready for.

'And I can't wait to be Mrs Moody,' she said, exhaling a big breath, wondering if she would ever get used to the mad idea. In a way, she hoped that she wouldn't, that it would always serve to thrill and amaze her.

20

'Bye! Love you. See you soon.' Sophie blew kisses as she walked backwards out of her mum's room. She always felt a mix of emotions whenever she left after a visit to the Rushgrove Lodge care home. Feelings of love, regret, sadness and guilt rushed up inside her. Guilt that she couldn't stay longer and regret that she was leaving her mum behind. It never got easier, but she could only reassure herself that her mum was safe, well looked after and relatively happy, and that was the most important thing. And today's visit had been one of the best yet.

'Thanks so much for coming today,' she said to Tom as she climbed into the passenger seat of his car. She laid a hand on his leg.

'No need to thank me. It was a good day and Nina is great fun.'

'She was on top form today. She has her good days and she has her bad days, and I'm never sure what I'll be walking into, so it was great to see her so bright and engaging.'

Sophie felt sure that Tom's presence had only added to her mum's high spirits. They'd loaded the wheelchair into the back of the car and put Nina into the front seat, before driving the short distance to Primrose Woods. Although it had been bitterly cold, it had been a clear day, and wrapped up in their coats, hats and scarves, they walked along the main track, which led through the woods and around the lake. At this time of year, with the trees bare of their leaves, the woods opened up to offer an insight into the deepest depths of the forest, which were usually hidden from view. There were lots of other people about, couples holding hands, families exploring the wooden sculptures and dog-walkers, but the woods were vast enough that you could easily believe that you were the only ones there. Tom took charge of the wheelchair, for which Sophie was hugely grateful. She would take her mum out on more day trips, but she found wrangling the unwieldy chair and having the sole responsibility for her a lot to bear. With Tom at her side, everything seemed more manageable and she'd been able to enjoy the day without her anxiety getting the better of her, and most importantly, Nina had enjoyed herself too.

Sophie let her head drop back on the seat and breathed a sigh of contentment, giving an appreciative glance to Tom in the driving seat. Seeing her mum so happy, chatting away with Tom and becoming animated noticing the dogs, squirrels, ducks, swans and coots in the park filled Sophie with joy. Nina had been through a difficult time, struggling with ill health for many years now, so any moments of light relief were welcomed all round. Sophie knew her mum would be absolutely shattered this evening, but that she would think it was entirely worth it after the lovely day they'd had, and would soon be tucked into bed after a light supper provided by the carers.

Now, she turned to watch Tom as he guided the car out of the grounds. His well-defined jawline, his distinctive cheekbones and his wide mouth were features that she'd become so familiar with, but still they attracted her gaze as though she was seeing them for the first time. Most of all she appreciated his kindness and patience in dealing with both her and Nina.

She felt a wave of gratitude for everything he'd done today. He would downplay his role, say that it was nothing, but it had made a big difference to her having him by her side.

'I'll cook supper as a way of thanking you for today,' she announced. It seemed only fair. They'd had tea and cake when they'd returned to the care home, but now Sophie's hunger was stirring in her stomach and her thoughts drifted to what they might eat tonight.

'No, you don't have to do that. Why don't we pop into The Three Feathers on the way back, have a drink and then we can pick up something on the way home.'

'How do you do it?' she asked with a grin. 'You always know exactly the right thing to say.'

'Well, you've had a full-on day, you don't want to be cooking. A takeaway is a much better idea.'

'Sounds good, if you're sure you're okay with that? I feel bad that I've taken up most of your day already. There's nowhere you need to rush off to?'

'Absolutely nowhere I need to be, other than here with you,' he said, turning to glance at her with that sexy half-smile on his lips. She knew she shouldn't compare, but she couldn't help but be reminded of Kyle and how uncaring and uninterested he'd been in her mum's welfare. There were only a couple of occasions when Kyle had gone with her to visit the home, but she'd quickly realised that it was better if she went without him. While her mum had never come out and said anything derogatory about Kyle, Sophie knew that she had never really liked him.

In contrast, it was clear how much Nina liked Tom. Her whole demeanour changed in his presence and Sophie might even go so far as to say that she caught her mum flirting with Tom, giggling and blushing when he spoke to her. Mind you, Sophie could understand her reaction completely. Tom had a way about him that made you feel cared for, supported and safe, and she counted herself lucky that she had him in her life now.

After a quick drink in The Three Feathers, they called into the fish and chip shop and picked up their dinner before heading back to Sophie's cottage.

'What a treat this is,' said Sophie, unwrapping the fish and serving it up onto plates. The aromas of the battered cod, chips, mushy peas and curry sauce made her mouth water. They sat down on the sofa together and tucked in.

'I meant to say we had an invitation from Pia to spend Christmas Day with them at the hall.'

'Again? That's so kind of them! How lovely. It was an amazing day last year, although getting to know a certain Moody brother over a delicious lunch and sipping on the ever-flowing champagne probably added to my positive view of that day. Can you imagine if someone had told us then that we would be in a relationship within a year? We would have called them mad!'

'I know. Definitely something mysterious at work, if you believe in those kinds of things, which normally I don't, but who knows, perhaps there's something in it after all.' He flashed her a sideways glance, and her stomach tumbled. She wasn't sure about fate either, but it was certainly a coincidence the way they'd found each other at a time when they were both starting over again, finding their place in a world that suddenly looked very different to the one they'd each known for years. Their friendship came at the right time, when they could simply enjoy each other's company without any undue pressure on either of them.

'Anyway, have a think about it,' said Tom, 'and see what you want to do.'

'Do I really need to think twice about that kind of invitation? I'd love to spend Christmas at Primrose Hall. I'll speak to Pia and see what I can take along. They are always so generous, it would be nice if I could help out in some way.'

'What about your mum?' Tom asked, genuinely concerned. 'You'll want to see her on Christmas Day?'

'She's going to my brother's for a few days down on the South Coast. They have a downstairs bedroom and bathroom where she can stay and it means she can spend some time with her grandchildren. He's coming up on Christmas Eve to collect her and then he'll bring her back on Boxing Day. She went last year and while it's a lot for her, she enjoys the change of scene. I'll worry about her, but then I always do, even when she's at the lodge, but Ian is very good with her and he'll make sure she's well looked after.'

'That will make a nice break for her, and for you, I'm guessing? I know how close you are, but it must be draining emotionally, being your mum's main source of support.'

'It can be. Not that I would change anything. I'll do whatever I can for Mum, but sometimes it doesn't seem enough,' she sighed defeatedly. 'I wish I could do more, but I've come to realise that it isn't always possible, that her illness and her care are out of my control. I mean, Ian is really good, and I'm pleased that he's there at the end of the phone to chat things over with, but because of his work he can only get up to see her every couple of months. I think that's one of the reasons he's keen to have her over Christmas so that it gives me a bit of a break as well.'

'That's understandable. Look, perhaps we can visit her together when she's back in the days after Christmas. And if you wanted to, you and I could do something together on Boxing

Day? Maybe we could go to the races, or the cinema, or if there's something else you fancy?'

'Yes, to all of the above,' said Sophie, laughing, wondering if she should have feigned a degree of coolness, but she hadn't been able to help herself. She was excited at the prospect of having Christmas plans and sharing them with Tom.

'Thanks for everything, Tom. You know, for being so kind and lovely.' Whoops, there went any vestige of nonchalance. 'It means a lot.'

After being with Kyle for so long, it was a revelation that a man could treat her with such thoughtfulness and appeared genuinely interested in her.

'Aw, Sophs, you don't have to thank me. It's what you do, isn't it... for someone you love.' Sophie quickly glanced at Tom, expecting him to laugh and correct himself, but he didn't. He simply fixed her with a gaze that was full of warmth and honesty. The words hung in the air around them and she gave an embarrassed giggle.

'Err... what did you say?'

'Yeah.' His head tilted to one side, his gaze travelling to the ceiling, as though what he'd said came as a surprise to him as well. Now it was his turn to give a soft laugh, before turning back to look at her. 'I suppose I hadn't expected to say it like that, but the words just slipped out. Don't get me wrong, I absolutely meant it, but sorry if that's taken you by surprise. I love you, Sophie, and have done for several months now.'

'Oh...' she said, feeling a heat rush to her cheeks, momentarily taken aback, as she struggled to find something to say. Tom must have seen her hesitation as he was quick to reassure her.

'I hope that's not too much.' He held up his palms to her. 'I don't want to put any pressure on you and have no expectation of you feeling the same way about me, but I'm not going to deny it, or pretend I didn't mean it. I love spending time with you, Sophie, and the more time for me the better.'

'That's lovely, unexpected, but... thank you,' she said, feeling a sense of joy as tears prickled in her eyes. 'And a huge relief as well, because... well, funnily enough, I love you too, Tom.'

'Really?' Tom's expressive brown eyes widened, her own happiness reflected in his features.

She nodded, biting on her lip, goosebumps running down the length of her arms.

'I love you, Tom,' she said, repeating the words aloud, putting them out there in the universe.

'Well, that is pretty darn special,' said Tom with a wide smile. 'I really do love you too, Sophie.'

21

'Thanks, bro,' said Jackson with a sidewards grin. 'This has been great, just what I would have organised for myself. I really appreciate all your efforts.'

'Ah, it's been a pleasure,' Tom said, nodding. 'I'm stoked that I could be a part of this, with you and Dad, and your friends. It's been a real privilege. When I think how I could have so easily missed out on all of this if I hadn't come searching for Dad and found you guys.'

'Well, I for one am really glad you did.'

They were sitting in a cocktail bar in town, waiting for the minibus, which would take them home after a full-on day of events. They'd started with early-morning clay-pigeon shooting, followed by some hot pork rolls and warming cups of coffee standing in the grounds of the shoot, before they went off on a brewery visit after lunch. There'd been a great deal of laughter and ribaldry, which continued into the evening when they went to an Indian restaurant, and it was fair to say there had been copious quantities of drink imbibed, apart from Rex, who was teetotal these days, putting the stags into high spirits all around.

There were about ten of them in total, the guys in Jackson's life who were most important to him. The earlier antics and banter were replaced now with an air of relaxed satisfaction and appreciation, mingled with weariness.

Rex, Mateo, Frank, Stu, Ash and Mike were seated on a leather sofa and a couple of the others had popped outside for some fresh air, leaving the brothers alone together.

'Should we have a round of espresso martinis to see us on our way?'

'I think we need to,' said Jackson with a grin.

With their order placed for their nightcaps, Jackson turned to Tom.

'What about you? Do you think you might ever want to get married one day?' he asked.

Tom nodded, reminded of his recent conversation with Sophie. He hadn't meant to admit his true feelings to Sophie for fear of scaring her away, but he was relieved it was now out in the open. He was even more relieved that she had admitted to feeling the same, but he wasn't making any assumptions. It was still early days for them.

'I'd like to think that it might happen. I want to settle down and start a family one day. Sophie and I are getting on well and growing closer so who knows where that might lead?'

'It's funny, isn't it?' Jackson leaned forward on the bar, steepling his fingers. 'I always swore that I would never marry. I mean, Mum and Dad were hardly the best example of a happy relationship and I couldn't see any reason why I would want to sign up for something like that. That all changed though when I met Pia. For the first time in my life, someone else's happiness became more important to me than my own. That's when I knew that she was the one. Everything I do now I have Pia at the forefront of my mind. I can't imagine my life without her.'

'That's what it's all about, Jackson. You two make a great partnership and I know the pair of you will go from strength to strength at Primrose Hall both personally and professionally.'

A satisfied smile spread across Jackson's face. Tom could see how Pia was a good foil to Jackson's sometimes abrasive personality, how she brought the whole family together and made everything turn over smoothly at the hall. Jackson was a lucky man.

'Well, if you want advice from your younger, better-looking brother, then I would say take that next step with Sophie. Honestly, it's not half as scary as you might think it is.' Jackson wrapped one arm around his brother's shoulder and took a sip of his espresso martini, which was in his other hand. 'And it's down to you and me to keep the Moody line going now. Although if it were up to Pia, I'm sure the first thing she would want to do is fill Primrose Hall with the patter of little hooves and paws.'

Tom laughed.

'Anyway.' Jackson pulled his stool up closer to Tom's, still resting his arm around his brother's. 'Are you still set on taking this new job after Christmas?'

'Yeah.' Tom nodded, feeling a sense of trepidation. He didn't want to talk about this. Not tonight when it should have been all about having a good time. 'In fairness, it's a pretty good offer. I couldn't afford to turn it down.'

'You know it's not too late, you don't have to take that job. I had hoped you'd get involved with the Rosewood Farm Cottages refurb. You've got all the right skills and experience to manage that project. And working locally in the beautiful countryside has surely got to beat driving up and down the motorway, selling drugs.'

Tom cast Jackson a withering look.

'Look, I really appreciate your faith in me, and you're right, if I didn't have this job then I'd jump at the opportunity, but I've got to think of my future. You must see that. You're telling me to make plans with Sophie, but I'm not in a position to do that right now. It's all right for you, Jackson, you're sitting on a country pile, with a ton of business interests. I'm not begrudging you your success. I think everything you've achieved is bloody amazing, but you're not seeing my reality.'

'Jeez, Tom, I'm trying to give you the opportunity to make a new reality. Don't you get it? Financially, I can help you out until you're back on your feet.'

'I don't want your bloody charity,' Tom snapped. 'I know I'm the poor relation, but you don't need to do me any favours. Believe it or not, I was pretty successful in my previous career without being given any handouts.'

'I don't doubt that for one moment, but that's not the point. The point is do you really want to be doing that for the rest of your life?'

'Yes!' Tom thought on that. 'Well, maybe not for the rest of my life, but for the immediate future at least.'

The brothers' raised voices drew some concerned glances from the other guys.

'You've got a chip on your shoulder, that's your problem,' Jackson said into the depths of his cocktail.

Tom gave a casual dismissive swipe of his arm, which accidentally caught the glass in front of him and sent it toppling over. In his haste to grab it, Tom fell off his stool and into Jackson's lap, while Jackson was on his own mission to save the glass from dropping to the ground. They both ended up clutching on to each other, stumbling onto the floor as they heard the sound of breaking glass behind them.

'Hey, boys, what's going on? Are you two all right?' Rex called from across the bar. 'We don't want any fisticuffs tonight,' he said with an uneasy chuckle.

'Yep, all fine, Dad,' Jackson reassured him. 'Just a little accident over here.' Luckily a barman dashed over to clear up the mess and Jackson ordered replacement drinks, although Tom realised in that moment they'd all probably had far too much already. When they'd cleaned themselves up, Tom sat back on his stool.

'Look, Jackson, I don't want to fall out with you, especially not on your stag night. You're my brother and I love you, but you're not right about absolutely everything. Yep, I realise this might come as a shock to you. But really, you need to trust that I'm making the right decision. You might not like it, but I have to take this job so that's an end to it. And one other thing. I most certainly do not have a chip on my shoulder.'

'Well, you're too stubborn for your own good, is that any better?' Jackson asked.

Tom shook his head and they both fell quiet, lost in their own thoughts. It had been an action-packed day, where all the guys had bonded, enjoying the high-jinks and banter, but especially so the two brothers. Now they were weary from too much of a good thing, booze, food and entertainment, and needed to get home to their beds.

Jackson, though, still had something else on his mind.

'Despite what you think, this isn't about me looking out for family and doing you a favour out of the goodness of my heart. You really don't know me, do you?' he said with a wry grin. 'For some time now, I've wanted to expand the property development side of the business. I must admit I enjoy being hands-on and even helping out with the build, but I need to be realistic. With everything else going on at the hall and my regular commitments up in London, I'm not in a position to devote the time required to stay on top of things. You know what it's like. You need someone on site every day so that you can pick up problems as they arise, otherwise you just run into more issues further down the line. That's a sure-fire way to lose a lot of money. I need a project manager to take control of that side of the business. Someone I can trust. I think that person's you, Tom, but if I can't persuade you otherwise, then I'll need to go and find someone else to fill the role.'

Tom could hear the passion in Jackson's words. It was hard not be swept up by his enthusiasm, especially with several beers, wines and cocktails sloshing around his veins, but Tom was determined to keep a level head.

'Rosewood Farm Cottages are just the start,' Jackson went on. 'There'll be other developments, mostly local I'm hoping, but I'm thinking we could work together to find those projects. If your main motivation is money then I'm telling you, you'll earn more money working with me on this new venture than selling drugs.'

Tom rolled his eyes and flashed Jackson a scornful look once again.

'I wish you wouldn't make it sound as though I'm doing dodgy deals on street corners.'

'Well, it's not far off it, is it?' Jackson had a glint in his eye, determined to prove his point. 'Do you want to be making money for huge pharmaceutical corporations or would you rather help build something of your own, for your future, to be in control of your own destiny? We would set up an independent business purely for the property developing, a partnership, me and you. A family business. Aren't you excited by that prospect?'

'Well.' Tom pressed his lips together, nodding, contemplating Jackson's proposal. They'd both had far too much to drink and maybe tonight wasn't the right time to be having this conversation. Although there was no doubting Jackson was incredibly persuasive.

'You want a new property?' said Jackson, warming to his

theme. 'There will be three cottages available soon at Rosewood Farm. You could be the one in a position to choose the bathroom and kitchen fittings. One of those cottages has got your name written all over it.'

Now Tom knew for certain. Jackson was pie-eyed drunk, talking nonsense, making promises he would never be able to keep. He would likely have forgotten this entire conversation by the following morning.

'Tell me you'll think about it,' pressed Jackson now.

'Sure thing,' said Tom, patting Jackson on the back heartily. He pushed his stool back and stood up, looking all round him. He really needed to get these stags home soon. 'Let's have a chat in the morning.'

22

'Pia! My gorgeous daughter-in-law! Well, very nearly... As good as, eh?'

Ronnie plonked herself down on the seat beside Pia and took hold of her hands. Pia smiled, feeling deliciously light-headed. She noticed a gentle slur to Ronnie's words, but then she wasn't entirely confident that she was making a lot of sense either. It was hardly surprising considering the number of pornstar martinis they'd been knocking back all evening. Pia should have known that she could rely on her friends. They'd given her the best hen night ever, everything she could have ever imagined or wanted. Go-karting had been highly contested but brilliant fun, before the group had headed off to a cocktail-making workshop where they'd sampled all of their concoctions, then eaten from the most exquisite tasting menu at a Michelin-starred restaurant where the maître d' and his waiters had fussed over them all night long, keeping their glasses topped up with champagne. Now they'd arrived back at The Three Feathers, where Rhi had organised a private disco in the barn at the back and the friends had been bopping to all the old classics from the eighties and nineties.

'Do you know, darling, what you've done for our family?'

Pia shook her head, a beatific smile on her face, knowing from the way Ronnie was peering into her eyes and the tight grip she had on her hands that Ronnie was about to tell her, whether she wanted to hear it or not.

'You've brought a joy and a light to the hall that was missing before. Jackson spent a lot of time and money restoring the hall and there's no denying everything he accomplished; he turned a derelict run-down building into a magnificent country house, but there was something missing. He'd admit that himself. It was effectively a beautiful shell and Jackson and I were like characters from a bygone age, wafting in and out of the rooms, not knowing what to do with ourselves. That's why I always preferred to live in the van. It was so much cosier. Then you arrived with Bertie and turned everything upside down. You made the hall a home. It was wonderful to see the place suddenly come alive, and of course I knew right from the outset that Jackson was smitten. He can be prone to his dark moods at times, as you well know, but it was clear that he was so much happier within himself as soon as you arrived. It was as though he'd been waiting for you to turn up.'

'Aw, Ronnie, that's such a lovely thing to say, but I honestly feel as though I'm the lucky one. I found my teenage love again when I wasn't even looking for him.'

Abbey, Katy and Ruby had pulled up some seats to join them, taking a break from their exertions on the dance floor.

'It's so romantic,' sighed Katy. 'To be reunited with your first love and then to end up marrying him on a beautiful country estate. It's like one of those Channel 5 movies that are shown in the run-up to Christmas.'

'Yes, the really bad ones! I love those and curling up on the sofa to watch them on a rainy afternoon. What you have to remember is that there has only ever been Jackson for Pia,' said Abbey.

'Uh? You've had other boyfriends though?' Katy asked, her head wobbling on her shoulders.

'No,' Pia admitted. 'After Jackson left the village, I spent the next few years looking after my parents. I didn't have time for boyfriends and then when I applied for the job and I ran into Jackson again, well, the rest, as they say, is history!'

'Oh my God, I didn't know that! That's amazing,' said Ruby. 'So you didn't have to kiss a load of frogs to find your prince then?'

'No,' admitted Pia, unsure if she should be proud or embarrassed of that fact.

'Well, tonight is your last chance to let loose as a single woman and what happens on a hen night stays on a hen night, isn't that right, girls? So come on, let's go and have some fun,' Ruby rallied, grabbing hold of Pia's hand, trying to drag her up on her feet, but Pia resisted, laughing.

'You go, I'm just going to have a chat with Ronnie first, but I'll come and join you in a moment.'

She dropped her head on to Ronnie's shoulder as they watched the girls bop onto the dance floor, thinking what an amazing day it had been, how she would remember it forever.

'I know how lucky I am. Not only did I find Jackson, but I also found a sense of family again with you and Rex, and Tom now too, up at the hall. I still have to pinch myself that it's actually my home.' She gave a low chuckle. 'I can hear my mum saying from on high, "Well, you've certainly landed on your feet, young lady!" They'd be so proud. It's such a shame that you and Jackson never got the chance to meet my parents.'

'Oh, I would have loved to have met them,' said Ronnie, 'and to sit around the kitchen table at Primrose Hall and share a drink with them.' She frowned, peering into the bottom of her empty glass. 'Well, maybe a cup of tea then. I'd have probably needed to be on my best behaviour,' she said with a chuckle.

'Not at all. They enjoyed a drink too and would have loved you. And Rex, and Jackson, but it wasn't to be,' she said sadly. 'Talking of which, do you fancy another?' Pia nodded to Ronnie's glass.

'We could have a nightcap. We've had everything else. Do you fancy an Irish coffee to see us on our way?'

'Good idea,' said Pia without thinking twice.

'Well, you sit, my lovely, and I'll go and see if the other girls want anything. I won't be a jiffy.' Ronnie dashed off, and left alone, Pia felt her head swimming and wondered why she'd ever thought it a good idea to let anything else pass her lips tonight, but soon Ronnie was back with a promise that the drinks were on the way. It didn't matter. The very last one, she told herself, and then she would definitely have to head for home.

Ronnie sat down beside her.

'It's been a fabulous day but I clearly haven't got the stamina that I used to have.' She giggled. 'Honestly, Rex and I are changed people these days. We used to be party animals, but now we both prefer a quiet night in, a couple of old farts, you might say. You know, I do love him, but it's never easy when you love someone as much as I love Rex.'

'Oh, Ronnie, why do you say that?'

'Well, being in love makes you vulnerable. The fear of losing Rex is never far away. It's that sense of dread you feel in the pit of your stomach that something bad might happen. I suppose it's the price you pay for love.'

Pia had experienced that same sense of dread for herself. Could it explain her own doubts about marrying Jackson? That she was scared her happy ending might not be guaranteed after all.

'It's understandable,' said Pia. Now it was her turn to take Ronnie's hand, interlocking her fingers with the older woman's. 'Rex gave us quite a scare in the summer and you don't easily forget about something like that. The thing is, at least he's receiving the best medical care now. Besides, he's looking great these days. I know it's hard not to worry but try to put it at the back of your mind and enjoy the time you do have together.'

'Oh, I'm not worried about him popping his clogs, if that's what you mean.' Ronnie's laughter rang out around the bar. 'Rex will see us all out, I'm sure about that! I suppose it's...' Her gaze drifted around the room. 'Well, he's been acting a bit oddly recently, don't you think? I've got a sixth sense about these things and I've always been able to tell when Rex is up to something. I'm wondering if his health scare has reawakened his wandering spirit.' Ronnie cast Pia a warning glance. 'If that man takes off again, breaks my heart for a second time, I honestly don't know what I'll do. I'll bloody well run after him and murder him properly,' she said with a raucous cackle.

'Rex adores you, that's one thing I do know. He wouldn't do anything to upset you, not intentionally at least.' Pia gave Ronnie's arm a gentle squeeze by way of encouragement.

'I do hope you're right.' Ronnie shook her head as though ridding herself of that line of thought. 'It's the booze, making me melancholic, and that's no good at all. Not tonight.' She exhaled a big sigh. 'What a lovely night we've had! I'm so pleased you invited me.'

'It wouldn't have been the same without you, Ronnie.'

'I felt a bit out on a limb before you arrived at the hall. Jackson tolerated me, but only just!' Pia gave Ronnie an indulgent smile. 'It's true! There was a bit of an atmosphere about the place and I think Jackson still held a lot of bad feelings towards me from when he was a kid. That boy certainly knows how to hold a grudge.'

'All I know is that he's incredibly fond of you, Ronnie. You'll probably think me mad, but I honestly believe that the hall was waiting for its rightful owners to arrive. Jackson had an emotional attachment to that old derelict building from when he was a teenager and he's put his heart and soul into bringing it right up to date, making it a home and bringing the Moody clan together as a result. He always says he's just the caretaker of the place, looking after it for future generations.'

'Ooh, well, I for one can't wait for the future generations to arrive,' said Ronnie, giggling. 'Not that I'm putting any pressure on you.' She flashed a look of innocence. 'I would absolutely adore to be a grandmother, even though I didn't make the best job of being a mother. Perhaps I'll get it right the second time around.'

'You're too hard on yourself, Ronnie. No one's saying you were a bad mother to Jackson. You did your best and that's all anyone can do. How can anyone else judge when they have never stood in your shoes? Jackson's upbringing has made him the man he is today and I'd say that he's done pretty well for himself. More than that though, he's the kindest man I've ever met with a beautiful soul. Most of what he does at the hall is for the benefit of others and he has to get those admirable traits from somewhere.'

'Probably his dad,' said Ronnie with a curl of her mouth. 'Well, I always say to Rex that you and Jackson seem to have your heads screwed on properly. You seem much more level-headed than Rex and I were at your age. We were a bit wild, a bit selfish, although we had plenty of good times,' she added wistfully.

'Are you suggesting Jackson and I are boring?' Pia asked in mock outrage.

'Not at all! I think you've got it exactly right. And this is only the beginning. You'll have so much to look forward to together. There'll be ups and downs, that's just life, but it's how you deal with the issues that will help build and bond your marriage. That's where Rex and I went wrong. At the first sign of trouble, we headed off in opposite directions. Hindsight is a wonderful thing, but I'm sure you won't fall into the same traps as us.'

Pia hoped not, but Jackson was like his dad in so many ways.

'It's good though that you and Rex found each other again after so many years apart. I always think how romantic that is, as though you were always meant to be together.'

'I always loved him, even when we were separated. He was the one who stole my heart, and he's the reason why I never pursued anything serious with anyone else. Not that I was a saint. I liked to enjoy myself, but no one could really compare to Rex.'

Pia saw so many similarities in the way she felt about Jackson. Would she get to Ronnie's age and have regrets about the choices she'd made, the things she hadn't done?

'Honestly, Ronnie, what are these Moody men like?' Pia took a breath and a sip of her creamy coffee, the whiff of alcohol meeting her nostrils. Up on the dance floor, Abbey, Rhi, Sophie, Katy and Ruby were still brimming with energy and Pia marvelled at their stamina. There would be a few sore heads in the morning, including her own, and the deliciously rich coffee in her hand was going to do little to sober her up.

Ronnie leaned across and whispered in her ear.

'I don't want to worry you, but there's a guy over there, up at the bar. He's not been able to take his eyes off you for the last ten minutes. Do you know him?'

Pia turned around to check and her eyes locked with the good-looking guy sitting astride a stool at the bar. Her heart filliped. She hoped this wasn't the moment when those male strippers that she had so dreaded made an appearance at her hen night. She'd been convinced she'd got away with that. Although... maybe at the end of the day, with several drinks inside her, it didn't seem such a terrible proposition after all. Ronnie had been right: despite Pia acknowledging the man, he still continued to stare, even perhaps rudely, clearly unable to takes his dark eyes off her.

'Do you want me to go and have a word with him? Send him off with a flea in his ear?'

'It's fine,' said Pia, getting to her feet, steadying herself for a moment. 'I have a way with handsome men. Leave it with me. I'll go and sort him out. See what he has to say for himself.'

'Well, be careful! And don't get into any trouble!' Ronnie called after her as she went off in search of the other girls.

23

Pia wandered over with a sense of inevitability, as though she was being pulled by an invisible thread towards the man at the bar. All those cocktails and glasses of champagne were conspiring inside of her to give her a boldness that she hadn't known she possessed.

It was something so fundamental and instinctive that she didn't think twice, her head turned by the guy, admittedly drop-dead gorgeous, whose intense attentions were hard to ignore. What had Ruby told her? That this was her night and a chance to really let go and celebrate. She would only have one hen night, after all. Wasn't she supposed to enjoy herself?

'Do you want a drink?' he asked when she joined him at the bar, his deep brown eyes inveigling her with a look that was full of promises. She nodded her assent. *One last drink*. She felt sure she had heard that before tonight. Wriggling up on the stool beside him, unable to keep that knowing smile from her lips, it was as if the two of them were on a collision course. She couldn't apply the brakes now even if she'd wanted to; they were simply hurtling towards each other, completely oblivious to everything else around them.

'So, have you had a good evening?' he asked, his voice low, warm and caressing.

'It's been great. My friends are...' Momentarily, she looked around. That was funny. They'd been here a minute ago, but now they'd disappeared from sight. She would find them. Soon. 'It's my...' Her voice trailed away. She didn't want to talk about that right now. She had the rest of her life to think about her marriage, her commitment, being a good wife. Tonight was all about losing herself to the moment.

'What about you?' she said, her hand instinctively reaching out to touch the man's knee, which sent a jolt of electricity along the length of her arm. 'Your evening?' she clarified. Her words sounded slurred to her own ears.

'It's just got a whole lot better bumping into you.' He placed a hand on top of hers and they sat quietly like that for a few moments. She closed her eyes briefly, considering the sensation of their bodies touching, even if it was only their hands entwined. So much electricity in the lightest of touches.

'Do you dance?' he asked her.

Pia wasn't sure that she could stand up, let alone dance, but she tuned into the soulful notes of Luther Vandross coming through the speaker system. He was one of her favourite artists, and his smooth words of love only added to the intensely claustrophobic atmosphere.

'Yes!' Often she would put music on in the kitchen and try to persuade Jackson to spin her around the floor, but he would always laugh off her advances. Now she took the proffered hand, an old-fashioned gesture that made her legs sway, as she stood up to meet him. He'd done this before, she could tell, his every move intended to disarm her, to impress and seduce her. He placed one hand on the small of her back, and the other took her hand in a loose hold, even though it felt as though their bodies were being magnetically drawn together. She longed to feel his lean, hard body against hers and to wrap her arms tight around him. She could so easily have melted in his embrace, reached up to feel the dark shadow of stubble across his jawline, stood on tiptoes to press her lips against his. The desire she felt deep down to her core was so overwhelming that she was thankful when the music changed to something more upbeat, the heady sensual atmosphere lifting just a little.

A smile spread across his features, as if he was aware of the power he held over her. With the rhythm of the music thrumming through their bodies, they danced at arm's length now, matching each other's movements, their gaze on each other not wavering. Pia relished the freedom, spontaneity and abandonment she felt, as though nothing else in the world mattered but being here, in the moment, and losing herself in the music. She was impressed by how he could dance. Most men would shuffle around a dance floor awkwardly or else throw themselves wholeheartedly into some dad-dancing, but he had all the moves, slow swaying hips and long arm extensions, which looked seductive and tempting in the dark shadows of the bar.

They sidestepped each other as they moved around the dance floor, deliberately avoiding each other, the electric pull between them growing in intensity all the time. Occasionally their bodies would brush together and the resulting frisson would send ripples along Pia's spine. He was taunting her, teasing her with a wicked smile on his face, but she was enjoying every single second. She didn't care if they might be seen, because everyone and everything else was forgotten. Her friends were long gone and it was just the two of them in the moment, dancing to the beat of the music.

It was inevitable that they would ultimately be drawn together again. However much they tried to resist, the magnetic pull was too strong and they ended up in each other's arms, still swaying to the soulful beat. He ran a hand through her hair, which was wild and messy now after all her exertions on the dance floor. Her breath came in short sharp gasps.

'Can I kiss you?' Dark brown eyes that glistened with intensity and desire roamed her face, and she felt her skin prickle with anticipation at the thought. To hold his face in her hands, to feel his lips upon hers, to inhale the scent of him, she was simply powerless to resist. She felt beautiful and alive and free, and she nodded as he pulled her towards him urgently, all his pent-up longing erupting in a flood of kisses that ignited an explosion of delicious sensations around her body. She kissed him back, the feelings so natural and all-consuming that she never wanted them to end.

'Should we get out of here?' he asked, his long lean body hard up against her. Her hand rested on his lower back, pulling him ever closer.

'I think we should, Jackson,' she said with a smile, taking the hand he offered and following him outside. Some things were simply meant to be.

24

Pia had deliberately arranged the charity coffee morning for a couple of days after her hen night, thinking that it would be enough time for everyone to have recovered from the excesses of the evening. While her thumping headache and lethargy had just about lifted, she still harboured a small worm of anxiety that had gripped her as soon as she'd woken up the following morning. She couldn't quite put her finger on what was troubling her, but she'd vowed, there and then, much to the amusement of Ronnie and Rex, that she would never drink again. Not that she could really complain. She'd had the best time ever, remembering clearly the fun they'd had during the day, the amazing food they'd sampled, the endless laughter and the free-flowing champagne. The events of the evening were a blur, small snapshots of time when she'd been laughing, drinking, dancing, being swept off her feet by Jackson. Had that really happened? She could hardly believe it, but they were memories she would cherish forever.

She shook her head and brought her focus back to the kitchen at Primrose Hall. Today was a thank you to everyone who had supported Jackson and Pia at the hall throughout the year: the whole team at Primrose Hall, their local suppliers and all their friends within the locality. She'd put on a similar event last year when the annual Christmas bazaar held in the village hall was cancelled due to asbestos being found in the roof. Pia and Jackson had stepped in to host instead and it had been such a success that Pia had been asked by several people if the event would become a regular fixture on the social calendar, and Pia had agreed that it should. If there was one thing she loved, it was a get-together of all her favourite people with tea and cake, and with Ivy and Ronnie on hand to help serving drinks, it made for a lively sociable affair.

The autumn wreath that had sat on the kitchen door for a few weeks had now been replaced with a Christmas one, brimming with frosted berries, holly, ivy and mistletoe, and the oak beams in the kitchen were decorated with garlands made from the foliage of noble firs and pinecones, the scent of the local woods transported into the country kitchen.

People came bearing gifts: Christmas cards, poinsettias, cyclamens, jars of homemade chutney, bottles of sloe gin and a sense of festive goodwill. Chatter and laughter rang out to the rafters and Pia made a point of speaking to everyone who had made the effort to attend.

'Not long to the wedding now then?' Sam Finnegan said with a big grin on his face, before taking a bite from the slice of gingerbread traybake in his hand.

'I know!' Pia's face lit up. 'It's feeling very real now.' For so long it had been a distant vision on the horizon and there was a part of Pia that thought the day might never arrive, but now it was within touching distance and her excitement was tinged with trepidation. Normal bridal nerves, she hoped.

'Anyway, Sam, thanks for coming and for all your help this

year.' With Sam being a senior ranger at Primrose Woods, their paths often crossed during the working week. He'd become a good friend to Jackson, who often consulted Sam about the maintenance of the trees on his land and borrowed equipment when it was needed.

'Absolute pleasure. The Christmas trees are looking good.'

'Aren't they? I know we can rely on you picking out the best specimens for us. There are definite perks to having you as our neighbour.'

'No problem, that's what friends are for, right?' He gave an amiable wink. 'Besides, it's what people come to see at the hall at Christmas so it's good for us all if they're looking their best,' said Sam with a smile.

'And how's my adorable little goddaughter doing?'

'Well, I might be biased, but I think she gets ever more gorgeous by the day. She's entranced by our tree at home. Her little legs kick excitedly and her hands reach out to grasp the baubles. Honestly though, there are so many presents around the tree already, and of course, they're all for Willow. I don't know how one small person can be quite so popular or need so many presents and clothes.' Sam laughed, looking bemused, although utterly proud. 'This Christmas is going to be a lot of fun, that's for sure. Anyway' – he took a glance at his watch – 'I think Abbey should be down soon. I think she's just about recovered from your hen do.' He gave a wide-eyed glance, a smile twitching at his lips. 'I hear it was quite the night!'

'It was great! The girls certainly made it an evening to remember,' she said, laughing. At that moment she spotted Jackson and Harry coming through the back door, their faces red and ruddy from the cold. 'Harry!' Pia went across and took hold of his hands, kissing him on the cheek. 'Ooh, you're freezing, come and sit down and I'll get you a cuppa and some cake. What would you like?'

A few minutes later, with Harry settled in the window seat with a warming mug of tea, and a selection of cakes and biscuits on a plate, Pia sat down beside him.

'So what did you think to seeing the alpacas in their new home? They seem to have settled in well. The vet came over a couple of days ago to give all the animals a welfare check and she gave your boys a clean bill of health. She said that they'd clearly been very well looked after.'

'I was saying to Jackson how pleased my Vera would be to know that the boys had found such a good home. They came running over to see me in the paddock. I'm sure they were telling me "thank you".'

'They've made themselves right at home. Everyone loves them and their inquisitive funny faces make us all smile. Remember, anytime you want to come down to see them, let us know and we can get something organised.'

'Thanks, sweetheart,' he said, patting Pia's hand. 'You've certainly got a lovely place here.' Harry looked all around him, soaking up the convivial atmosphere in the kitchen.

'It's not bad, is it?' She giggled, always appreciative of seeing the hall through the eyes of any visitors. 'Anyway, much more importantly, how have you settled into your room at Rushgrove Lodge?'

'So far, so good. People told me I would find it hard to move, but quite honestly I was pleased to get away from that place. Don't get me wrong, it holds lots of happy memories, but that's all they are, memories. The cottage was never the same once I lost Vera. It lost its heart and soul and I knew it was crumbling down around me. I didn't get to see anyone down there, only the carers, and I was worried about everything that needed doing, and of course the alpacas too. You made it possible for me to forget those worries and think about myself. As much as I might not like it, I have to face up to the fact that I'm not getting any younger and I can't do the things I used to. I'm unsteady on my feet so it's a relief to be somewhere I can move around a bit more freely.'

Pia nodded, listening to Harry intently. Already he appeared so much brighter in himself. His curly white hair had been tamed into shape, he was now clean shaven and his clothes were unstained and neatly pressed.

'Well, you're looking good on it, Harry. About ten years younger, I'd say.' Pia patted his knee.

'I'll tell you something. I've spoken to more people in the last week, since moving into the lodge, than I reckon I did in the previous five years. It's been exhausting but suddenly I feel a part of life again, as though I belong somewhere. And I get an endless round of teas and meals made for me. Something else I don't have to worry about.'

'That's great, Harry. I'm really pleased it's working out. Oh, look, here's Wendy.'

Pia's old next-door neighbour and fellow resident of Harry at Rushgrove Lodge came over, a big smile on her face.

'Is there room for a little one on there?'

Pia shuffled up closer to Harry.

'Of course!'

'I've been to see Bertie. He's as daft as ever and we had lots of fun in the other room, throwing his tug toy. I do love that boy! You see, Bertie was my dog originally,' Wendy explained to Harry. 'Well, actually, he was my son Simon's dog first and then when he went to live abroad, I offered to look after Bertie, not realising quite how energetic he was and how much walking he required. It soon became clear that I couldn't manage him, but luckily Pia stepped in to help. I honestly don't know what I would have done without her. She lived next door then, you see, and she would come in every day to check on me and Bertie.'

'It was no hardship. I always loved walking Bertie, and you're one of my dearest friends, so I was always going to look out for you.'

'That's Pia, all over. She's such a kind and caring soul. She looked after the house and Bertie when I was in hospital and then gave him a home here when I had to move into the lodge,' Wendy said, addressing Harry. 'Rest assured your alpacas will be very well looked after.'

'I've seen them. They've got better living quarters than me,' he said, chuckling. 'I couldn't be happier with the arrangement.'

'You know Jackson and Pia are getting married soon? They deserve all the success and happiness in the world. They do so much for other people.'

'Aw, Wendy, that's such a lovely thing to say, but let me tell you a secret: it really doesn't feel like work at all. It's a privilege to be a part of the events here, and it's very much a team effort. We're all working towards the same common goal. As for the animals, they're part of our rapidly expanding family now.' Pia's attention was distracted by more visitors coming through the door. 'Look who's here! Let me go and say hello and I'll catch up again with you later.'

Leaving Wendy and Harry to chat, Pia swooped over to see Abbey, who came in from the cold with little Willow in her arms.

'Hello, you two. You've just missed Sam.'

'We saw Daddy on the way out, didn't we?' she said to Willow. 'How are you? Not long to go now!'

It was a standard greeting from everyone that she met now, which only added to the air of excitement and trepidation. 'Any pre-wedding jitters?' asked Abbey, unceremoniously dumping the baby into Pia's arms.

'Yes, lots,' said Pia, 'but that's normal, right?' She attempted to remove Willow's puddle suit, which proved to be a much more difficult task than she'd anticipated. There were little limbs everywhere that refused to move in the right direction and Willow was no help whatsoever, she just looked up at Pia, cute and bemused at her godmother's incompetence. 'There!' Pia exclaimed after struggling for what seemed like ages, managing to free Willow from her suit. 'Crikey, that was a proper work-out.' Pia giggled, hugging Willow tight and kissing her on her forehead.

'As long as it's only nerves and not second thoughts,' said Abbey, which did nothing to allay Pia's concerns.

Her gaze travelled across the room to where Jackson was chatting with some visitors. He was easily distinguishable in a crowd, his tousled dark hair and tall and broad frame easy to pick out across the room. More than his undeniable good looks, though, it was his energy, a certain composure and self-assurance, the way he held himself, that drew attention from all quarters. She loved him with all her heart. That much she did know.

'Thanks again for organising the other night. It was great, although there are whole swathes of the evening that I simply can't remember.'

'I think that means I must have done a good job then,' said Abbey, laughing.

'You did! It was amazing, but I had far too much to drink. I just hope I didn't say or do anything stupid. I can't even remember how I got home.'

'Oh, I know exactly how you got home. You were whisked off into the night by a tall, dark, handsome stranger...'

Pia put her hand up to her brow.

'It's all coming back to me now,' she said with a small shake of her head, her gaze travelling across in Jackson's direction. 'I feel a bit guilty actually.'

'Why?' asked Abbey, concerned.

'Well, you'd given me such a fantastic day and evening and then, at the last moment, I deserted all my lovely hens for the sake of a man! Without thanking you properly or even saying goodbye.'

'Ah yes, but not just any man,' said Abbey, her gaze following Pia's across to Jackson. 'It's allowed when it's your future husband, and I can perfectly understand why. What woman's head wouldn't be turned by the lord of the manor?'

Pia giggled at the memory.

'As long as you know how much I appreciated everything you did. I couldn't have wished for a better night, and sorry for abandoning you all at the midnight hour!'

'Don't worry, honestly. The main thing is you had a good time and you got home safely in one piece. That's all I was worried about!'

Pia knew she could trust Abbey with her life. She'd supported her through all her ups and downs, the good decisions and some bad ones. There wasn't anyone else she would want at her side as her maid-of-honour.

'It will be all right, won't it?' Pia asked in a moment of uncertainty.

'The wedding? Your marriage?' Abbey pulled an arm around Pia's shoulder. 'It will be absolutely fine, you'll see.'

25

Pia closed the kitchen door on the last of the coffee morning visitors and exhaled a sigh of relief and satisfaction. She looked across at Ivy, who had been a complete star as usual and had unloaded and reloaded the dishwasher, washed up some of the remaining crockery and put away what was left of the cakes and biscuits into Tupperware boxes. The kitchen looked almost back to normal, aside from the profusion of plants and gifts on the dresser. Pia would go through them each individually, making a note of who had brought them, and would find the perfect spot for them later around the hall.

'Come on, Ivy, you haven't stopped all morning. Sit down with Ronnie and we'll have another coffee. We should do our best to eat some of these goodies too. It's a shame to see them go to waste.' Pia bit into a bar of Christmas rocky road, which was filled with biscuit, marshmallows, nuts and dried fruit, and made an appreciative groan of delight.

'I need to get off actually,' Ivy said, 'I've got a big pile of presents waiting to be wrapped at home, but I'll take some mince pies and fruit cake with me. See you both tomorrow!'

'Thanks for your help,' Pia called out after her. 'My goodness, these are really moreish, Ronnie. Will you have one? I shall have to have another slice because, well, someone's got to eat them,' she said, laughing.

'Don't worry,' said Ronnie. 'With our lot, they won't last long at all so I should get in while you can. Talking of which, where is everyone?'

The kitchen had been a hive of activity all morning with chatter and laughter ringing out around the room, a definite air of Christmas goodwill, but now Pia relished the sense of peace and calm.

'Well, Jackson has gone into the office to make some calls and Rex... ah... talk of the devil.'

As if he'd heard his name mentioned, Rex wandered in through the back door, a smile on his face.

'We were just wondering where you'd got to,' said Ronnie.

'I've been surveying my estate,' he said with an extravagant flourish of his hand, making them laugh. 'It's blooming cold out there, but a beautiful day and the grounds look first class, just right for a winter wedding.' Rex gave Pia a friendly wink. 'I had a word with Twinkle and Little Star, and the alpacas, whilst I was out there. They seem to be settling in well.'

'Definitely. It's as though they've always been here,' said Pia, gesturing to Rex to come and sit down at the table, while she went to fetch him a coffee.

'A bit like me then,' he said, laughing. 'Thanks for having me, love. Not everyone would relish the idea of living with their in-laws, especially when some of them can be quite tricky and difficult. No names mentioned, of course.' Rex stuck his tongue into the inside of his cheek and widened his eyes, deliberately avoiding Ronnie's gaze.

'Hey, talk for yourself, Rex Moody!' she said good-naturedly.

'This is as much your home as it is ours,' Pia reassured him. 'Can you imagine the two of us rattling around here on our own? I wouldn't like that. There's so much space that it seems only natural we would want to fill it with the people we love. The hall should feel like a home, not a museum.'

At that point, Teddy decided to take a friendly swipe at Bertie's tail, which sent the spotty dog into a frenetic whirl of giddiness, as he leapt down on his front paws, his behind wagging in the air. The two of them bounced around the kitchen like a couple of puppies, banging into chairs and skidding across the floor.

'Steady, you two!' Pia chastised them, but they were having far too much fun to listen, their antics making them all laugh.

'That's the thing. Looking at this place from the outside, you might think it would be stuffy inside, but it's not. It's a proper family home, warm and welcoming,' said Rex, who was obviously having a sentimental moment.

'Yes, well, that's all down to Pia,' Ronnie chipped in. 'All we need now is a few kids running about the place and we'll be set!' Ronnie had a mischievous glint in her eye and Rex immediately chastised her.

'Stop it. That's none of our business. For all you know, Jackson and Pia might not want to start a family. You shouldn't be putting pressure on them.'

'Oh...' Ronnie put a hand to her mouth, looking suitably contrite. 'I was only teasing. I didn't mean anything by it...'

'It's fine,' Pia laughed. Why shouldn't Ronnie have been thinking along those lines? Pia certainly had, and maybe one day they would be lucky enough to have some cute children to fill the spare bedrooms at the hall, but there was plenty of time ahead for that. At the moment, Pia was busy enough with managing the social calendar of events and looking after their family of animals.

'Hmmm, I always manage to put my foot in it, one way or another,' Ronnie muttered.

'That's true, love,' said Rex, helping himself to a berry muffin, 'but we wouldn't have you any other way.'

'Actually, I've been thinking,' she said airily, lifting her chin. Pia suppressed a smile, recognising the gesture. Ronnie was about to say something provocative, something for Rex's benefit, no doubt. 'I expect it's time I moved back into the van.'

Rex and Pia both turned to look at Ronnie, aghast.

'Why would you want to do that?' Rex's brow furrowed and he gave a questioning look.

'Well, I only moved in to keep an eye on you while you were recovering. And, well, look at you, you're better now. Back to your independent self. I just thought you probably don't want me cramping your style.'

'Why would you think that? We don't need a formal arrangement to sleep in the same room together, do we?' He glanced across at Pia, who gave a barely perceptible shrug. 'Besides, I thought you liked snuggling up with me of a night. There would be a big empty space in that bed if you were to leave. How would I keep my feet warm?'

Rex threw an arm around Ronnie's shoulder, and Pia was relieved to see her grinning, obviously buoyed by his reassurance.

'I mean, I know how much you're attached to that ruddy van of yours so if you really want to go back out there, then don't let me stand in your way, but I can't promise I'll come with you. I'm rather fond of my creature comforts these days.'

'Especially at the moment, Ronnie, when it's so cold out

there?' Pia wasn't certain if Ronnie meant what she'd said or if it had been a cry for some attention from Rex.

'Well, no, but I was thinking of Rex. I moved in without a proper invitation; you didn't really get much say on the matter. I don't want to overstay my welcome.'

'Oh, darling, you don't need an invitation. You're welcome in my bed anytime, you know that.' Rex chuckled and his laughter was so infectious it was hard not to join in with him. 'Besides, I look upon it as our bedroom now.' He took her face in his hands and planted a kiss on her mouth and Ronnie seemed appeased. Pia gave a smile and eased herself up from the table, thinking it was probably time to leave Rex and Ronnie to their smooching and canoodling.

She didn't know about having children of their own yet; she had enough on her plate dealing with these two big kids.

26

The biggest night of the Primrose Hall social calendar had arrived and Pia felt like she had as a small child waiting for Christmas to arrive, full of expectation and wonder. Wrapped up in her winter coat, gloves and hat, she stepped outside the kitchen door, where Jackson was waiting for her on this bitterly cold December evening, and took hold of his hand. Along with Rex and Ronnie, they wandered around to the front of the house to stand for a moment to admire the hall, which was looking resplendent under the glow of the floodlights. The huge Christmas tree to one side of the portico was lit by a profusion of fairy lights and Pia gasped at its beauty as though seeing it for the first time, even though she'd admired it on a daily basis ever since it had been put into place by Tom, Frank and Mateo. She would never grow tired of looking at it in awe like a small child, entranced by its twinkling magnificence. She turned to look along the length of the driveway where sculptures of woodland creatures, deer, squirrels and rabbits were illuminated against the night sky.

Jackson pointed into the distance, spotting cars turning into the grounds through the gates, and people walking in groups along the path, an air of excitable anticipation preceding their arrival.

'Come on, we should get over there before the crowds arrive.'

Pia snuggled up closer to Jackson, the cold of the December night air biting at her cheeks and making her eyes water, the cool crispness playing at her nostrils. This had to be her favourite of all the events held at the hall, the last one of the season, and with it came a real sense of accomplishment. It was a culmination of all the hard work of the team throughout the year, a celebration that brought so many people in from the local villages and beyond, where there was something for everyone to enjoy. The light trail around the grounds was one of the main attractions and Pia loved to see people's reactions as they took in the sights and had their photos taken against the displays. As Jackson and Pia reached the stables, the joyful sounds of the carollers greeted their ears and a shiver ran down Pia's spine hearing the tones of 'Good King Wenceslas' ring out.

Pia waved, seeing Tom and Sophie, while Jackson peeled away to chat to one of the rangers from Primrose Woods. Everyone was in high spirits and wanted to come and pass on greetings for the festive season.

'This is fab!' Sophie said. 'It's my first time at the trail. I'd heard so much about it and it's as brilliant as everyone told me. The lights, the trees, the carols, it's just so Christmassy. Look at this.' Sophie pulled out a brown paper bag from her jacket pocket. Inside was a hand-painted wooden decoration of a jolly Santa Claus, with intricate and colourful detailing. 'I've bought it for Mum. She's got a table-top tree in her room at the lodge and I know she's going to love this.'

'It's gorgeous,' said Pia, hugging her friend tight, knowing how much Sophie missed her mum's presence on occasions like these. 'Send her my best wishes, won't you?'

'Ah, I was hoping to catch you.' Rex arrived and put an arm around Tom's and Sophie's shoulders. He looked around him before saying in hushed tones, 'You'll be coming back to the hall later, won't you, as I have a bit of news I'd like you to hear.'

'We were planning to, yes,' said Tom. Pia and Jackson had already invited them. It was becoming a bit of a thing that they would all congregate in the kitchen of the hall after an event for a debrief and a celebratory coffee or nightcap.

'Well, that sounds very intriguing,' said Pia, who was only slightly put out that this was the first she'd heard of it. She gave Rex a sidewards glance, ignoring the sense of concern she felt in her chest. He had a mischievous look in his eye and a hint of a smile playing at his lips, so she could only hope that it was good news, for everyone concerned.

They huddled together, joining in with the Christmas songs, through a repertoire that included 'O Come, All Ye Faithful', 'Hark! The Herald Angels Sing', 'God Rest You Merry Gentleman', and a rousing edition of 'Ding Dong Merrily on High' that left them breathless and high-spirited as they gave their best efforts to reach the high notes.

Pia glanced at her watch, her gaze travelling around the crowd to see if she could spot a certain someone, and was relieved finally to pick out Luke's blond hair peeking out from the hood of his zipped jacket. She caught his eye and he gave a small nod of his head, confirming that everything was set for the big moment. It was still a little while until the pre-arranged time, but Pia would be ready in position, not too close so that she would intrude on their intimate moment, but close enough to catch the moment on film. She could only imagine how Luke was feeling, as her own nerves and excitement were running away with her.

Jackson came up behind Pia and slipped an arm around her waist.

'Well done,' he whispered in her ear.

'Hey! What for?' she asked him, turning to look into his face, his dark eyes shining in the glow from the lights.

'For organising all of this. Anyone turning up tonight can see what a fantastic show this is, but they don't get to see all the hard work that goes on behind the scenes. Each year this event gets bigger and better, and I know that because people keep coming up to tell me so.'

'Aw, thanks, Jackson, but you know that it's a real team effort. I couldn't have done it without the rest of you. I think we should all be proud.'

He pulled her to him and kissed her on the lips and she revelled in the moment of intimacy, feeling part of something much bigger, amongst so many people gathered together in the magical festive celebration. Couples, families with little tots in pushchairs, pensioners and teenagers, all enjoying the sights and sounds. In Jackson's embrace, Pia had never felt happier, safer or more valued.

'Oh, and by the way, happy anniversary,' Jackson said.

'Yes, of course, how could I forget?' Pia hadn't really forgotten; it had flittered through her mind earlier, as her beautiful diamond ring had sparkled in the rays of the sun filtering through the kitchen window. Jackson was out in the grounds at the time and so the moment was missed as she was quickly swept up in everything that needed doing for this evening. Then, along with a constant flow of visitors and deliveries coming to the door in preparation for the festivities, the day had run away from her.

'Happy anniversary, Jackson,' she said, kissing him on the lips. 'I can hardly believe it was a year ago! That evening will stay with me forever, it was so romantic.' She sighed, conjuring up memories. 'And it looks as though you've set a precedent with your proposal,' Pia whispered, 'because it won't be long now until Luke pops the question too!'

27

'Peee-aa!' She looked round and greeted Katy, Brad, Pip and little Rosie, who was suitably attired in a faux-fur animal print winter coat with matching hat and mittens. 'Look what I've got from Father Christmas.'

Gleefully, jumping up and down on the spot, the small girl held up a craft set, still half covered in its Christmas wrapping, for Pia to see.

'And Pip did get a dinosaur! Mummy says I can use the stickers when I get home.'

'Well, that looks brilliant.'

'And we did see Twinkle and Little Star in the stable!'

The animals always took a starring role in the nativity display, proving a big hit with all the visitors, young and old alike.

'Have you heard that we've got some new animals now, some alpacas?'

Rosie nodded her head, wide-eyed.

'Mummy told me. Can I go and see them, please?'

'Well, they'll be fast asleep now, but you'll get to see them at the wedding because we're going to have some photos taken with them in all our finery.'

'What are their names?'

'There's three of them: Humphrey, Marvin and Jack.'

'Pah, they're silly names,' said Rosie disapprovingly.

'Don't be rude,' Katy gently chastised her daughter, although Pia thought the little girl probably had a point, even if she couldn't imagine them being called anything else now. In the short time that she'd got to know the alpacas, Pia had realised that they each had distinct personalities and suited their names perfectly, although Humphrey was definitely the main man and very much in charge.

'Not long to go now to the big day,' Katy said with a smile. 'How are you feeling?'

The number of times she'd been asked that question, Pia would have expected to be able to come up with a coherent answer, but still she stumbled over her words, unable to get her thoughts into order.

'I don't know. Scared, excited, nervous. To be honest with you, I'm a bit of a mess, but I'm looking forward to it. I can't wait, in fact.'

'Me too! I can't wait.' Rosie jumped up and down on the spot in her excitement. 'I'm going to wear my princess dress and I'm going to hold your hand all day so that you don't feel nervous or sad.'

Pia's heart swelled and she exchanged a look of affection with Katy.

'That will mean the world to me,' Pia told the little girl. 'It will make all the difference knowing that you'll be there at my side.'

'Come on, kids, we should be getting home,' Katy said, taking Rosie by the hand. 'We'll see you next weekend, Pia, but if there's anything you need me to do in the meantime then just let me know.'

It was the same message from everyone Pia chatted to that night. People shared their good wishes for Jackson and Pia's upcoming wedding while friends who would be attending spoke of their anticipation and excitement for the big day.

Over by the stables, Tom and Sophie huddled together as they soaked up the glorious festive atmosphere. They both had a warming mug of mulled wine in their hands, the aromas of cinnamon, spices and fresh oranges playing at their nostrils.

'It's been a lot of fun working on this,' admitted Tom, who had helped with the set-up of the stalls, the light display and the signage. The team had worked incredibly hard, right up until the last minute, to get the hall looking absolutely first class for tonight's event, so it was good to see that everything had come together as they'd planned. Now, Tom looked all around him. 'Tomorrow, we'll take down the nativity display, get Santa's grotto removed, ho-ho-ho, and start the preparations on the barn and stables ready for the wedding.'

'You do realise that when you're in your new job and they ask for volunteers next year to sort the Christmas party, you're going to be the go-to man with your knowledge of grottos and donkeys!'

Tom laughed.

'Transferable skills, definitely.'

Sophie still felt apprehensive about the steps Tom was about to take in his career, and what it might mean for their relationship, but outwardly she tried her best to show him her support and encouragement. It was her own insecurities that taunted her, but she couldn't let Tom know how she really felt. It would be an adjustment for them both, her especially, knowing he wouldn't be there at the craft days, as her safety blanket, and inevitably seeing less of him because of the travel involved in his new work schedule. They would find a way to make it work. They were growing closer, creating a deeper bond all the time, and hopefully their relationship was strong enough to navigate this change in their circumstances.

'Hello, you two.' Ronnie appeared at their side. She cut a flamboyant figure in her long, fur-trimmed sheepskin coat and wide-brimmed hat. 'There's something about hearing beautifully sung Christmas carols on a cold winter's night that sends goosebumps along my body. It reminds me of being a small child, and going to church with my mum and dad, knowing Christmas was just around the corner.'

'And is there any better place to spend Christmas than Primrose Hall?' Sophie held her mittened palms up to the sky. 'It's so kind of Pia and Jackson to invite me for Christmas lunch again. I had such a wonderful time last year, although of course I didn't really know any of you then. I was in complete awe of you all, thinking what a vibrant, colourful bunch you were.'

'Now, that's a very polite way of describing us.' Ronnie's distinctive laugh rang out in the cold air. 'You mean noisy and dramatic really, don't you? Dysfunctional, perhaps? Anyway, you're part of the clan now so you'll always be welcome at the hall.'

'Aw, thanks,' said Sophie, giving Ronnie a squeeze. While it was a lovely thought, Sophie knew that she and Tom came as a unit at the dinner table at Primrose Hall and if their relationship should ever falter then she would lose not only a good friend in the man she adored, but also the close connection she'd built with the rest of his family. She exhaled a breath, seeing it gather in front of her face, realising that she didn't want that to happen. She'd found a happiness and contentment with Tom that extended beyond their own connection and she would hate for anything to impact upon that.

'So what's Dad being so cryptic about, Ronnie, do you know?'

Before Tom had finished his question, he'd felt the full force of Sophie's elbow in his side. He whipped his head round to see what had caused such a reaction, but by then his head had caught up with his mouth, especially as he had Ronnie's puzzled expression observing him closely.

'What do you mean?' she asked, her brow furrowing.

'Oh, Dad was just saying that he hoped we were going back to the hall because there was some news he wanted to tell us.'

'Did he now? I wonder what that's all about then. No, he didn't mention anything to me, but then he has been acting a bit secretively these last few weeks.' She shook her head. 'Hmm, I knew that man was up to something!' she announced as though solving a mystery.

'Look, I'm sure it's nothing. It's probably something to do with the wedding. Maybe a surprise for Jackson and Pia,' Sophie suggested, hoping Tom hadn't just dropped his dad in it.

'Hmmm, possibly,' said Ronnie, sounding unconvinced. Her lips pursed together as she contemplated what might be going on with Rex. She'd sensed for weeks now that he was up to something. He'd been distant and evasive with her and she recognised that behaviour from old. And why hadn't he said anything to her about this news? Perhaps he thought there would be safety in numbers if he got the rest of the family around when he was announcing whatever it was he had to say.

Ronnie lifted her face up to the night sky, revelling in its sharp coldness and the feeling of energy it brought to every inch of her body. She adored Rex, loved him with all her heart, but she was too old to have her heart broken again. Surely he couldn't be contemplating one of his escape manoeuvres, not when he'd been through so much this year and had found, or so she thought, a contentment at Primrose Hall? Or else perhaps his close brush with his maker had given him a new lease of life and he was making plans to take off on his travels again, on his own. She suppressed a sigh. That man would never cease to surprise her.

When Jackson arrived and placed an arm around his brother's shoulder, engaging him in conversation, Sophie steered Ronnie to one side.

'So are you all ready for Christmas?' Sophie put her arm through Ronnie's. 'It's such a busy time and you've had so much going on at the hall this year.'

'Yes, all my presents are wrapped. I just have to put the finishing touches to the wedding present and then I shall be done. I hope they like it after all the hard work I've put into it.'

'I'm sure they're going to love it. Come on, let's walk.'

They wandered arm in arm, soaking up the festive atmosphere, looking around the stalls, stopping to chat to people that they met.

'Look at those two,' said Ronnie, turning to watch the Moody brothers in animated conversation, clearly sharing some good-natured banter judging by their body language and the back slapping. 'They're so much like their dad, taller and broader, of course, but the family resemblance is striking. What a blessing it is that they've found each other. If you'd asked Jackson a year ago, he would have been totally indifferent to welcoming a new relation into the family, but I think it's surprised him how his relationship with Tom has developed. They'll be a huge support to each other as they grow older; it's good to have someone to confide in about business or families or children.'

'Absolutely, I know how much it means to Tom having found

his family,' Sophie said, knowing it was also the reason why he would stay living in the local area. His new job might take him away for days or weeks at a time, but the pull of home and family would always bring him back. She hoped that she may have played a small part too in Tom wanting to stay close to Primrose Hall.

28

'Well, Tom, thanks for all your help.' Jackson rested his arm around his brother's shoulder. 'We couldn't have done it without you.'

'Cheers, Jackson. It's been an honour and a privilege.'

He knew Jackson was being kind; the event would have run just as smoothly if Tom hadn't been involved, but he appreciated Jackson's sentiment, and his own words had been entirely truthful. He wouldn't have missed the experience for the world. There was an added dimension to this evening, with it being the last event of the year before Jackson's wedding and before Tom started the new job in January. He hadn't given too much thought to his new role. There was no real preparation that needed to be done; the company had organised some internal training for the first week and then he would be right back into a world he was extremely familiar with. He had no regrets about accepting the position; his reasons for doing so hadn't changed, but he would be lying to himself if he didn't admit that he would miss the camaraderie of working with his brother and as part of the hall team.

'So, as best man, I think it's my duty to ask if you're entirely happy with your upcoming decision to marry Pia, although I'm pretty certain that I already know the answer to that one.'

Jackson grinned.

'I've never been more certain of anything in my life. I'm looking forward to the wedding, exchanging our vows and having a bloody good party with all our friends and relations, but most of all I'm looking forward to getting on with spending the rest of my life with Pia.' Jackson shook his head wryly. 'Honestly, what's happened to me? That sounds really corny, doesn't it?'

'Not at all,' said Tom, laughing. 'It sounds perfect. Pia's a great girl and you both deserve all the happiness in the world.'

'Cheers, Tom. That means a lot. Now, not to put any pressure on you, but I don't suppose you've had a chance to think over our last conversation?'

Tom turned to look at his brother, trying to think what he might be talking about.

'On my stag night? We spoke about us going into business together as a partnership. You looking after the development of Rosewood Farm Cottages. Making one of those cottages your home. Come on, Tom. Surely you weren't that drunk that you can't even remember the conversation.'

'Woah, I can remember it all right, but I thought you were completely wrecked, some of the stuff you were coming out with. I thought you would have forgotten it all by the following morning.'

'Surely you know me well enough by now to realise that I can handle my drink. I'm not going to lose control to the extent that I don't know what I'm saying.' Jackson's distaste at that idea showed in his expression and Tom wondered if he might have offended him. 'And I certainly don't go round making promises I can't keep. That conversation we had, I meant every single word. I want us to go into business together, Tom. We'd make a bloody good team.' Jackson slapped Tom on the top of his arm, trying to make him see sense, and Tom heard the passion and enthusiasm in Jackson's words. 'I've loved having you on board and I'll do everything within my power to make you stay. It makes complete sense to me to keep the business within the family. But as I told you before, we would get everything drawn up properly, with solicitors, fifty-fifty down the middle, with us both taking an equal share of the profits. In the meantime, I'd pay you a salary to match that of your new job.'

That grabbed Tom's attention and he whipped his head around to look at Jackson.

'Come on! How can you possibly do that?'

'I've costed it out. That's what I've been trying to explain to you. I certainly don't want you to be out of pocket so while we're setting up a formal arrangement and working on our first project, the cottages, then it makes sense that I pay you a competitive salary through the existing company. And this is not me being charitable, or doing my brother a favour, or acting like the big I-am.' He cast Tom a sidewards glance. 'I'm doing it because I want to do this with you. I can't think of anyone else who I would rather do it with. And it's exciting to think that we could build something together. Come on,' said Jackson, jiggling Tom's arm with his hand. 'Aren't you even the slightest bit curious about the prospect? You can't tell me that your life's dream is to work for that drugs cartel?'

'Hey, come on, don't belittle what I do. I know it might seem uninspiring to you, but this is my career, it's what I'm good at.'

'Sorry! I'm not playing down what you do. Not at all.' Jackson was animated, unable to keep still, constantly leaning a hand on Tom's shoulder and arms to elicit a reaction. 'I know you're bloody good at your job, and that's exactly the reason why I want you to come and work with me. I think I know you, Tom. You're like me. You want that freedom to be in control of your own destiny. Look, in three months' time you could be moving into one of the refurbished cottages if you want to. Or you might decide you want to go and find somewhere of your own, but that's entirely down to you.'

Jackson looked at Tom expectantly as he fell silent, his gaze drifting off into the distance, clearly struggling with his own thoughts. The last thing he wanted was to make the wrong decision, to do something that would impact negatively on his future. He wasn't going to pretend to anyone that the thought of going back to his previous career filled him with joy, but then he wouldn't be the only person to ever be in that situation. He had accepted the role for a specific reason. To gain some financial security, to provide a future for himself and Sophie. It went beyond his personal aims and desires.

'Tell me what's worrying you? What's stopping you from biting my hand off at this deal?' Jackson jumped right in Tom's line of sight, grabbing hold of his shoulders, almost as if wanting to shake some sense into him.

'Honestly? It seems... well, it almost seems too good to be true.'

'That's because it's a great deal. And no, it's not too good to be true. You need to trust your little brother. Come on, Tom, this will be just the beginning in this new venture for us. I promise you, if you decide to come aboard, then six months down the line you won't be regretting your decision.'

Tom took a breath.

'You don't know that. It might not work out. You and me in a formal work arrangement. Admittedly I've enjoyed my time working at the hall, but...'

'Exactly! So, what's stopping you?'

'Look, more important to me than my job, my living arrangements and my future is family; my relationship with Dad and
you, and the whole dynamic here at the hall. I spent so many
years unhappy, knowing instinctively that there was something
wrong, that I really didn't belong in what I thought was my
family. Now, having found you and Dad, I don't want to do
anything to jeopardise those relationships. We've had our ups
and downs already, I suppose that's only natural, but working
together, seeing each other every day, might put an unnatural
strain on our relationship.'

'I get what you're saying, but we'll make this work. To be fair,
it's me who's been the idiot, not you, and that's just my nature. I'm
hot-headed, reactionary, but that's why we'd make a good team.
We complement each other. Like brothers should. You'll know I
wasn't looking for a long-lost brother and I admit I was slightly
put out by the idea when you first arrived on the scene. I didn't
think that we'd have anything in common and I couldn't see the
point in getting to know you better. I'd done okay without a
brother for thirty years, why would I need one now? It was only
Dad and Pia persuading me that it was the right thing to do that
made me go through the motions. I'd assumed, hoped, I suppose,
that you wouldn't hang around. That you would satisfy your
curiosity and then leave again.'

'Sorry that I didn't live up to your expectations,' said Tom
with a wry smile.

'Honestly, I'm glad you didn't because as soon I got to speak to
you and spend some time with you, I realised there was a bond
there, something instinctive, something I could never have anticipated. It surprised me and it made me want to get to know you
better. Seeing too how Dad was buoyed by your arrival made me
appreciate what a gift it was having you come into the family.

Everyone loves you: Mum and Dad, Pia, all the team; it's as though you've always been a part of the clan.'

'Wow!' Tom bit on the inside of his cheek. 'That means a lot because it's changed my life finding my real family. It's as though I found my true self, the person I was always destined to be. I mean, I'm grateful to you all for being so warm and welcoming, even if you didn't really feel the love in the first place.' Tom chuckled.

'Family is important. When I was younger I had this idea that I didn't need them, that I could get by without them, but that was clearly a defence mechanism. Now, I'm grateful to have all you guys around.' There was a passion and intensity as Jackson spoke. 'Talking to Harry, the guy from Rosewood Farm, made me realise how lucky I am. He had a brother who he fell out with years ago, over the running of the family business. They went their separate ways and he never saw him again. How sad is that? It's made me realise that I want to do everything to keep our small family unit together.'

Tom nodded, encouraged by Jackson's words, his gaze drifting around him.

There was a wonderful collective atmosphere in the grounds of the hall on this dark December night. The plethora of sparkling lights created a stunning winter scene, and seeing everyone milling around, chatting and laughing, enjoying the festivities, somehow made it easier for the brothers to talk candidly and openly. Their attention was taken by the buzz of activity around them, but their thoughts and minds were very much focused on the conversation unfolding between them.

'Look, it won't be a problem us working together. We've not had any serious issues up until this point and Pia, Dad, Mum and Sophie will keep us in check if anything crops up between us, but honestly, Tom, I can't see that happening. Come on, take that step. I promise you, you won't regret it.'

Tom inhaled a big breath of the cool night air.

'I don't like letting people down,' he uttered.

'Well, don't then!' Jackson chivvied him.

'I don't mean you!' Tom said exasperatedly. 'I mean the job that I've already accepted. They'll be expecting me to start in the new year.'

Tom saw a light shine in Jackson's eye, as if he realised in that moment that all his cajoling and persuading had finally paid off and that Tom was on the verge of coming to the right decision.

'I know you don't. That's because you're a decent and honourable guy, but they'll get over it.' Jackson gave a dismissive wave of his hand. 'They'll find someone else to step into your shoes. That's the trouble with those big corporate entities. You're just a hamster on the wheel. Dispensable if it suits their needs.'

Tom smiled. He had to give it to Jackson. He'd done an excellent sales pitch on the role at Primrose Hall, although he'd never really had any qualms about the position as he knew exactly what would be expected of him. The new property-developing venture sounded right up his street and Jackson would allow him the freedom and responsibility to take the role in the direction he saw fit. Besides, the package that Jackson was offering was too good to refuse. To work with his family, to have his own place to live within a couple of months, to be close to Sophie and to continue his role at the stables, it was everything he would have hoped for himself. And if he was being honest, he'd never really relished the idea of selling drugs for a living. He turned to Jackson.

'Did you always know that I was going to say yes?'

Jackson's face beamed, the reflective glow from the myriad of sparkling lights around them glistening in his eyes.

'Really? It's a yes then?'

Tom nodded.

'Honestly, bro, how could I ever refuse?'

Jackson swept Tom up in his arms, which was no mean feat, as Tom was over six feet tall and broad and muscular, but there was no way that was going to stop Jackson. He swung Tom round in his arms, laughing all the time.

'Put me down, you bloody idiot!'

Jackson didn't need telling twice and dropped Tom with an unceremonious thump so they both stumbled, grabbing hold of each other to keep upright, falling into laughter.

'You know it makes sense,' breezed Jackson, giving Tom a hearty slap on his back. 'It'll be the best decision you've ever made.'

Tom laughed, feeling a huge sense of relief that the decision had been made, and agreed with Jackson. First thing tomorrow he would send an email to the pharma company to explain that he wouldn't be accepting their offer after all. It might cause some small inconvenience, but as Jackson had said, they would quickly find a replacement for Tom. He wouldn't lose any sleep over it. His mind was now focused on working with his brother to build a successful property-developing business and he couldn't wait to get stuck in.

'Hey, what are you two plotting?' said Pia, who arrived with Sophie, having both witnessed the high spirits and ribaldry between the brothers.

'Ah, we've just been working some stuff out. Making plans. It's all good though.'

'Great, well, I'm pleased to hear it, but we need to get over to the Christmas tree now.' Pia tapped at her wristwatch by way of explanation. 'The other big event of the evening?' she emphasised with a none-too-subtle wink.

'Oh, yes, of course! I'd forgotten. Come on, Tom, Sophie.' Jackson linked arms with them both and walked them in the direction of the Christmas tree. 'This evening keeps on getting better and better.'

29

'Are you happy?'

Rhi turned to look at Luke, who was observing her closely, warm affection flickering in his always expressive eyes.

'Yes!' She held her arms open wide. 'You know this is my happy place! Just look at the tree and the lights, and that smell.' She inhaled a deep breath. 'It's so Christmassy. It reminds me of being a little girl and being swept away by the magic of it all, honestly believing that if I looked long and hard enough, I might be able to see Santa Claus and his reindeer up in the sky.' She grinned, tipping her head back to look upwards.

'Look over there!' Luke turned and pointed into the night sky and Rhi laughed, shaking her head.

'I am not falling for that one again.'

He played that trick on her before during the snowstorm that had fallen on Christmas Eve a couple of years ago when they'd been visiting Lizzie's for drinks. Along with Bill, Abbey, Sam and Katy, they watched in awe as the heavy downfall covered the ground, making a picture-postcard effect outside and the roads impassable. Lizzie insisted that everyone stay overnight to avoid any accidents and they'd all hunkered down with blankets and duvets, chatting and laughing over the unexpected turn of events. Later, when the others were asleep, Luke and Rhi had slipped outside, making footprints in the thick deep fresh snow and when Luke spotted something in the distance, Rhi had been totally invested in his wonder. When he'd urged her to look, asking her if she'd seen the lights trailing across the sky, the big fat guy in the red suit pulled along in a sledge by nine reindeer, her mouth had dropped open and she'd laughed uncontrollably, realising she'd been totally duped.

Memories flooded her mind, happy memories, knowing even then that she'd fallen in love with this kind, sweet-hearted guy, but not knowing if their fledgling romance would ever come to anything, when Luke was due to move away to start another job in the new year.

Now, as she snuggled up closer to him, she was very glad they'd been able to make it work. She felt a blast of happiness at being in the moment with the man she loved, seeing all her friends around her who, funnily enough, had all gathered in the same spot as them.

'You know I love you, right, Rhi?' Luke's declaration distracted her and she turned to face him, taken by the intensity of his words. Luke had his romantic moments, but normally they came with his cheeky tell-tale grin and a wisecrack, but now she could tell he was being deadly serious.

'Yes, of course I do. And I love you too, Luke,' she said, trying to see beyond his earnest expression, to find any hidden meaning behind his words. 'What's got into you tonight?' she said with half a smile. 'You're being all soppy.'

'Well, I suppose it's a big occasion. Two years of being together as a couple. Who'd have thought it, eh?'

'Not me, that's for sure. Not when we first met at work, and when you used to go out of your way to annoy me.'

'Ha ha, I was being friendly, Rhi, but you didn't want anything to do with me back then!'

'Don't remind me!' Rhi grimaced, digging Luke in the side. He pulled her closer. She was only grateful to him that he'd stood by her when she'd made some very dubious decisions, like getting involved with that guy at work who turned out to be a liar and a cheat. When she discovered the truth of that situation and she'd walked out on the relationship and her job, nursing her embarrassment and shame, Luke had never judged her. Never said 'I told you so', even though he'd tried to warn her about that sleazeball. When it had imploded all around her, Luke had been there, checking up on her, making sure she was okay. Luke's offer of friendship had meant the world to her when she'd been at her lowest point. He'd provided a listening ear, which had marked the beginning of a deeper connection for them both.

'I'm just grateful that you never gave up on me, Luke. It makes me shudder to think that we might never have got together because our timings were out, that we could have gone our separate ways, oblivious to what could have developed between us. It's mad when you start thinking like that, isn't it?'

'I think we were always meant to be,' he said, squeezing her hand tight. 'It was probably written in those stars twinkling up above us,' he said, pointing up into the dark sky.

'Aw, that's so romantic. I'm not sure what's got into you tonight, but all I know is that I like it.' She giggled.

He pressed his lips against hers and his touch sent a warm feeling running around her veins, in spite of the cold taste of winter she detected on his lips. He pulled away, his gaze roaming her face.

'You look beautiful tonight,' he whispered. 'Look, I should take a photo of you by the Christmas tree. Go on,' he urged.

'We should take a selfie.'

'We will but let me take one of you first. We want to capture this moment for posterity, Rhi. It's such a great backdrop.'

She walked forward towards the imposing sparkling tree, only feeling the slightest bit self-conscious as she glanced at Pia and Sophie out of the corner of her eye, standing to one side, giving them a wave. She turned round, dropped the hood of her coat and ran her hands through her hair to tidy away the wayward strands, adopted a pose and faced Luke who was... tying up his shoelaces? What exactly was he doing down there? It took her a moment or two for the whole scene to compute in her head. For her to realise that he wasn't tying up his shoelaces, but that he was actually kneeling down, on one knee. She could have sworn her heart stopped in her chest at that moment. Luke looked up at her with a light in his eyes, an uncharacteristically heartfelt expression on his features, before it was replaced with that cheeky, irrepressible half-smile on his lips that she knew so well.

'Rhianna West, I love you. With all my heart. I have not stopped smiling since the day I met you and I never want to imagine a time in my life when you're not at my side. Would you make me the happiest man in the world, Rhi, and agree to be my wife?'

'Oh my God! Stop it! Is this really happening?' Rhi's eyes widened and her mouth dropped open as she looked to Luke and then to the small group who had gathered to witness the proposal. 'Do you mean it?' Rhi rushed over to view the little black box that Luke was presenting.

'Yep, I absolutely mean it, Rhi,' he said, wobbling on his knee, looking as though he might fall over at any moment.

'Oh, Luke, I love it!' she said in a breathy whisper as he climbed to his feet, and they drew together, clasping hands. Carefully, he extracted the ring from its box and slipped it onto Rhi's finger. He'd taken no chances and borrowed one of her rings from the dressing table to find the correct size. The ring, a halo of brilliant diamonds with a striking centre gem on a platinum band, slipped easily onto Rhi's finger.

'I love it,' she repeated, gazing at the stone, still with a sense of disbelief and awe. 'And I love you! And yes! Yes, yes, yes! I'd love to marry you,' she said, jumping into his embrace, so that her legs wrapped around his body. Luke laughed and swung her around to a huge round of applause and a cheer of congratulations from the assembled crowd.

30

'I'm not sure I'll ever recover from the shock.' Rhi fanned her heart, which was still thumping nineteen to the dozen. 'It was the best surprise ever. Did you all know?'

After the celebrations outside they'd retreated to the comfort of the kitchen at Primrose Hall, the Aga emanating a warm and hearty welcome. The dogs had greeted the returning revellers with a great deal of excitement and wagging tails but had now settled back in their beds.

Jackson had opened a magnum of champagne that had been on ice and poured a glass each for Rhi and Luke, then poured glasses for the rest of group. Sophie and Tom were there, along with Abbey and Sam, and little Willow, who was fast asleep in her buggy, oblivious to the sounds of laughter and chatter around her. Ronnie had popped the kettle on and made a mug of tea for Rex.

'Jackson and I knew, yes,' Pia explained to Rhi. 'Luke wanted to arrange some fizz to celebrate the moment and we were so happy and honoured to play a small part in the proceedings. We were just thrilled that he chose the hall for his proposal.

Honestly, Rhi, I've been more excited and nervous about this than anything else tonight.'

Jackson nodded, confirming Pia's assertion.

'We should have a toast,' he announced. 'To our dear friends, Luke and Rhi, huge congratulations on your engagement. It couldn't happen to a nicer couple!' Best wishes rang around the kitchen and Rhi beamed. She hadn't stopped smiling since Luke had dropped down onto his knee to surprise her.

'It was so romantic,' she sighed, looking up at Luke, who had his arm wrapped around her waist. 'I wouldn't have wanted it to have happened at any other place on earth. Not on the sandiest beach, or under the sunniest sky. Luke knows me so well,' she said, grinning. 'This spot means so much to me, and this will stay in my memory forever.'

'Well, I took lots of photos so I'll let you have those,' said Pia. 'I hope you didn't mind us gatecrashing your big moment.'

'No, not at all. When I realised what was happening and looked around to see all your smiling, happy faces looking at me, it just made the moment even more special.'

'Well, I think it's very romantic,' said Ronnie. 'Young men these days seem so lovely and thoughtful.'

'Oh, blimey,' grimaced Rex. 'I hope you're not casting aspersions in my direction.'

'Well, you know, if the cap fits and all that,' she said, pursing her lips and sweeping a gaze in his direction. 'Anyway, when are you going to tell us your big news that you've been keeping to yourself?' She widened her eyes at him expectantly.

'Bloomin' heck, who told you?' he said gruffly. 'You weren't supposed to know about that.'

Ronnie noticed Tom's stricken expression from the other side of the table, but she wouldn't let him take the blame.

'Well, that's neither here nor there, but whatever it is, why don't you just come out and tell us? I can hardly bear the suspense.'

Rex leaned across towards Ronnie and lowered his voice.

'Not now, Ronnie. There's a celebration going on in case you hadn't noticed. And my news, well, it can wait until later.' His eyes chastised and reassured her in equal measure, but she couldn't help thinking that he was up to something and, impatient at the best of times, she wouldn't be happy until she knew exactly what it was.

'Let's have a top-up,' said Jackson, offering a much-welcomed distraction as he grabbed the bottle of fizz from the fridge.

'I won't, thanks,' said Luke reluctantly. 'Much as I'd like to, I need to drive this one home.'

'And while I could quite happily stay here all night long and drink champagne,' said Rhi, who was high on the fizz and the events of the evening, 'I should probably get home and speak to my mum. I can't wait to tell her! She's going to be so excited.' Rhi dropped her gaze to her empty glass. 'Perhaps I'll have a little top-up before we go though,' she said, laughing. 'I mean, it's not every day you get engaged, is it?'

Jackson went round and refilled the glasses, chatter and laughter rang out and everyone was caught up in the celebratory atmosphere. Later, after Rhi and Luke had left for home, amidst a chorus of good wishes, and Abbey and Sam had reluctantly said their goodbyes too, anxious to get Willow home and into her bed before she stirred, the Moody family congregated around the kitchen table where Pia and Ronnie had put on a wonderful buffet of cold meats, cheeses and breads.

Sophie exhaled a quiet sigh of satisfaction. Every time she came to the hall, she could imagine she'd been whisked away to a grand hotel on a country estate for a romantic weekend. Especially with Tom sitting at her side, casting her that wide smile of his as he tucked into the food on offer. The farmhouse kitchen was straight out of the pages of a glossy magazine, but with the dogs mooching about, the warmth of the Aga radiating around the room and the oak beams festooned with Christmas garlands, it was cosy and welcoming too.

'What a gorgeous moment it was tonight,' she sighed. 'I've never witnessed a proposal before and Rhi's face was a picture. She obviously had no idea! I'm so happy for them both.'

'Well, you know, we are in the business of making dreams happen here,' said Jackson with a wry smile, intended entirely for Pia. He was sitting back in his seat, his arm resting on her chair, his hair sticking up from where he'd run a hand through it to tidy it up, which only had the opposite effect entirely, making him appear weary but so very sexy.

'The whole evening was great,' she said. 'I wouldn't have changed a thing about it. We had our biggest turnout too and to see everyone having such a great time, well, it makes it all worthwhile.'

'Yep, a good night's work, I reckon. Scrap that. A good year's work.'

'That's all down to your hard work and vision,' said Tom, raising his glass in the direction of Jackson and Pia. 'We should definitely have another drink to that. To Pia and Jackson!'

'Aw, thanks,' sighed Pia, who was in danger of becoming emotional from the air of goodwill that had been radiating around the grounds of the hall all night long. There was a huge sense of satisfaction knowing they'd survived a particularly challenging year, coming through it not totally unscathed but certainly stronger, more resilient and with a determination to push forward and build on the hard work and success of the last twelve months.

'Now, you need to take a couple of days to recover,' Ronnie

said, 'before getting ready for the wedding. You've worked so hard, the pair of you, and now's the time for you to really unwind, so that you can fully celebrate and enjoy the upcoming weekend. No one deserves it more,' Ronnie said with a kindly smile.

'I still can't believe that I'm getting married next weekend. It doesn't feel real. This is all a dream, isn't it?' Her gaze ran round the room past Sophie, Ronnie and the others, who gave indulgent smiles, before it landed firmly on Jackson's face. Nothing stood in their way now. The countdown to the wedding was well and truly on.

'You'd better start getting used to the idea,' said Jackson with a smile, 'because it's far too late to back out now. The champagne's on ice, the canapés are ordered and my new suit's hanging in the wardrobe. I had so many people tell me tonight how much they're looking forward to celebrating with us so we can't let anyone down.'

'I know.' When he said it like that, it sent tingles down her spine. 'I've already picked up a whole bunch of wedding cards from well-wishers. I've put them on the dresser. We'll have to open them, the evening before, perhaps.' She fell quiet, thinking about all the preparations that had gone into their day; the invitations sent, the outfits planned, the drinks and food ordered, the flowers arranged, the disco booked, the guests expectant. Such a big undertaking for a single day.

'I mean, you're not having second thoughts, are you?' asked Ronnie, who'd noticed that Pia's attention had drifted.

'No, not at all,' Pia said, realising everyone had been waiting on her reply. 'I was just thinking, that's all.'

Thinking was it the right decision, would she make a good wife, would everything change once they were a married couple?

'Well, that's a relief because in just over a week's time you'll be Mrs Moody.' Jackson sat back in his chair and nodded his head.

as though trying that out for size in his head, his smile latching on to Pia's. 'It can't come a day too soon as far as I'm concerned. Oh, and on the subject of good news, there's been another exciting development this evening.'

Ronnie's eyes flashed as she looked from Jackson to Rex, expecting to hear the snippet of news that Rex had been nursing to himself all night long, but she quickly discovered that Jackson was talking about something else entirely.

'I've not even had a chance to tell you this yet, Pia, but I'm delighted, more than delighted actually, to announce that my big brother has finally seen sense and has agreed to join me in the new property development business. We'll be equal partners and we're really looking forward to working together on a more permanent footing, starting in the new year with the project up at Rosewood Farm Cottages.'

'That's amazing,' said Pia, clapping her hands. 'And such a relief too. Jackson's being wondering what he could do to persuade you to come and work with us,' she added good-naturedly.

'Really?' Sophie squealed, the news taking her entirely by surprise. She grabbed hold of Tom's leg, unable to hide her excitement. 'So does that mean you won't be taking up the new job and you'll stay at the stables?'

'It does.' Tom nodded, having never looked more pleased about anything in his life. 'I thought about it long and hard, and Jackson can be very persuasive when he wants to be. Tonight, well, we talked it through again, and it seems like too good an opportunity to miss. Working within the family business here at Primrose Hall, well, I can't think of anything better, can you?'

Rex eased himself up out of his chair and went across to hug both his sons.

'I certainly can't. That's brilliant news, lads. The pair of you will be unstoppable together and it's great to see you two looking out for each other. It means a lot to your old dad, that's for sure.'

'Oh, Rex!' Pia was sure she spotted tears brewing in his eyes so she went across and gave him a big hug, rubbing his back fondly. Whether it was the aftereffects of the festive celebrations or the romance of Luke's proposal, emotions had never been far beneath the surface this evening.

Tom turned to Sophie.

'Thank you, by the way,' he said, pulling her to one side.

'What for?' she asked, perplexed.

'For being so encouraging and enthusiastic about the job even though it would have meant a compromise for us both.'

'Aw, Tom, I tried to be happy for you, really I did.' She lowered her voice, focusing all her attentions on Tom. Not that the others could hear as they were all too involved in refilling their glasses and their own conversations. 'I'm sorry if I wasn't always very convincing, but I really couldn't imagine you going back into that world.'

'Well, being honest with you, neither could I,' he said with a wry smile. 'I would have done it, though. I was trying to put a positive spin on it so as to convince you, and Jackson, and myself mainly, but I can't tell you what a huge relief it is having made the decision to join the family firm.' Sophie laughed, thinking how he made it sound like a mafia outfit, but the tight bond between the two brothers and their dad couldn't be denied.

'I'm really happy for you, Tom, and purely from a very selfish viewpoint, I'm thrilled that you're going to work locally. Knowing that you're nearby gives me a sense of security, if that doesn't sound daft. I suppose I worried we might drift apart once you got settled in your job, that the travel and the hours might create an emotional distance between us.'

'Are you mad?' He looked at her, his gaze roaming her face as though she just might be. 'I would never have wanted or allowed that to happen. My heart is very much here, with my family, but mainly with you, Sophie. I've found you,' he said, taking hold of her hand and threading his fingers through hers, 'you don't really think I'd want to let you go now.'

Sophie's chest filled with a sense of pride and happiness. So much for telling herself that she was happy being single, that she didn't need a man, that she would keep her relationship with Tom on a friendly basis. Despite all her best intentions, she'd fallen in love with Tom and there was nothing she could do about that, even if she'd wanted to.

Tom leant forward and kissed her on the lips, sending delightful sensations the entire length of her body, before she reluctantly pulled away, hearing Ronnie's distinctive voice ring out.

'Well, it's clearly the night for good news,' she said airily. 'But I'm not certain we're finished, are we, Rex?' she asked pointedly. 'Didn't you mention you had some news of your own you wanted to share with the family?'

'Look, I was going to, but do you know, I'm sure it can wait until another day.'

'Oh, come on, Dad,' said Tom, 'don't be shy. It did sound as though you might have something important to tell us. What is it?'

Ronnie looked at Rex wide-eyed, her expression brooking no argument. She hated any kind of secret so if there was something Rex was keeping to himself then she needed to know what it was.

'Okay, okay!' he said, looking around him at all the expectant faces. 'If you must know, it's something I've got for you, Ronnie. A present.'

'A present?' she repeated. Rex's response had completely wrong-footed her.

'Yes, I originally thought of giving it to you tonight, but then I wondered if Christmas Day might be more appropriate.'

'What sort of present? A going-away present?' she asked, looking around the kitchen table to see if anyone else could shed any light on the mystery.

'No, you silly bugger. Not a going-away present. Where on earth would I be going?'

'Oh, I don't know, I just thought...' Her words trailed away, the pent-up emotion held in her shoulders evaporating with that idea. She immediately brightened. 'Well, you've mentioned a present so now is a good a time as any, don't you think? Otherwise, I will never be able to bear the suspense. What is it?' She clapped her hands together excitedly. 'Do you know, Pia? Sophie?'

Her question swept around the table to include everyone, but she was met with a sea of blank faces and shrugs.

'Wait a minute then,' said Rex with an indulgent smile. 'I'll go and fetch it.'

With Ronnie brimming over with excitement, trying to engage everyone in guessing what it might be, those couple of minutes seemed to stretch interminably, but soon Rex was back carrying a beautifully wrapped package, which he handed over to Ronnie.

'Oh, my goodness, this is it,' she gasped, taking the parcel from him, her fingers stroking the luxurious glossy paper, which had a matching gold bow tied around the middle. 'It's almost too special to open!'

'Come on,' urged Pia, 'we're all dying to find out what it is now.'

Tentatively, Ronnie untied the bow, pulling it straight and folding it up neatly to use it for another time. Her hands felt through the paper, pressing and squeezing to see if it would offer any clues. It was soft, with no hard edges, so Ronnie thought it might be a scarf or a top. Unable to contain her excitement any longer, she pulled back the sticky tape and the paper fell open, revealing the contents of the gift. It took Ronnie a moment while she simply stopped and stared, her mind working overtime, words escaping her, before she realised what it was.

Her hands reached out to feel the flowing cream material of the dress that she recognised instantly. With its long and flowing skirt, shirred front and pretty daisies embroidered over the lace fabric, she gasped at its beauty. On the mannequin in the shop window the dress had been eye-catching, but in the flesh, her hands stroking the delicate softness of the material, it was absolutely stunning.

'What is it?' asked Jackson, who was unable to see it properly from the other side of the table.

Ronnie carefully pulled it out from its wrapping, holding it up to show the others.

'It's a dress. The most exquisite dress ever. We saw it in a shop window in town a few weeks ago. I can't believe you actually went back and bought it for me, Rex.'

'Well, from the moment I saw it, I knew it was meant for you, Ronnie. It had your name written all over it. I couldn't leave it in the shop. I had to go back and buy it. It's around about your size, but we can go and get it altered by a seamstress so that it fits you perfectly.'

'Oh, Rex, I don't know what to say!'

'Blimey,' said Jackson. 'For once Mum is speechless. That's some achievement right there.'

'Oh, stop it! It's so thoughtful of you to do that for me.' Was this the news he'd been so intent on telling though? She still didn't understand. She cast her gaze towards Rex, totally overwhelmed by the gesture. Of all the things that she might have been expecting, this certainly wasn't one of them. She stood up and held the dress against her for everyone to see and there was a collective sigh of appreciation.

'Goodness me, that's stunning,' said Sophie.

'I love it,' agreed Pia. 'It's very bohemian. Very you, Ronnie.'

'I could wear it to the wedding,' Ronnie announced. 'That's if you wouldn't mind, Pia?'

'No!' Rex was quite insistent. 'It's not for the wedding. You already have your outfit sorted for that. This is for you... to wear... to wear on another occasion. On another wedding day.' Rex took a deep breath. 'On our wedding day. I thought we might like to get something sorted in the new year. What do you reckon, Ron?' Rex fumbled in his pocket before pulling out a box and handing it across to Ronnie.

She looked at it, then at him and then at the bemused faces of Jackson, Pia, Tom and Sophie.

'Are you having a laugh?' she asked him.

'No, I am not having a laugh,' he said crossly. 'I think we should get married, Ronnie.' He threw his hands up in the air, a big grin on his face, and she heard a gasp of astonishment from the others. 'I've been looking at Jackson and Luke and seeing how these youngsters do things. They've got the right idea. They know what they want and they go right after it. No messing about. You've always been the girl for me, Ronnie. It's just a shame that it's taken me all these years to realise it. I was a pretty rubbish husband the first time around, but I want to make it up to you now, love. Neither of us are spring chickens, so I don't want to waste any more time.'

Ronnie's eyes widened as she nodded her head, still struggling to find any words.

'I want people to know that you're my wife. Not my ex, or my partner, or my girlfriend. We're too old for all that kind of stuff.

He reached out to take Ronnie's hand. 'I don't want you thinking I'm going to do a bunk every time I disappear out of sight for ten minutes. I want us to have a bit of peace together. Having that heart scare brought home to me what's important in life. And that's my family and you, Ronnie. You really took care of me then and I realised how much it means to me to have you in my life. I don't know what I'd do without you now. None of us know how much longer we've got, but what I do know is that I want to spend that time, however long it may be, with you. So, what do you say, sweetheart?'

A huge smile threatened to spread across Ronnie's face, but she kept it at bay, still not entirely sure that she was fully understanding what he was telling her.

'Are you absolutely 100 per cent serious about this, Rex? This isn't one of your silly pranks?'

'One hundred and ten per cent serious, Ronnie. I've got you the dress and the ring, what more could a girl want? You do like the ring, don't you? If not, I'm sure we could get it changed. Come on, Ronnie, please don't make me get down on one knee. I mean, I can probably get down there, but there's no way on earth I'll be getting back up again.'

Rex chuckled, looking round at Jackson and Tom for some moral support, but all the others had fallen into an expectant hush waiting for Ronnie's response.

She pulled out the ring from its box and slid it onto her finger, the memory of Rhi having done exactly the same thing only hours earlier uppermost in her mind. She picked up the dress and buried her face in the fabric, before holding it up against her body again, doing a twirl in the middle of the kitchen floor.

'Well, bloody hell, Rex, you've taken your time getting round to this, but of course I'll marry you, you daft old sod. I've always

loved you, even if you have put me through the wringer at times.'
She carefully put the dress back in its wrapping before throwing
herself into his arms. 'I love you, Rex Moody. Always have done
and always will, and we've still got plenty of years left to spend
together so don't go making out that the pair of us are on our last
legs.'

Pia's chest filled with happiness as she bit on her lip to try and
stem the tears that were threatening to fall. She needn't have
worried, though, because taking a look around her, she noticed
Jackson, Tom and Sophie were struggling to contain their own
emotions too. The Primrose Hall effect had definitely worked its
magic tonight.

31

Pia had tiptoed down the stairs first thing in the morning to let the dogs outside. She'd expected to be exhausted after the activities of the last week, but instead she felt entirely energised as she'd gazed out of the kitchen window, watching as the boys larked about, sniffing at the ground. The bare trees were tipped with frost, the cold of the day shimmering in the air. After the hectic energy of yesterday, a peace and calm had descended over the hall. The dogs came running inside, bringing a touch of winter with them. Pia quickly closed the door and warmed her hands on the mugs of tea and they made their way back upstairs to the bedroom, the dogs racing to get ahead of her. They pitter-pattered around the bed, just as impatient as Pia was for Jackson to properly wake. She sat down on the edge of the bed next to Jackson, whose eyes were just beginning to open as he stirred from what was an uncharacteristically long lie-in.

'I've brought you a cup of tea,' she said, placing the mug on the bedside cabinet and leaving a kiss on his cheek.

'Thank you,' he muttered through half-opened eyes.

It was the morning after the night before and still Pia couldn't stop herself from smiling as images of the previous evening flooded her mind.

'Well, that was quite a move by Rex last night. Did you not have the slightest idea what he was planning?'

'No.' Jackson shuffled up the bed, rearranging his pillows to sit upright. 'He didn't whisper a word to me, but then again, my parents have always been full of surprises.'

'Your mum's reaction was so sweet, it made my heart melt. They are made for each other, those two, and I really hope it means your mum won't feel so insecure in their relationship now. Something else it means is that we'll probably have two more weddings on the calendar for next year. That's if Ronnie and Rex, and Luke and Rhi, decide to hold their weddings here, of course.'

Jackson dropped his chin and cast her a gaze.

'Well, we know that's a given, but can we not start thinking about next year's schedule just yet,' said Jackson with a lazy smile.

They'd made the decision early on, or else Jackson had, that he didn't want to make the barn a dedicated wedding venue, as he'd realised that they could quickly book out every single weekend, as well as additional days during the week. Instead they reserved that facility for close friends only.

'At the moment the only wedding I'm concerned about is our wedding. I don't want to think beyond that. Anyway, tell me, what are you doing up so early when we could legitimately be having a well-earned lie-in?'

'The dogs woke me and to be honest I couldn't sleep. My mind was full of everything that happened last night so I thought I might as well get up.'

'You're mad, do you know that? Let's make the most of the peace and quiet while we can. Why don't you come back to bed?'

Jackson patted the space beside him and Pia thought how tempting it looked. In her head, she'd thought she would go down to the office, open up her laptop and deal with her emails and job list, but she breathed a sigh of relief, knowing that there was nothing that pressing and if there was, she could deal with it tomorrow. She jumped up and walked around to the other side of the bed, wriggling out of her cotton pyjamas, before pulling back the duvet and climbing into bed to snuggle under the covers with Jackson. He pulled her into his embrace and kissed her on the head, and she stretched out her body along the length of his long limbs, wrapping her arms around him. She loved his solid, masculine form, the scent of him, both when he was wearing his familiar citrusy aftershave or like now, when his natural earthy aroma toyed with her senses.

'Great news about Tom and the new business,' she said, twisting her head to look up at him.

'I know, right?' His hand aimlessly stroked her head. 'Tom held out on me for a long time, and I was beginning to think I might never be able to persuade him to come and work for us, so I was pretty relieved when he finally said yes. The reason it was so important to me was because I knew it would be the right thing, not only for me and the business, but for him as well. All those things he tells me he's been striving for, financial security, a place to live, a future, will be achievable for him as the business develops. I'm even more invested now in making it work for Tom's sake.'

'Well, I know someone else who was especially pleased by his decision: Sophie. And your dad. I think it's good news all round.'

Jackson exhaled, his eyes fluttering closed again, and Pia rested her head on his body, enjoying the sensation of his chest rising and falling in a steady motion beneath her.

'I hope Rex and Ronnie don't decide they want to go and find a place of their own once they're married. I'm so used to having them around now that I would miss them if they were to leave.'

'Knowing Mum like I do, the only place she'll ever want to go is back to her van and I'm not sure that holds the same appeal these days. You know Ronnie. She won't want to feel as though she's missing out on anything and she'll want to be around to help out when we have some children.'

'Is that right?' said Pia, with an air of mischief to her voice. 'So that's when now and not if?' she teased. 'I remember a time when you were indifferent to the idea of kids.'

'Well, that was before I met you,' he said, running a trail with his finger up and down her arm. 'All I want is to make you happy, Pia, so we'll have to see what happens.'

'If you'd told eighteen-year-old me, all those years ago when I was nursing my broken heart, that one day we would get back together, and make a life and home together, then I would never have believed you.'

'Hmm, are you ever going to forgive me for walking out on you?'

'I forgave you a long time ago, but sometimes it strikes me just how far we've come together. I only wish Mum and Dad were here to see everything we've achieved, to meet Rex and Ronnie, and Tom, plus the animals. It would have been lovely to share all this with them. They would have been amazed to see this place.'

'I'm really sorry that I didn't get to meet them. I know they'd be so proud of how you've turned your life around. If they were still here, I would want to thank them for bringing you into my life.'

'Ah, that's such a lovely thing to say. I love you, Jackson.'

'Yeah, but I love you more,' Jackson insisted as he hooked his leg over hers, turning to face her, hovering his body weight over her so that she could look into his dark brown sparkling eyes, which always held the power to seduce her.

Pia smiled as he leant down to press his mouth against hers, and she accepted his sweet, gentle kisses readily, a swirl of anticipation and desire travelling around her body as she felt the touch of his hand as it ran along the curves of her bare skin.

32

Pia had always intended to have an afternoon tea with Wendy as an alternative hen do. When they'd been neighbours, there was barely a day that had gone by where they didn't share a cuppa with a biscuit, or on high days, a slice of cake too. So it seemed only fitting that their own low-key pre-wedding festivities should involve tea and cake. This event, though, which was being held in the spacious guest room at the lodge, had taken on a life of its own when Pia thought it would be nice to include some other residents too including Stella Darling and Reg Catling, who were great supporters of the literary festival. Then there was Sophie's mum, Nina, who was delighted to receive an invitation, and Harry too, as Pia thought it would be the ideal opportunity for him to get to know some new people. Abbey, who had not yet returned to work after maternity leave, also popped in to join in the festivities.

'This is a first for me,' said Reg, laughing, sitting in a comfy armchair next to Wendy. 'I've not been to a hen do before, but I suppose there's a first time for everything. Harry and I are very honoured to be invited, aren't we?'

'Honestly, my social life has improved immeasurably since I've come here. I've been to more parties in the last couple of weeks than I have in an entire lifetime. Not that I'm complaining. I'm having a great time.'

'Well, I'm very pleased that you're here, Harry. That you're all here,' Pia said, addressing the rest of their small group. 'I've already had one hen night, which was a bit wild, if I'm being honest with you, but now I'm having a second celebration with you lovely lot. This is a much classier do,' she said, laughing. 'Anyway, how lucky am I? I can definitely recommend getting married. Although I'm obviously not going to be making a habit of it. This will be my one and only wedding, hopefully,' she added with a grimace.

'And on that note, let me go and collect the fizz,' said Abbey. 'It's not a proper celebration without a glass of bubbly.'

Moments later, Abbey was back with a tray of glass flutes and a couple of chilled bottles of Buck's Fizz to a round of appreciative oohs and ahhs. She eased off the shiny orange foil and then popped the cork, filling up the glasses, handing one to each of the people in the small gathering.

'We should have a toast to our dear friend Pia, wishing her and her husband-to-be Jackson all the happiness in the world on their forthcoming marriage.'

'To Pia and Jackson!' They all raised their glasses, a sense of excitement rippling around the circle of guests like a round of Chinese whispers.

'I think it's marvellous,' breezed Stella. 'You're young and you're starting out on your married life together and I'm sure the future has wonderful things in store for you both.'

'Thanks, Stella. Jackson was the first boy I fell in love when I was a teenager. When we broke up, I was devastated and thought that I would never see him again. So you can imagine my surprise when I applied for a job almost ten years later and came face to face with the man who had broken my heart all those years ago. I wanted to turn and run in the opposite direction, but obviously I'm really glad I didn't now.'

'That's so romantic,' said Stella, fanning a hand in front of her face.

'It was the best thing I ever did, finding my Vera,' Harry said. 'We were very happy. We led a simple life with our work and our animals, but we never wanted for anything. It's a blessing to find that special person who loves you, warts and all. I often look back and think Vera was a saint to put up with me and all my funny ways.'

'It's what marriage is all about, isn't it?' said Reg. 'I remember...'

And they were off, reminiscing about their younger days, the good times and the bad times, and Pia was happy to listen to their stories as they all enjoyed the fizz and the selection of cakes and sandwiches. She wondered what stories she and Jackson might have to tell in forty years' time. If they would still be living at the hall? If either she or Jackson had anything to do with it, then they definitely would. She gave a thought to the animals they might have given a home to. Already Pia had in mind to increase their herd of alpacas, although she was keeping that idea to herself until the new year. And the hall was so big that they could easily accommodate another dog or two. As for children, who knew what was in store for them?

In reality, nothing would change in their daily life in the immediate future. They would continue to host their regular events on the social calendar, welcoming their friends and family and the wider community to the hall. Nothing would change and yet everything would change.

Pia took a moment to speak to Abbey whilst the others were deep in conversation.

'What's it like to be back here? How are you feeling about returning to work after Christmas?'

'In two minds. Obviously it's great to catch up with everyone, but I honestly feel as though I'm missing my right arm. I'm so used to having Willow at my side, in my arms or on my hip, that I keep thinking I've forgotten something.' Abbey put a hand to her chest. 'I know I'm going to miss her when I come back to work, but it will only be three days to begin with, and I'm sure we'll quickly establish a routine. Dad and Lizzie will be having her for one day a week, and the other two days she'll be going to a childminder, someone who comes highly recommended.' Abbey grimaced as though saying the words aloud made it so much more of a reality.

'Ah, Abbey, I can imagine how you must feel, but try not to worry. Those first few days will be hard, I'm guessing, but at least you know Willow's going to be in safe hands.'

'Exactly. And I want to get back here and pick up where I left off so I'm sure we'll find a way to make it work. Other people manage it so I'm sure we will too.'

'You know you can always bring the little one in here,' suggested Stella helpfully, 'if you're ever really stuck. You wouldn't be short of volunteers to look after the baby.'

Abbey laughed.

'Well, there's an idea, but I'd never be able to concentrate with Willow here, and I'm sure there'll be all sorts of rules and regulations that would prevent me from doing that, but don't worry,' she reassured Stella, seeing her hopeful expression. 'I'll be bringing Willow in on a regular basis so that you can all get to see her growing up.'

'That's what I was angling for,' said Stella, laughing.

Abbey knew how much the residents at the lodge gained from visits from the arranged speakers who came to talk about their areas of expertise, but especially they enjoyed the less formal visits from animals and children alike that always lifted the atmosphere within the lounge. In fact, even before she'd got together with Sam, he'd brought along his springer spaniel, Lady on one of his visits when he spoke about his work as a park ranger at Primrose Woods. The dog proved a big hit with the guests, even if Lady's behaviour had been questionable once the tea and biscuits arrived, scrounging for titbits, before snaffling a slice of cake from the table, much to Sam's mortification and the amusement of everyone else. Not that it precluded her from being invited back again. Lady had been such a star attraction that she'd since made several more visits to the lodge.

'Well, this bunch will welcome you back to work with open arms,' said Pia. 'I know that.'

Abbey was pleased she'd come along today. It had eased her back into a work mindset, and she'd made a point of saying hello to each of the residents, and informing them of her return-to-work date. She'd spent some time in the office with Lydia too, going through the diary and discussing the current issues. It seemed like a lifetime ago when she'd last been here, running the show, but she also saw how easy it would be to step right back into her role when she returned after Christmas.

'Well, with Pia's wedding now just a couple of days away, I wondered if any of you had any words of wisdom to offer her with your broad wealth of experience?' Abbey looked around the assembled group. There was a rumble of nodded assents that went around the room.

'"Never go to bed on a row." That's what my Ivy always used to say,' Reg piped up. 'Even if we'd had a big falling out in the day she would always make sure we'd kiss and make up before lights out. I think it's good advice, because a lot of the time you'll have forgotten whatever it was you were arguing over the next morning.'

'I'd tell you to have a running-away fund,' Stella added. 'It's what my mum always told me. And she was right. It's always handy to have something stashed away just in case.'

Pia gave a gentle chuckle. In case of what, she wasn't quite sure.

'Well, hopefully I won't need a running-away fund, Stella, but I think that's sound advice. It's good to have some financial independence.'

'I'd say you need to have a good laugh together. Oh, and dance together too. Vera and I were always jigging around the kitchen. We used to know all the steps to the ballroom classics.'

A wonderful image of Harry and Vera waltzing around their cottage popped into Pia's mind, making her smile.

'I think that's a lovely idea, but Jackson's never been very keen on dancing.' Although considering what she'd recently discovered about him, she wasn't certain if that still held true. Her thoughts drifted off to a different time and place, when they'd been caught up in the beat of the music, abandoning their bodies and soul to the rhythm. It had been completely mad and unexpected and thrilling, and she still had to pinch herself to believe that it had actually happened. 'Although I have told him he will have to dance with me on our wedding night, whether he likes it or not. There will be no excuses permitted!'

'I'm probably not the best person to ask for advice about marriage,' admitted Nina, 'my husband left me when the kids were small, but I suppose I'd say don't listen to other people, however well-intentioned, when it comes to your relationship. Trust your own instincts.'

Pia nodded.

'I understand that. Thanks, Nina.'

'What about you, Abbey?' said Wendy. 'You're newly married. Us lot can barely remember what it's like to be young and in love. What advice would you give to Pia?'

Abbey gave a warm smile.

'Well, I suppose Sam and I are still very much in the honeymoon period, which I hope will never end. He's my best friend in the world, along with Pia, of course,' she said, laughing. 'I think communication is the key. Sam listens to me and hears what I'm saying, so I would say, along with all those other things that you lovely people have mentioned, to keep talking, keep listening and keep supporting each other. Although I'm not sure Pia really needs any advice from us. She's found her soulmate, who clearly adores her, and they've created something special already. All I would say is keep on doing what you're doing.'

Pia lifted her glass to her lips and took a mouthful of the refreshing Buck's Fizz, bolstered by the affection shown from her friends. She looked all around her and smiled.

'Thank you. You're all so kind, and I'm going to make sure I pass on all your great advice to Jackson. Whether or not he will take any notice, well, that's another thing entirely,' she said, laughing.

33

Pia had intended to have a quiet couple of days to start the week, recovering from the excesses of the weekend, safe in the knowledge that all the public events were behind them now. Her head was still abuzz with excitement after the success of the Carols by Candlelight evening, Luke's proposal, Rex's proposal and now the prospect of her own wedding. She took a deep breath, reaffirming to herself that there was no need to panic. Everything was in place; it was simply a case of checking that the flowers would be delivered on time, and confirming with the caterers, the photographer and the band the timings for the day.

Today she was going to meet Tom and Frank over in the barn to brief them on what needed doing to transform the space into the perfect wedding venue, ready to welcome their guests. Just as she was about to head out the kitchen door, Jackson physically stopped her.

'Hey, where do you think you're going?' he said, shaking his head. 'Absolutely not.'

'What do you mean? There's still a lot to do yet, and I need to make sure Tom knows the layout for the tables and the decorations. Rex and Ronnie will be helping too so I don't know why you're looking so glum. It's going to be fun.'

'I might have agreed to us getting married here, but there's no way I'm letting you do all the hard work getting the barn ready for your own wedding. Nope. I'm sending you away for a few days.'

'What? No, you can't!' Why had Jackson suddenly taken on the harsh tone and manner of an upright Victorian gentleman? 'Don't be ridiculous. I need to be here, Jackson. I've got so much to do.'

'It's all organised,' he told her. 'You and Sophie are going away for a two-night spa visit. No arguments. Sophie has the details. I think she's planned massages, manicures and pedicures for you both. A chance for you to properly unwind.'

'What, but...?' Pia wasn't sure whether to be annoyed or delighted. She had a schedule, a table plan and a whole box of fabric and garlands to decorate the barn with.

'Don't worry about a thing,' he said, as if reading her mind. 'We've got it all covered between us. You've worked so hard this year, looking after me, the hall, the animals and my folks, that you need some time for yourself, to recover, to be your absolute best self for the wedding. Otherwise you'll be in a walking trance come the day of the wedding. Leave it in our capable hands.'

'What about the dogs and the animals, they'll need...'

'I know exactly what they need. And I know exactly how you want the barn to look. We have spoken about it in quite a lot of detail, remember.'

Her every protestation was met with a firm rebuttal from Jackson so that she quickly ran out of reasons why she should stay.

'Did you say Sophie would be coming?'

'Yes.' He glanced at his watch. 'In about an hour's time actu lly, so you need to pack a bag, get on your way and don't give a second thought to what is going on here. I promise you' – he took her face in his hands – 'that we will make sure everything is perfect for Saturday. You do trust me, don't you?'

'Yes, of course I do!' As much as she would trust anyone with her wedding plans.

It didn't take her long to get used to the idea though. On Jackson's urgent shooing, she ran up the stairs to their bedroom, where her small suitcase was already opened on the bed. She hastily threw in some underwear and casual clothes, a swimsuit plus her toiletries, and her excitement built with every moment so that by the time she got back down to the kitchen, any reservations she may have had about leaving the hall in the days leading up to her wedding had completely evaporated. Especially so seeing Sophie's grinning face when she arrived shortly afterwards to drive them to the spa.

'Was this your idea?' Pia asked as they set off on their leisurely journey. She was still shaking her head, hardly believing this was actually happening.

'I'd love to take credit for it, but it was all Jackson's doing. When he mentioned what he had in mind, I thought it was a brilliant idea and I was delighted to be asked to be part of his secret plan.' She grinned. 'It's so kind of him, and just what you need before the wedding. You haven't stopped all year and this will give you the opportunity to properly unwind. You're going to come home pampered and preened.'

'Oh, he's not all bad, Jackson, is he?' said Pia, with a smile of relief. 'It's so thoughtful of him. Otherwise, I would have been hastily painting my own nails and toenails on the morning of the wedding! He obviously knows me better than I know myself.'

Although it was only two days away, it felt much longer and Pia was able to relax, with only the occasional moment of panic when she wondered what she might possibly have forgotten and how they were getting on back at the hall, resisting the urge to get straight on the phone to check. Instead she made the most of the peace, enjoying some one-on-one time with Sophie, chatting and laughing and sharing stories about their respective Moody men. It was the much-needed rest that she hadn't even realised she'd needed.

Arriving home two days later, she was welcomed warmly by Jackson and marginally more enthusiastically by the dogs, but with strict instructions from Jackson that she wasn't to take a peek inside the barn. That delight would have to wait until Saturday, the day of the wedding.

* * *

Pia was superstitious by nature so had insisted that she and Jackson spent the night prior to the big day apart. She remained at the hall with Ronnie, while Jackson, Tom and Rex stayed overnight in a local hotel.

Waking up on that crisp December morning, Pia could quite easily have believed that it had been snowing overnight because as she pulled back the curtains and peered outside she saw that the ground was covered in a thick frost, the bare branches of the trees tipped with white icing. There was a serene calmness to the morning even if she could feel the anticipation hanging in the air as though the trees and shrubs were aware of the enormity of the day. Pia glanced across at the barn, the Christmas tree now sporting the addition of a myriad cream bows, which would be shown off to magnificent effect when the lights were turned on before the arrival of their guests. There were beautiful natural garlands, made from spruce and eucalyptus intertwined with holly, ivy and mistletoe, running the length of the stables, and Pi couldn't help thinking how magical it looked from the outside. In a few hours she would be stepping inside the barn to be greeted by Jackson and the thought sent goosebumps travelling the length of her body.

'Knock, knock!'

'Come in,' she called excitedly, hearing Ronnie's familiar voice.

'Good morning!' There was a big smile on her mum-in-law-to-be's face. 'How are you feeling today?' Ronnie asked as she wandered through the bedroom door carrying a tray with a small vase of flowers, a welcome mug of coffee and a glass of orange juice.

'Ooh, what a treat, thank you!' When Ronnie placed the tray down on the beside cabinet, Pia stepped towards her for a hug, squeezing her tight. 'I'm so pleased you're here, Ronnie. I'm so nervous. Part of me wants to crawl back under the duvet, but I'm excited and happy too. Once I'm in my dress and I see our friends and family waiting for us, and spot Jackson as well, I know I'll feel so much better. It was weird waking up without him this morning, but tonight when we go to bed we'll be Mr and Mrs Moody.' Pia tilted her head to one side in contemplation. 'That's so funny. I've just realised you and Rex will be Mr and Mrs Moody again soon.'

'I know, I haven't got used to it myself.' Ronnie eyelashes fluttered involuntarily, and a dreamy look crossed her face, before she gathered herself. 'I have to keep checking my ring to remind me that it's true. Anyway, all that is for another time. Today is about you and Jackson. As his lordship's mother, I can't tell you what a relief it is to know that he's found you, Pia, because I know how much you love and care for him and I can see how happy you make him.'

They must have sat there chatting, laughing and hugging for

at least an hour, until Ronnie jumped up from the bed where she'd been sitting.

'I've got something for you. A wedding present. Can I go and get it and give it to you now?'

'Of course,' said Pia, clapping her hands excitedly. 'You didn't need to do that though. I hope people don't think they have to buy us a present. We have everything we need, but it's so lovely of you.'

'It's from Rex as well, and I didn't wrap it, but we hope you'll like it.'

Ronnie came back into the room holding the neatly folded crochet blanket that she had poured all her heart, time and soul into over the last few weeks. She'd only finished it in the early hours of the morning, sewing in the last remaining ends, and giving it a gentle press, before tying it with a big red ribbon.

Pia's eyes lit up as she accepted the blanket, fascinated by the colours, the intricacy and the craftsmanship of the piece. She opened it up and held it above her, her gaze taking in every detail of the cream and gold blanket, which was a patchwork of individually designed squares with hearts, and bobbles, and with hers and Jackson's initials entwined at its centre.

'Oh, my goodness, it's beautiful. You're so clever, Ronnie!' Pia buried her nose in the blanket. 'We will treasure this forever. I can't thank you enough.'

It was big enough to cover their king-size bed and Pia couldn't wait to show it to Jackson, knowing that the blanket would be a constant companion to them through their married life.

'Anyway, I shall get in trouble,' said Ronnie, looking at her watch. 'We need to start getting ready. How about some breakfast first? Abbey, Katy and Rosie will be arriving soon.'

The morning passed in a whirl of excitable chatter and laughter, glasses of champagne and a breakfast of scrambled eggs and smoked salmon, until it was time for Pia to step into her wedding dress. As she spent most of her days in jeans and a sweatshirt, Pia had eschewed some of the more elaborate fussy gowns she'd tried on and instead opted for a simple sheath dress in soft ivory that swept her curves, the beaded detailing on the cap sleeves adding a touch of elegance and glamour.

'Well, look at you!' Ronnie gasped, seeing Pia in her dress for the first time. Pia had to avoid her gaze as she'd glimpsed the emotion in her eyes, matching her own bubbling feelings inside. 'You look stunning!'

It was the same reaction from little Rosie who had looked at her in awe, her big eyes growing wide, seeing Pia in all her finery.

'You look like a princess, Pia.'

'Thank you, Rosie, and so do you!' Pia took hold of the little girl's hand and twirled her around the floor. 'I'm so grateful you're here today to help me. I've got flutters in my chest so I wouldn't be able to do this without you. And you too, Abbey,' she said, clasping her best friend's hand. Rosie and Abbey, in their dusty pink dresses in complementing styles, were the perfect assistants and Ronnie took some spontaneous photos in the bedroom as they put the final touches to their make-up, with Rosie insisting on having a dusting of blusher, in the kitchen as they sipped on Buck's Fizz, made with lemonade for Rosie, and then out on the patio beside the stone balustrade with the trees of Primrose Woods providing a perfect backdrop.

'Come on,' said Abbey, taking her matron-of-honour duties very seriously, 'we need to get you across to the barn. Jackson will be wondering where we've got to.'

They made the short walk across the stony path, holding hands all the way, gasping as the cold air took their breath away, but it didn't matter because they were all filled with excitement. For Pia there was every other emotion too; happiness, trepidation and a pang of sadness, thinking about her parents and missing them hugely, but gaining solace from the fact that she was certain they were looking over her today from high above.

'Mum and Dad would be so proud, you know that, don't you? And I'm proud too,' said Connor, who had joined them and who was doing her the honour of escorting her into the barn.

'Thanks, Connor, that means a lot. Having you here, your arm to hold on, has stopped my legs from shaking!'

'Glad to be of service, sis!'

Stepping into the barn, Pia was in total awe and she might have been forgiven for thinking she'd been transported into a winter wonderland with the myriad taper candles and fairy lights, the swathes of green foliage and white blooms creating a magical effect. She had to give it to Jackson and the gang; they'd done a far better job than she could ever have managed. Exhaling the breath she'd been hanging on to, Pia immediately relaxed seeing all her friends and family gathered to greet her. She spotted Abbey and Sam first with little Willow, Wendy and Simon, Lizzie and Bill, Luke and Rhi and so many others, all dressed up to the nines with smiling faces. She heard an appreciative gasp of delight and a ripple of spontaneous applause break out as she made her entrance. Her gaze searched out Jackson, and spotting him in the crowd caused her entire being to fill with love, pride and happiness as his eyes snagged on hers, a smile spreading wide across his face. His hand reached out to grasp hers.

'You turned up?' he said, looking relieved.

'Yes!' She laughed. Was it ever really in question? There'd been moments when she'd wondered if they were doing the right thing, if she was doing the right thing, but any lingering wisps of doubt evaporated in that instant as her fingers threaded with Jackson's. 'Nothing could have kept me away.'

'You look beautiful,' he said, taking a step backwards to run his gaze appreciatively along the length of her body.

'You look very handsome too,' she said in the understatement of the year, the sight of Jackson in his grey silk Italian suit, pristine white shirt and purple polka-dot tie bringing her out in goosebumps.

'Shall we do this?' he asked her, looking at her intently, his dark brown eyes glistening with emotion.

'Yes, please.' She nodded, with a smile.

* * *

The ceremony, presided over by a jovial registrar under the oak beams of the old barn, was simple, intimate and touching, with Jackson and Pia exchanging their personally written vows in a heartwarming and emotional moment for every single person in the room. When the formalities were over, the registrar prompted the happy couple to seal their marriage with a kiss and as they did so, a little voice piped up from behind.

'Thank goodness for that. Can we have some food now, please?'

Everyone erupted into good-natured laughter at Rosie's off-the-cuff comment, which cut through the hushed atmosphere. Several of the other guests admitted they were of the same mind as Rosie, eager to get the party started with a drink and some enticing-looking canapés.

The day passed in a haze of love, laughter and good wishes as Pia and Jackson made a point of speaking to each of their guests, and it was only then that Pia could fully relax into the celebrations.

'All of this, it's amazing, thank you, Jackson,' Pia said, gesturing around her, only noticing some of the finer details of

the sumptuous decorations in that moment: the gold ribbon
adorning the backs of the chairs, the pinecones along the centre
of the trestle tables and the mistletoe hanging from the beams. 'I
couldn't have done it any better myself.'

'See, what did I tell you? You need to learn to trust your
husband,' he said, his eyes shining with affection and love, his
hand touching her cheek. 'But I'm very glad you approve.'

She took another sip from her glass of champagne and an
attentive waiter immediately refilled it to the top. She smiled
thanking him, but she wasn't going to make that mistake again.
She needed to keep a clear head today to ensure she could
remember every single exquisite moment of what already had
become the best day of her life.

'It's all perfect,' she uttered.

'Hmmm, kind of,' said Jackson, his face crumpling in distaste.
'Although I'm not sure about the disco. What kind of music is
that exactly?'

Pia laughed.

'I'm surprised you don't recognise it, Jackson. Everyone knows
this one. By special request from one of our younger guests.' She
nodded towards the centre of the room where Rosie, arms wide,
was spinning around on the spot, perfecting a princess pirouette.
Pia suspected that, like her, Rosie was having the best day of her
life.

34

'So, where did you learn to dance?' Pia asked Jackson, when the music had switched to something more acceptable to Jackson's ears, and he proceeded to twist and turn her expertly around the barn floor. Aware of the eyes of all their friends and family on them, she felt as though she was floating on air, as though she was, in that moment, the most beautiful woman in the world. In fact, she was certain it must be true because Jackson had kept telling her so all day long.

'I'm a man of many talents, did you not realise that?' he whispered in her ear as he pulled her up close, before spinning her away again.

'Honestly, Jackson, you never cease to amaze me. You have so many skills,' she said, 'but I never believed for one moment that I would actually see you tripping around this dance floor as though you were born to dance.'

'Well, I couldn't let you down, could I? And with my two left feet, I knew I would need some help, so I'll let you in on a secret: I may have taken one or two lessons.'

'I knew it!' she said, laughing, catching her breath as he took her in his arms, placing a hand on the small of her back, sweeping her around the floor with a mastery she could never have imagined. 'That night in the bar, after my hen night, it was like meeting a stranger. It was wild and thrilling and I was literally swept off my feet. I kept replaying it over in my head afterwards and wondering if it really had been you.'

'Err... what was that then? I'm not really sure what you're talking about, Pia. Is there something you need to tell me? Another man?' He narrowed his eyes at her, his brow furrowing.

'Stop it,' she said, laughing. 'You definitely led me astray that night. You bad, bad man!'

'You're not complaining, are you?'

'No, it was totally unexpected, that was all.'

'Well, you know I always aim to please.'

'I suppose there was a part of me that worried that perhaps it was unlucky to see the groom on my hen night or if it was a bad omen for our marriage.'

'What?' He pulled back to look into her eyes, sweeping a hand over her hair. 'We make our own luck, Pia, and nothing's going to change that.'

'Yes, you're right, of course,' she sighed.

'Always. And I for one thought that night was bloody magical,' he said, his eyes shining, clearly remembering the romantic intensity of the moment. 'Once I'd got past your eagle-eyed friends and my mother. Honestly, I had to swear on my life to them that I would get you home safely.'

She laughed, entranced by his warm brown eyes.

'The dancing definitely fooled me. I couldn't believe that my boyfriend suddenly had the moves of a Latin Lothario. It was honestly like being with another man.' She giggled. 'You know, I think I could sign you up for *Strictly Come Dancing* next year, you're that good.'

'I don't know about that, but I do think it's important never to take anything for granted in a relationship and to hold on to a few surprises, don't you?'

Pia nodded. She was certain she'd received similar advice from one of her friends at Rushgrove Lodge recently and she was in no doubt that her marriage to Jackson would have plenty of surprises in store for her.

'Only good surprises, I hope.'

'Absolutely,' he said, laughing, taking her in his arms as the music slowed. She rested her head on his chest, closing her eyes, revelling in the closeness and intimacy from having exchanged their wedding vows, at becoming being Mr and Mrs Moody, in front of all their family and friends.

'You know, I think this has been the best day ever, certainly the best event we've ever held at the hall.'

'Oh, by a country mile,' agreed Jackson.

As the music changed again, and everyone joined them on he dance floor, they melted into the middle of the room, surrounded by all their loved ones.

'So have you finally forgiven me for running out on you when we were kids?' he asked her, running a hand over her cheek.

'There's nothing to forgive, Jackson. I loved you then and I love you now, and I will love you forever more.'

'Good answer, Pia, because I never stopped loving you either.' He held her face in his hands and kissed her on her lips, sending ripples of delight the length of her body. 'The teenage girl I fell in love with always had a part of my heart, and finding her again, well, it was as though this, us, it was always meant to be.'

She allowed her head to fall back onto his chest, a beatific smile spreading across her face, in total and utter agreement. With Jackson at her side, she knew that her future at Primrose Hall was destined to shine very brightly indeed.

EPILOGUE

In the darkest, wettest days of January, when Pia was gearing up to get back into the office, after the glorious celebrations of December, Jackson came up with one further big surprise.

'What on earth have you done now, Jackson?' she said looking at him aghast as he waved a couple of tickets to the Maldives in front of her nose. 'We can't go gallivanting off to the other side of the world. We need to get back to work. We've got a busy season ahead of us and I need to make a start on the arrangements.'

'There's nothing that can't wait for a couple more weeks. Besides, it's all booked now. It's our honeymoon, Pia. You can't possibly deny us that.'

'But what about the dogs and the animals and...' Pia felt anxiety grip her tummy at the thought of leaving the hall for an extended length of time.

'All sorted. Mum and Dad will be here, of course, but Tom is stepping in to look after the estate and the daily care of the animals.'

'Wow.' She shook her head. He promised there would be

surprises, but she hadn't expected anything like this. 'The Maldives, you say?'

For someone who had only ventured as far as the South Coast, the golden sandy beaches and the vibrant blue skies of the Indian Ocean provided a perfect distraction that made it easy for Pia to forget entirely about the demands of her inbox. Despite her reservations, it turned out to be the holiday of a lifetime where they spent their days scuba diving, island hopping, drinking cocktails and lounging in their overwater villa, relishing the intimate time spent together.

As much as she loved the honeymoon, gathering memories that she would cherish forever, she was just as pleased to return home to Primrose Hall. She'd missed Bertie and Teddy far too much, all the animals in fact, and she missed Ronnie and Rex too. Joining them again round the kitchen table at home, for that first cuppa after their holiday for a full debrief, was the highlight of a memorable trip, although she would never have admitted as much to Jackson.

For Pia, home was definitely where her heart was and, back in the fold, she was eager to make a start on planning the calendar for the year. Already she had two weddings to schedule, one for Luke and Rhi, who had opted for the August bank holiday weekend and were planning on a festival theme, making the most of the wild meadows that surrounded the barn, and one for Ronnie and Rex, who, impatient to waste no further time, were married in March in a rumbustious affair that had all their guests rocking and rolling until the early hours of the morning. Ronnie announced that their second wedding was a much classier affair than the first, helped this time around by foregoing the curled sandwiches and instead opting for a sumptuous three-course lunch. She was also delighted to have in place a professional photographer, who took some unblurry snaps for posterity.

As everyone suspected, Tom took to his new role heading up the property-developing business with enthusiasm and confidence, delivering the completion of the Rosewood Farm Cottages on time and within budget. The homes were unrecognisable from the crumbling old buildings that had first greeted Pia and Jackson, transformed into beautiful dwellings for contemporary living. As agreed with Jackson, Tom had first pick on the cottages and he decided on Harry's old home, which offered scenic views over the local countryside. The other two properties were rented out to local families, who Jackson knew through his charity work. Tom was already making plans and pricing up their next project, a barn conversion in a neighbouring village.

His relationship with Sophie continued to grow now they were able to spend even more time together, with Tom enjoying cooking and entertaining for her in his new home. Sophie ended up staying over most nights of the week, only going home for the occasional evening and at weekends to work in her studio, where she was developing a new range of products to add to her jewellery collection.

The craft fairs at the stables were as popular as ever with the numbers of visitors increasing significantly on the previous year. Due to demand, Tom had scheduled in another two workshop sessions for later in the year and this time Sophie had no hesitation in signing up again.

As for Pia, she was kept as busy as ever, but she would never have had it any other way. The arrangements were well under way for the classic car show in the summer, with Jackson and Reg determined that they wouldn't miss out on any of the action this year. Dates were set too for the writing festival, the bonfire night display and the Christmas carols evening. There was another event that had crept onto the calendar too: an Easter Sunday celebration, with an Easter egg hunt for the children, with chance to meet and get to know the animals of Primrose Hall, which Pia had personally overseen. It had been planned as a low-key family event, but the day had been more successful than they could have hoped. With the sun shining brightly, highlighting the golden hues of the daffodils, it had been a relaxed friendly affair which had brought out all the familiar faces.

Katy and Brad were there with Rosie and Pip, eager to say hello to the animals, Bill and Lizzie came along too, Luke and Rhi obviously, because they would never miss an opportunity to visit the hall, and Pia was always thrilled to see her dear goddaughter Willow with Abbey and Sam, and her gorgeous nephew Freddie with his parents Connor and Ruby.

A minibus with a group from Rushgrove Lodge, including Stella, Reg, Harry, Wendy and Nina, also put in an appearance, with the whole group appreciating and enjoying the delights of Primrose Hall on a sunny afternoon. On their advice and urging, it had already been agreed that the Easter Day celebration would become an annual event on the calendar.

Pia needn't have worried that marrying Jackson would bring about unwelcome changes to their relationship and the daily life at the hall. With her friends and family, her adored animals and the continuing support of the local community around her, she knew that she was absolutely where she needed to be, with the man she'd loved, ever since she was a teenager, at her side, ready for all the challenges that lay ahead of them.

Pia was delighted to discover that life went on in the same way as it ever did at Primrose Hall. Only, as Mrs Moody and Lady of the Manor, it was infinitely better.

ACKNOWLEDGEMENTS

All good things must come to an end and so it is with this sixth and final book in the Primrose Woods series. I've had such a wonderful time creating these characters, who have been constant and friendly companions to me, and I hope to you as well, over the last couple of years. It is bittersweet saying a final goodbye knowing I will miss them hugely, especially the four-legged friends, although it pleases me immensely to know they all found their happy endings!

A big thank you to my publisher, Boldwood Books, for their continued support and hard work behind the scenes in producing and promoting the books, and continually striving to find new markets and avenues to reach more readers. Thank you, Amanda, Nia, Claire, Jenna, Marcela, Ben, Issy, Niamh and the entire Boldwood team for everything that you do.

In particular, special thanks to my lovely editor, Sarah Ritherdon, whose patience, understanding and guidance through the writing process is always very much appreciated.

Thanks too to Cecily Blench for her expert copy-editing skills and to Jennifer Davies for proof-reading.

It's wonderful to see the series in its entirety sitting on my digital and physical bookshelf and I'm indebted to Clare Stacey at Head Design for creating such a wonderful and fitting cover for the last book in the series.

I'm always grateful to the bloggers who sign up to take part in the blog tours as I know how much work is involved in writing such detailed reviews and posting them across the internet. A big thank you to you all and to Rachel at Rachel's Random Resources for organising and coordinating.

To Nick, Tom, Ellie and Amber – thank you, as always, for your love and support. I really couldn't do it without you all.

Finally, thank you to all my lovely readers, for joining me through this series. I always appreciate hearing from you, and knowing that you have enjoyed spending time with the gang in the beautiful setting of the woods makes all the hard work worthwhile.

Thank you so much for picking up this book to read and really hope to see you again next time!

Much love

Jill xx

ABOUT THE AUTHOR

ill Steeples is the author of many successful women's fiction itles – most recently the Dog and Duck series - all set in the close ommunities of picturesque English villages. She lives in Bedfordshire.

ign up to Jill's newsletter to read her short story Take a Chance or FREE, originally published in Best Magazine

'isit Jill's website: www.jillsteeples.co.uk

ollow Jill on social media:

 facebook.com/jillsteepleswriter

x.com/jillesteeples

instagram.com/jill.steeples

ALSO BY JILL STEEPLES

When We Meet Again

Maybe This Christmas?

It's Now or Never

Primrose Woods Series

Starting Over at Primrose Woods

Snowflakes Over Primrose Woods

Dreams Come True at Primrose Hall

Starry Skies Over Primrose Hall

Sunny Sundays at Primrose Hall

A Winter Wedding at Primrose Hall

Dog & Duck Series

Winter at the Dog & Duck

Summer at the Dog & Duck

Wedding Bells at the Dog & Duck

Happily-Ever-After at the Dog & Duck

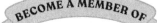

THE
SHELF
CARE
CLUB

The home of Boldwood's
book club reads.

Find uplifting reads,
sunny escapes, cosy romances,
family dramas and more!

Sign up to the newsletter
https://bit.ly/theshelfcareclub

Boldwood

Boldwood Books is an award-winning fiction publishing company seeking out the best stories from around the world.

Find out more at www.boldwoodbooks.com

Join our reader community for brilliant books, competitions and offers!

Follow us

@BoldwoodBooks

@TheBoldBookClub

Sign up to our weekly deals newsletter

https://bit.ly/BoldwoodBNewsletter

Printed in Great Britain
by Amazon

49194678R00149